PIE À LA MURDER

PIE À LA MURDER

MELINDA WELLS

**WHEELER
CHIVERS**

This Large Print edition is published by Wheeler Publishing, Waterville, Maine, USA and by AudioGO Ltd, Bath, England.
Wheeler Publishing, a part of Gale, Cengage Learning.

ALL RIGHTS RESERVED

The text of this Large Print edition is unabridged.
Other aspects of the book may vary from the original edition.
Set in 16 pt. Plantin.

LIBRARY OF CONGRESS CATALOGING-IN-PUBLICATION DATA

Wells, Melinda.
    Pie à la murder / by Melinda Wells. — Large print ed.
      p. cm. — (A Della cooks mystery) (Wheeler Publishing large print cozy mystery)
    ISBN-13: 978-1-4104-4309-0 (pbk.)
    ISBN-10: 1-4104-4309-4 (pbk.)
    1. Carmichael, Della (Fictitious character)—Fiction. 2. Cooking—Fiction.
3. Santa Monica (Calif.)—Fiction. 4. Large type books. I. Title.
PS3623.E4765P54 2011
813'.6—dc23   2011032978

BRITISH LIBRARY CATALOGUING-IN-PUBLICATION DATA AVAILABLE

Published in 2011 in the U.S. by arrangement with The Berkley Publishing Group, a member of Penguin Group (USA) Inc.
Published in 2012 in the U.K. by arrangement with the author.

U.K. Hardcover: 978 1 445 87887 4 (Chivers Large Print)
U.K. Softcover: 978 1 445 87888 1 (Camden Large Print)

Printed in the United States of America
1 2 3 4 5 6 7 15 14 13 12 11

To Norman Knight

ACKNOWLEDGMENTS

I am grateful to the following:

Editor Kate Seaver, I appreciate (immensely) your excellent suggestions, which make these books better. It's a pleasure to work with you.

Priscilla Gilman and Morton Janklow, thank you for your continuing support and for your expert guidance. You couldn't possibly have a client any happier than I am.

Claire Carmichael, a terrific novelist and a brilliant instructor, I'm a better writer than I would have been without your "athletic" eyes.

D. Constantine Conte, mentor and treasured friend, I've learned so much from you.

Carole Moore Adams, thank you for creating another great recipe for this book!

To the other generous people who have allowed me to share their recipes in this book: Mira Waters, Fred Caruso, John Bonhert, Freda Small (via Abigail Shrier), Jaclyn Carmichael Palmer, and Julie-Anne Liechty. Thank you all.

To the test readers who give me their invaluable reactions: Arthur Abelson, Carole Moore Adams, Hilda Ashley, Gina Anderson, Penrose Anderson, Christie Burton, Rosanne Kahil Bush, Jane Wylie Daley, Ira Fistell, Lynn Harper, Nancy Koppang, Judy Tathwell Hahn, Jaclyn Carmichael Palmer, and Anna Stramese.

Wayne Thompson of Colonial Heights, Virginia, who continues to inspire me and make me laugh.

Berry Gordy, thank you for making me an "honorary Gordy," and for all that I've learned from you.

1

"Della, I've got something to tell you. . . ."

In my experience, nothing good ever follows a statement like that.

"You know I was married before, a long time ago."

"Yes. Why are you bringing it up now?"

"What you don't know is that I have a daughter. . . . She's eighteen."

"What!" I stared at Nicholas D'Martino, the man in my life. He'd never even hinted that he was a father, and certainly not one who had a teenage daughter. His striking Sicilian face with eyes the color of black coffee, high cheekbones, and a nose broken during his years as a college boxer was topped with a full head of dark hair that never quite managed to look combed. A thick lock of it curled down onto his fore-head like a question mark, emphasizing his uncomfortable expression. He was looking at me as though he didn't know how I would take this news. I wasn't sure myself.

"You're a journalist," I said. "Isn't telling me this after more than a year of our being together called 'burying the lead'?" I was surprised at how calm I sounded.

His wry smile acknowledged my attempt at humor. He cleared his throat. "I haven't seen Celeste since she was a baby. Tanis, my ex-wife, lied to get sole custody. She convinced me that it was best for the child, that it was only a technical thing, that I could see Celeste every day. I believed her. Then she left for Europe as soon as our divorce was final."

Nicholas had taken me on what he'd billed as "a teenage date" in the carnival atmosphere of the Santa Monica Pier, just a few blocks west of my little house on Eleventh Street. First, a mobile dinner of fish and chips wrapped in newspaper and seasoned with a sprinkling of malt vinegar, after which we rode the Ferris wheel and the whirling cups, and tried to work off our meal by climbing the Pier's rock wall feature. Nicholas beat me to the top by only one foothold — my new personal best.

We were sitting on the beach below the Pier, listening to the music and laughter floating down from above as we watched little diamonds of moonlight sparkle on the surface of the Pacific Ocean. It had been a wonderful evening, up until now. The cone of chocolate frozen yogurt I'd been devouring with such pleasure a moment ago dripped in my hand. Dollops of melting yogurt splattered onto my new tan slacks. Raw silk. The pants were cut so artfully that they managed to make my hips look smaller, and they were the perfect shade with my new butter yellow cashmere sweater. I laid my cone down in the sand and dabbed at the dark spots with a napkin, but I knew the slacks were ruined.

Nicholas put his cone beside mine and carefully covered them both with sand. I wondered if that counted as littering.

"Celeste called me from Vienna, where she's living with her mother," he said.

I filled the awkward silence that followed with a question. "Is this the first contact you've had with her since she was a baby?"

He nodded. "Over the years I tried to talk to her countless times, but Tanis made sure I was always one step behind them." He half smiled. "Del, Celeste wants to see me."

"That's marvelous," I said, genuinely happy for him.

His face split into that grin he saved for special triumphs, as when one of his crime stories in the *Los Angeles Chronicle* was

11

nominated for a Pulitzer Prize. "My daughter's coming to LA. She arrives tomorrow. And she wants to live with me."

"Don't you watch daytime-TV talk shows? It's a known fact that the biggest threat to a romantic relationship is a man's daughter from a previous marriage." Liddy Marshall shook her head as she reached down to pet my big black standard poodle, Tuffy, who was lounging next to her chair at my kitchen table. "Mark my words," Liddy said, "this girl will be trouble."

"I know you mean well, but I don't believe that." I was thinking of my honorary daughter, Eileen O'Hara, and the joy I've had being her "mother-person," as she calls me, during the years that her own mother was ill and couldn't be with her. "I'd like to be her friend. With her mother so far away, she might need an older woman to talk to."

"Hah!" Liddy threw up her hands. "Good luck! You and Eileen are close because you're not in love with her father. Teenage girls are more territorial than hungry lionesses."

I smiled at her with affection. "Have you been watching Animal Planet, too?"

"Scoff if you like, but you heard it here first: your 'love boat' is heading for choppy waters."

"Nicholas and I have been through a lot and our relationship has only gotten stronger. We're going to be fine," I said.

I hope.

Liddy had been one of my closest friends for more than twenty years, and she had the kindest heart of anyone I knew, but I reminded myself that she was inclined to be melodramatic. An attractive natural honey blonde — a former Miss Nebraska — Lydia Nelson had come to California to be an actress, but had fallen in love with a cute young dentist named Bill Marshall. She traded movie dreams for a happy life as a wife and mother of twin sons. Now that the boys were away at college in the East, Liddy amused herself by working as an extra in TV shows and movies. As she liked to say, it gave her the fun of being on sets and around actors, but she didn't have to stay superthin or worry about aging.

Liddy turned toward the computer on my desk in the corner. It was in the kitchen because I used it to plan my TV shows and the cooking classes I taught on weekends. She asked, "What did you say his ex-wife's name is? It was something weird."

"Tanis."

"What did you find out when you Googled her?"

"I didn't. That's spying. There is no way I would invade Nicholas's privacy like that, and I don't want you to do it either. Promise me."

"Okay, I promise." Liddy sat down and clicked onto the Internet. "I'm all for scruples, but we still need information of a nonspying nature."

Peering over her shoulder, I saw what she was typing.

"Oh, Liddy — you're not going to look up what her name means. That's not information."

"I believe that names are predictors of personality. Della means 'cheerful' and 'happy.' That's you. 'Lydia' means 'life.' Do you know anyone who enjoys life more than I do?"

"Coincidence. Names are given to infants before they show any traits."

She ignored my argument, found a meaning-of-names site, and scrolled through the "Ts." "Does she spell her name with one 'N' or two?"

"No idea. It sounds made-up to me."

"I've heard it somewhere before. Oh, right — here it is. One 'N.' It's from the Greek name 'Tanith.' " Liddy jabbed at the screen.

"Ah-ha! It's derived from Semitic roots meaning 'serpent lady.' "

"It's also the name of the Phoenician goddess of love, fertility, the moon, and the stars," I read from the screen. I was instantly sorry I'd seen that part.

Liddy exited Google and returned to the kitchen table and her coffee. She had to step over Tuffy, who was watching us with the intense interest he displayed when he and I were on my bed, watching a movie with a dog in it.

"What did Nicholas say about his wife?"

"*Ex*-wife," I said. "Not much. She was a rich girl — inherited a fortune — but he didn't want them to touch her money. He got her to promise they would live on what he made as a reporter."

Liddy gave a cynical snort. "I bet that didn't last long."

"As far as he knows, she kept her word, until they had the baby. Then she started buying all kinds of luxuries for herself and Celeste. She told him she was leaving because she didn't want to have to keep lying to him about what things cost, or feel guilty about having money."

"That doesn't seem like a good enough reason to divorce when you have a baby," Liddy said.

"Nicholas didn't think so either. He was willing to forget her promise not to spend her money, but she said that wasn't good enough any longer because she'd come to see that they were incompatible personalities. Nicholas told me that he tried to talk her out of the divorce, but he had to admit that she was right. They had different views on almost any subject."

Liddy grimaced. "You'd think they would have figured that out before they got married. Sometimes I think love is not only blind but deaf, too."

I didn't want to think about their *love*. "Nicholas wanted to spend time with their child, but the day the divorce was final she moved to Europe. It broke his heart. He said that's why he hadn't told me about his daughter until now."

"Tanis is a bitch. Did he tell you how they met? Or what made him fall in love with her?"

"I didn't ask."

Liddy looked at me narrowly. "Does he still have feelings for her?"

"I don't think so. . . . No, I'm sure he doesn't."

"And his daughter knows about you?" Liddy asked the question as though expecting her worst suspicions were about to be

16

confirmed.

"Nicholas wants to introduce us 'casually.' He's going to bring her to the taping of the live show Thursday night."

Liddy raised her eyebrows. "To achieve exactly what?"

I'd wondered the same thing, and didn't like the thought that had occurred to me. "He didn't say explicitly, but I believe he thinks that if she sees me doing a TV show it will impress her."

That got another snort from Liddy.

"I admit it hurt a little when he told me how he wanted to introduce us, but he hasn't seen the girl since she was a year old. I think he's nervous. He wants everything to be perfect."

"The poor fool."

"Come on, Liddy. I want this to work out for him."

"I know, and I do, too," she said. "I like Nick — so I'm going with you. To be your second."

"My second what?"

"Like in the old days when people had duels. Each of the duelists had a second. You know, to hold their coats."

"What you mean is that they were there to cart off the body of the loser."

"Let's not think negatively." With forced

optimism in her voice, she added, "Thursday night might go very well. But whatever happens, I'll be there with you."

After Liddy left I took Tuffy for a long walk. While he explored the neighborhood and visited his favorite trees and bushes, I thought about Nicholas and what the arrival of his daughter might mean to us as a couple. I had meant it sincerely when I told him it was marvelous that she'd broken a seventeen-year silence and called. In spite of Liddy's grim warning, I really was looking forward to meeting Celeste.

Two weeks ago, in early October, Nicholas and I reached the one-year anniversary of the day we met. Recalling how enthusiastically we'd celebrated that milestone sent a shiver of delight through me. Late that night, Nicholas again brought up the subject of marriage. As I had when he'd asked me before, I told him I was partial to the idea, but we agreed there was no rush. While we managed to spend a satisfying amount of romantic time together, we both had busy careers and separate homes. That lack of pressure had produced a happy relationship composed of sexual compatibility, mutual respect, and love.

Now I wondered if I should have done

what Nicholas had wanted, and rushed off
to the nearest minister.

2

Nicholas didn't call that day, or that night. I was sure Celeste had arrived — otherwise he would have let me know — and I hoped that things were going well between those two strangers who were father and daughter. Still, I was disappointed, and a little miffed, that I hadn't heard from him.

On Wednesday, I kept myself busy planning the next four-week cycle — twenty episodes — of *In the Kitchen with Della,* my cable TV cooking show on the Better Living Channel.

While I was going through recipes and choosing themes for the broadcasts, an inspiration struck. I phoned Phil Logan, head of publicity for the cable network.

When I got through to him, he answered with a sunny, "How's the best-looking cook on television?"

"Giada De Laurentiis is seven or eight years younger than I am and probably twenty pounds thinner, but I appreciate the compliment."

"It was meant sincerely. What can I do for you, Della?"

"Project pies."

"Pardon me?" Phil said.

"Tomorrow night's live show is about pies. Millions of people don't realize that baking a pie is really easy, it tastes better and — depending on what's it in — is cheaper than buying one. I'd like to encourage a series of bake sales all around the country to raise money for good causes."

"Explain."

"Imagine teams of four, in hundreds of cities and towns, all baking pies — and cakes and cookies and brownies — to sell for whatever charity or cause they care about. Then on a date we pick we'll announce the name of the team that's raised the most money. We'll show their photos on TV. Is this something I'm allowed to promote on the air?"

" 'Promote' — that's my favorite word." I heard excitement in his voice. "It's a great idea! We can do *well* by doing *good.*"

"I'm not sure I follow you."

"Let's think big," Phil said. "You promote — 'champion' is a nicer word — bake sales around the country, and what we do at the

BLC is offer a nice prize for the group that proves it raised the most money. Wait a minute, I'm about to be brilliant! The prize will be a three-day trip to Hollywood for the winning team. They'll appear on your show, and we'll get them a VIP tour of Universal Studios, and send them to Disneyland."

"That sounds expensive," I said. "Do you think Mickey will go for it?"

Our boss, Mickey Jordan, billionaire owner of, among other businesses, the Better Living Channel, could be inconsistent in his generosity. He'd never balked at improvements in equipment, but sometimes he pinched pennies until they screamed.

"I think I can sell him on the basis that it'll get us free national news coverage. Mickey loves 'free.' Hey — we could make a documentary about the sales, focusing on a few groups in major TV markets as they organize, bake the stuff, sell it, and count the money. There's bound to be at least a couple of fights and kitchen disasters. Maybe some backstabbing and sabotage. Reality TV. I love it!"

All day Thursday I baked pies for the live show that night. I would be making an apple, a lemon meringue, and a chocolate cream on the air, but there wouldn't be

22

enough time in the hour to have all three ready so that viewers and the people in the studio audience could see the ready-to-serve finished product. I also planned to pass out slices for the studio audience to taste. To provide for that, I had to bake two of each at home.

Tuffy watched me take the last pie out of the oven and stood up. He always knew when I finished cooking or baking.

"You can't come with me tonight, Tuff," I said. "Sorry."

He seemed to understand, and settled back down on his cushy L.L.Bean dog bed next to the refrigerator. Nights, he slept in my bedroom, but he seldom left my side during the day, so I made sure he was comfortable while I worked long hours in the kitchen.

On Mondays and Tuesdays, when I pre-taped four half-hour shows, Tuffy came to the studio with me. He was a fixture on the set, which had been built as an exact replica of my basically low-tech yellow and white home kitchen, right down to a duplicate L.L.Bean dog bed. The camera operators photographed Tuffy watching me curiously, ready to taste anything I might drop. Those shots resulted in Tuffy getting his own electronic fan mail. One of Phil Logan's assistants answered the e-mails and signed them with paw prints.

Just as I finished washing the mixing bowls and the measuring cups and spoons, my gray and gold calico cat, Emma, strolled into the kitchen and went right to her food bowl. I glanced up at the wall clock and saw that it was three o'clock, her preferred time to dine.

"You must have a watch in your stomach," I said to Emma. She didn't look up at the sound of my voice, just crunched happily.

While the pies cooled, I let Tuffy out into the fenced backyard, took a bath, put a few hot rollers in my hair to fluff it out, and did my best to "glam up," as Liddy called it.

Apparently I didn't do it well enough, because when she came to my house to help transport the pies, she looked at me critically and then went back outside to her car for her professional makeup kit.

"Always carry it," Liddy said. "When you do extra work you don't get the top rank makeup artists, so I learned to do my own." She steered me toward the bathroom and handed me a towel from the rack. "Sit down, put this around your neck, and don't move your mouth."

I did as instructed. While she was using her skills on my cheeks, brows, lashes, and lips, I was doing a mental run-through of that evening's show. Cooking live on TV had begun as a publicity gimmick a year ago, when I suddenly went from being a cooking school teacher on the verge of bankruptcy to a TV cooking show host. Phil Logan's initial plan was to have me do live shows once a week only for the first two months. His theory was that the novelty of it would get the public's attention and help to establish me, an unknown. After the first two months, all the shows would be pretaped. But so many people began writing in asking for the free tickets that Phil persuaded our boss to keep the Thursday night live show on the schedule. Recently, Phil had found money in his budget to buy twenty extra seats, expanding the size of the studio audience from thirty people to fifty.

"Have you heard from Jolly Ole Nick?" Liddy asked as she applied eye shadow.

"No. But I didn't expect to."

"You sure he's coming tonight?"

"That's what he said he wanted to do. He would have let me know if he'd changed his plan."

"When we get to the studio, have one of your people tape off three reserved seats."

"Liddy, I don't have 'people,' but I was going to have seats saved for Nicholas and

25

Celeste. Why three? Oh, Lord." I felt a flash of dread and turned my back to the mirror in order to stare at Liddy. "You don't think his ex-wife came here with Celeste, do you?"

"I hope not. The third seat is for me. I'm going to sit next to them and try to get acquainted with the girl. See if I can do a little positive PR on your behalf."

I squeezed her hand. "You really are worried about Celeste ruining my relationship with Nicholas, aren't you?"

"Yes," she said softly, "I am. Now turn around again and tilt your head back so I can make you gorgeous."

When I could move my mouth again, I said, "I'm going to start exercising."

"Except for walking, you hate exercise."

"I like that climbing wall at the Santa Monica Pier."

Liddy nodded in approval. "Climbing's good for all parts of the body." She was silent for a moment. "When you think about it, it's also a kind of metaphor for life."

I wasn't thinking about metaphors. My mind was on Nicholas. With the sudden arrival of his eighteen-year-old daughter, was our relationship really heading for the choppy waters Liddy had predicted?

3

Because we planned to drive to the studio in my Jeep Compass, Liddy had parked her ivory Range Rover on the street. It was a beautiful day, this second of November. Sunny and just slightly crisp. Swimming weather — or it would be if I'd had a pool. I hoped the weather was a good omen for meeting Celeste tonight.

It took Liddy and me three trips back and forth from kitchen to vehicle, but we finally loaded the pies into the special boxed shelves I'd had installed behind the rear seats. They'd been made specifically for the purpose of transporting finished dishes to the TV studio, as well as the groceries and portable equipment I needed for teaching classes on Saturdays at my little cooking school in the back of a Santa Monica appliance store.

To avoid getting stuck in rush-hour traffic on the 101 Freeway, as usual I took Beverly

Glen Canyon through one of the several man-made clefts in the mountain range that separated the west side of Los Angeles from the San Fernando Valley. From either side it was called "going over the hill."

Once across the canyon and onto Ventura Boulevard I turned east. It was only another few minutes before we reached North Hollywood, and the corner of Chandler and Lankershim boulevards where the Better Living Channel's West Coast broadcast facilities were located.

As always, the first thing I saw was the billboard on the corner, just outside the high security fence that surrounded the airplane hangar–shaped structure that was my second home two days and one night a week. The huge sign featured caricatures of the BLC's four West Coast hosts. I liked the artist's rendering of me because he'd given me a smaller waist, bigger eyes, and hollow cheeks.

At the security gate I touched my finger to the "Call" button. Through the microphone I heard the jovial voice of Angie Johnson, one of the guardians of the entrance.

"Hi, Della. Whatcha makin' tonight?"

"Pies. How late are you working?"

" 'Til nine."

"I'll put a plate in the on-set fridge with your name on it."

"Yummy! Who's that in the car with you?"

"It's Mrs. Marshall."

"Okay, I'll log her in." Angie pushed the release on her side of the security camera. I watched the tall iron gate swing open.

"Angie, I'm expecting two special guests tonight. You know Mr. D'Martino?"

I heard her bawdy chuckle. "Oh, yeah. That man is *electric.* When you get tired of him, put in a good word for me."

"Don't hold your breath," I joked. "He's coming tonight, and he's bringing his daughter. I don't know exactly when they'll get here, but will you be sure to let them in, even if they're late?"

"Count on it."

"I will. Thanks." I waved at the camera's lens, drove onto the grounds and around to the rear of the building to my parking space near the big, sliding double doors into the studio. Members of the audience would enter through another door adjacent to the front of the building and the visitors' parking lot. I hoped two of those people would be Nicholas and Celeste.

I made myself stop thinking about them and parked the Jeep. As soon as Liddy and I opened the rear door to begin unloading,

29

George, one of the studio's uniformed security guards, came up to us at a trot.

"Let me get that stuff for you." He inhaled the aroma coming from the pies. "Smells good enough to eat."

"Hands off until after the show," I said, laughing.

Liddy and I carried one pie box each, while George, hefting the four biggest ones, followed us into the studio.

The Better Living Channel building was divided into two sections and housed four permanent sets. The workshop set for *That's Not Junk,* where the host demonstrated how to rescue and repurpose everything from broken can openers to butt-sprung sofas, shared space with the design studio for the channel's newest offering: *Decorating for Dimes.*

My kitchen was on the far side in the back half, next to *The Car Guy*'s automobile repair shop. Car — as we called the man who'd changed his name legally to "Car Guy" — had the spot next to the big sliding doors because he needed to drive his demonstration vehicles in and out.

Six PM. An hour to broadcast. I checked that my cell phone was on. Still no word from Nicholas.

One gaffer up on a tall ladder tested the lights above the preparation counter and stove top that faced the audience, while another technician adjusted the lights over the oven and the long display counter against the kitchen's back wall. Because Tuffy didn't appear in the live shows — too many people around for his safety — his dog bed had been moved to the storage room behind the set.

My favorite camera operators, Jada Powell and Ernie Ramirez, were checking their equipment and getting shot instructions from our TV director up in the glass production booth above our heads. Tonight, Jada's cloud of soft, curly hair — "Diana Ross hair," Ernie called it — was tamed into cornrows and accented with tiny red and white beads. Ernie was wearing his usual Los Angeles Dodgers baseball cap and blue satin team jacket. It hadn't been a great year for the Dodgers, but win or lose, Ernie was loyal.

While I was organizing the ingredients and utensils I would need for the show, Liddy was out in the audience, taping large white cards that said "RESERVED" in block letters onto the three seats in the front row closest to the entrance.

■ ■ ■ ■

Six forty-five PM. From a narrow opening behind the set, I watched audience members, guided by security guards George and Harold, chattering with excitement as they filed in to find seats. I saw Liddy in her chosen place: the third seat in row number one. To make it extra clear that the two seats next to her were taken, she'd placed her handbag on one of them and draped her jacket over the other. Every few seconds she glanced at the audience entrance. So far, no sign of Nicholas and Celeste.

Six fifty-nine PM. I tied the white chef's apron around my waist. Through the earpiece concealed under my hair, I heard the familiar voice of my director. "Thirty seconds, Della."

"I'm ready."

My theme music began to play. On the small backstage TV monitor I saw the program's logo. In my ear I heard the director's countdown begin.

"Ten . . . nine . . . eight . . ."

I came out from backstage, smiled, and waved at the audience.

". . . seven . . . six . . . five . . ."

Taking my place behind the prep counter, I surveyed the audience. In the semidarkness, I saw that the two seats beside Liddy were still empty.

". . . four . . . three . . . two . . ."

The audience door opened. In the sudden slice of bright light from the lobby, I saw George escorting two figures who hurried in and took the seats next to Liddy.

The man in my life and his long-lost daughter had arrived.

". . . one. Go!" Theme music faded down.

"Hi, everybody. Welcome to *In the Kitchen with Della*. I'm Della Carmichael, and tonight is all about dessert. I'm going to show you how really easy — and how much cheaper — it is to bake your own pies. We'll be making three that use the least expensive ingredients: apple, lemon meringue, and chocolate cream. If you like cherry or pecan pies, just realize that those ingredients are pricier."

I held up a basket of green apples. "So let's get cooking. Granny Smith or Pippin apples are the best to use for pies. These are Pippins. You'll need at least six for a nine-inch pie, but I use eight because I like to stack the slices high."

I measured granulated sugar into a mixing bowl and picked up a jar of cinnamon.

"I use a lot of ground cinnamon." I put in two teaspoons. "And a tablespoon of all-purpose flour for a little thickening. Mix this up and set it aside until we're ready to combine it with our apples."

As I peeled, cored, and sliced, I said, "Pies have been around for thousands of years. Really. The ancient Egyptians kept detailed records and many of them mention pies. The Egyptians filled theirs with honey and fruits and nuts. The ancient Greeks liked what the Egyptians were doing and took recipes home with them. Ancient Romans were so enthusiastic about pies that they made offerings of pie to their gods. A pie was originally a simple cooking and serving *container.* The crusts were pretty hard. At that time, when a pie had a top crust it was known as a coffin. If a pie didn't have a top crust, it was called a trap. . . ."

When the voice in my ear told me it was time for the first commercial, I said, "We've got to take a little break. I'll just keep slicing apples, and when I come back I'll show you how to make a piecrust so light and tasty that there won't be any of it left on the plate. I experimented the other day and combined the Crisco I ordinarily use with chunks of cold, unsalted butter. Don't worry if you can't write down the amounts because you'll find all the recipes on my Web site."

During that break, and the next three, I kept busy organizing for the following segment. While I frequently lifted my head to smile at the audience, I scanned what I could see of their faces without giving special attention to my three guests. I wished I could get a good look at Celeste, but it wasn't possible because her head was either turned to her father, or she was listening to something Liddy was saying.

The live hour shows usually went by fast for me, but this one seemed to last an eternity. I wanted it to be over so I could see Nicholas to get a sense of how he was feeling, and to meet Celeste.

Finally, the last segment. My eight-inch-high apple pie was out of the oven, the meringue on the lemon meringue had been lightly browned, and the chocolate-cream filling poured into its baked pie shell to cool.

After the cameras took their "beauty shots" of the pies, I began bringing those I'd made at home forward to the prep counter. "The pies I baked right here aren't quite ready to eat, but I brought the ones I made at home today so you could all have a taste."

As prearranged, I saw Phil's two young

male interns come down from the control booth with serving trays and make their way carefully over the electrical cables on the floor and toward the set.

I greeted the boys and turned back to the audience. "Meet Jerry and Cliff. They are about to be the most popular people on the show tonight, because they're going to pass among you with wedges of pie for you to taste. While they're getting the slices ready, I have an announcement to make."

Jada Powell moved Camera Two in for a close up of my face.

"The Better Living Channel has allowed *In the Kitchen with Della* to sponsor a National Bake Sale for teams of four. The objective will be to raise money for the good cause or charity of their choice. The team that bakes the best goodies and donates the most money by the day before Thanksgiving will win an all-expenses-paid trip to Hollywood."

While I outlined the details that Phil and I had discussed, and that he'd had Mickey Jordan approve, Jerry and Cliff loaded the trays with paper plates of pie and baskets of forks and napkins. "Details of this contest will be up on the Web site tonight. So pull out those recipes, heat up your ovens, and start planning what you can do this holiday season for people in need."

As I finished the announcement, Jada pulled the camera back to show me loading up a tray of my own.

"Okay, folks," I said. "Let's start tasting."

Lights were turned full up on the audience. The cameras followed Jerry, Cliff, and me into the audience with our trays. End credits rolled as people in the audience began to taste the pies.

Thank God — they're not clutching their stomachs in pain.

I'd made it a point to do my distributing at the opposite end of the audience from where Nicholas, Celeste, and Liddy were sitting.

Finally, the show was over and most of the audience began to leave the studio. I had been chatting with some of the people closest to me, thanking them for coming to the show, and — this was still a surprise to me — signing a few pieces of paper. For years the only time my autograph had been requested was on a credit-card slip.

I was back at the prep counter, instructing Jerry and Cliff about putting aside plates of pie for Angie and the security guards when I heard Liddy's voice behind me.

"That was a great show — and the pies were so good they were positively *evil*."

She was accompanied by Nicholas —
who, I was thankful to see, was beaming —
and an exquisite girl with perfectly spaced
features, large brown eyes, and hair the
color of corn silk. A little taller than my five
foot seven and considerably more slender,
she looked like an artist's rendering of a
princess from a fairy tale. She was so beautiful it was almost jaw-dropping.

My first thought was that her mother must
have been beautiful, too.

And probably still was.

Nicholas introduced us.

"Hello. I'm glad to meet you, Celeste. I
hope you enjoyed the show."

"You seem to cook quite well," she said.
Her voice was soft and had the tiniest trace
of an accent — one that I'd heard before, in
film clips of Grace Kelly after she married
the ruler of Monaco, or Madonna right after
she married a British movie director. A mid-
Atlantic accent, it was called. Although
Celeste's words were inoffensive, there was
a suggestion of superiority in her tone.

This eighteen-year-old girl, this breathtak-
ing vision, was being condescending to me,
and it didn't look as though Nicholas had
noticed.

I felt the first trickle of the "choppy

waters" Liddy had predicted lapping against my feet.

4

Liddy must have caught the girl's tone, too, because she filled the momentary silence with bright enthusiasm. "Why don't the four of us go out to dinner?"

Celeste frowned.

Nicholas said, "We'll do that soon, but tonight I promised to take Celeste around to check out some of the hot clubs."

"Hot" was not a word I'd ever heard Nicholas use about an establishment. I suspected the only reasons a teenage girl would want her father to take her out were that she didn't have a car, and didn't yet know anyone else.

"I've got to tell you something exciting, Del," Liddy said. "Celeste wants to be an actress."

"You certainly are beautiful enough for movies," I told Celeste. "Liddy's an actress."

Celeste looked at Liddy with interest. "What have I seen you in?"

"Most recently, I was the passenger in first class sitting next to Brad Pitt in *Flight Path*. I hid his revolver so the terrorists wouldn't see he had one and realize he was an air marshal."

"Oh," she said, losing interest fast.

Liddy was undaunted by Celeste's unenthusiastic response. "Della and I are going to the Hollywood Film Society luncheon tomorrow. Major people in the movie industry are always there. We'd like you to come with us, Celeste."

This plan was news to me.

Suddenly animated, Celeste said, "I'd really like to start meeting people."

"That's nice of you." Nicholas's tone was pleasant, and he smiled at Liddy and me, but I could see that the smile didn't reach all the way to his eyes.

I wondered if he'd known about Celeste's desire to be an actress before tonight. I didn't think he would be pleased. Nicholas had told me stories about what he called the "girls around town" who thought their good looks were a no-limit Visa card. Very few of those actress-wannabes had happy endings with the Hollywood men who used them.

Later, in my Jeep on the way home, Liddy

said, "You should have seen Nick's face when he heard Celeste tell me she wanted to be an actress. He looked as though he'd just been sucker punched."

"She has the looks." My newly awakened suspicious nature made me think that she could act, too — at least offscreen. I prayed silently that she was sincere in wanting to be with her father, and that she hadn't come here only because he lived in Hollywood.

"What's this about the Film Society luncheon?" I asked. "You'd never mentioned it to me. And don't you have to buy tickets in advance?"

"I go every year, but as soon as you told me about the daughter coming to town I bought two more tickets. She'll have the excitement of seeing some famous faces, and I thought if she believed it was both our ideas it might help your relationship with her."

"That's very generous of you, but I don't want to buy her goodwill toward me."

"Don't be silly. Stepparents do it all the time. Once Celeste gets to know you, she'll love you for yourself, but there's no reason not to use whatever we can to start things off on the right foot. Between Bill's celebrity patients, our social life, and what I laughingly call my own career, I do have a few important contacts. Tomorrow, when we're at the luncheon, I'll introduce Celeste to some people who could help her. She might even" — Liddy made quote marks in the air — " 'be discovered'!"

At my house, Liddy picked up her Range Rover and drove to her home in Beverly Hills, taking with her the big piece of apple pie I'd saved for Bill, her husband of twenty-plus years.

Using the remote control clipped to my sun visor, I opened the garage to put my Jeep away and saw that the little red VW wasn't there. It belonged to Eileen O'Hara, my semipermanent houseguest and partner in our walk-in and mail-order business, Della's Sweet Dreams. Eileen had lived with me for much of her life, during her mother's periods of mental illness. Now, thankfully, Shannon was on medication that kept her stable, but because Eileen and I worked together, Eileen still spent most nights at my house. I really hadn't expected to see her car there; usually on Thursday evenings she did the inventory with our store's manager and made up the list of what needed to be ordered.

As usual, Tuffy and Emma were in the living room, waiting for me. I greeted them both with affectionate petting, and checked their food and water bowls to see what needed refilling. After changing into my "Tuffy-walking" shoes, fastening his leash to his collar, and slipping the house key, my cell phone, and plastic bags into my pockets, Tuffy and I went out into the crisp night air.

While Tuffy decided which bush, tree, or patch of city grass was worthy of his attention, and I scooped up anything he deposited, I thought about Nicholas.

When I first met him, Nicholas had been dating a succession of twenty-something blondes. Seeing Celeste tonight had been a bit of a shock because she was a slightly younger version of those young women he had dated. I wondered if he had been drawn to blondes before he and I fell in love because they resembled his ex-wife. Had he been trying to recapture what he'd lost? Liddy's question, "Does he still have feelings for her?" came back to me.

Inside my pocket, I felt my cell phone vibrate.

Before I saw the caller ID I knew it was Nicholas.

"Hey, babe. Where are you?"

"Enjoying the night air." I heard loud music in the distance behind his voice.

"Where are you?"

"In the parking lot outside Cuba Libre."

"Isn't that a drink?"

"We're on the far side of the generation gap, honey. It's a Latin dance club Celeste wanted to check out. I miss you." He made his voice low and husky. "What are you wearing?"

"What I usually wear when I walk Tuffy: a white see-through nightie, black stockings, a garter belt, and stilettos."

"I wish I could rush right over."

"Me, too. How are things going with Celeste?"

"She's amazing, Del. Speaks four languages." Pride warmed his voice. I imagined his full lips curling in a genuine smile. "It was a little awkward, because we don't know each other. I wasn't happy to find out she wants to be an actress, but she's serious about it. She told me when they were living in London last year she studied at the Royal Academy of Dramatic Arts. Probably the best drama school in the world. I would have preferred it if she wanted to go to UCLA, but she's not one of those empty-headed girls who think they can become stars without bothering to learn the craft."

I wondered if he was trying to convince me or himself.

Before I had a chance to respond, he said, "I better go back in and check on Celeste. Make sure nobody's coming on to her."

"Go ahead."

"I promise we'll see each other soon, but you understand that I've got to spend as much time as I can right now with my daughter?"

"Of course I do."

"Until she settles in and learns her way around LA. For one thing, I've had to teach her how to drive on our side of the road — she got her driver's license in England."

"It's all right. Really. I agree that you need to get to know each other."

"I love you," he said, and disconnected.

"Back at you," I said to the dead line.

5

On Friday Liddy arrived at my house at noon. Half a minute later, Nicholas drove up with Celeste in the four-door Maserati he'd bought at an FBI confiscation auction.

Celeste looked spectacular in a short brown leather skirt, knee-high brown leather boots, and a sleeveless vest that looked as though it was made out of red fox fur, worn over a cream silk shirt. I hoped the fur was faux — there are some that look amazingly real — but I hadn't known her long enough to ask, nor to share my negative feelings about wearing real fur south of the Arctic Circle.

As always, Liddy resembled a fashion magazine cover, today in an authentic navy blue Chanel suit, with the also authentic shoes and classic bag.

For my part, I'd put on my best skirt suit: an apple red lightweight wool that I'd bought when Neiman Marcus had one of its rare sales. The suit didn't have a famous label inside, unless you counted Neiman Marcus, but Liddy had approved of the color and cut. I admit that I did feel pretty. The first time Nicholas saw me wear it, he said I reminded him of Sister Sarah, the Salvation Army heroine in *Guys and Dolls,* and that the outfit gave him the urge to undo my buttons. I had batted his hands away and told him to wait until after dinner.

I didn't expect any such romantic exchange today. When he got out of the car to follow Celeste up my front walk, he addressed all three of us collectively.

"You look gorgeous," he said. "Who's driving?"

Liddy raised her hand with the keys to the Range Rover in it. "I am."

"I've got to go to the paper for a while. After the lunch, do you mind taking Celeste back to my place?"

"Not at all."

He said to Celeste, "I'll try to get home before you do, but if not, you've got a key and your phone and all my numbers?"

"Yes, I do, Daddy. Don't worry about me." She gave him a light kiss on the cheek.

Nicholas told us to have fun. With some reluctance, he gave us a good-bye salute and

48

got back into the vehicle I called his silver Batmobile.

Celeste watched him drive away. "He's going to buy me a car tomorrow. I need one for going to auditions."

Surprised, I asked, "Oh? Have you met someone in the business?"

"Not yet," she said.

Behind Celeste's back, Liddy rolled her eyes. "Then we'd better get going," she said.

This year's Hollywood Film Society luncheon was being held in the main ballroom of one of the most glamorous hotels in Southern California, the Olympia Grand, on Wilshire Boulevard, in Westwood. Secretly, I hoped that this location wasn't a bad omen, because the last time I'd been in the ballroom, a few months ago, it had been the scene of a murder.

Liddy turned off Wilshire Boulevard and steered her Rover into the driveway leading to the hotel's entrance. A few chauffeured Town Cars — Liddy called them "daytime limos" — and a stream of expensive private vehicles were ahead of us, but the hotel's parking staff was so efficient that we had to wait only a few minutes before she handed her car over to one of the valets.

A doorman in a dark green uniform coat stood in front of the glass and brass entrance. Even though I'd read that the hotel had acquired a new owner, the name remained the same, as did the large entwined letters "O" and "G" etched onto the glass door in ornamental script.

The first visible indication of new management was the lobby. Gone were the pagan temple scenes and the wall frescoes depicting Greek gods and goddesses at play. They had been replaced by live trees and wall paintings of a lush forest and men in Shakespearean costumes. I realized that we'd walked into *As You Like It* when I read the words on the large scroll on the wall among the painted trees:

And this our life exempt from public haunt
  Finds tongues in trees, books in the
  running brooks.
  Sermons in stones and good in every
  thing.

What the name "Olympia Grand" had to do with Shakespeare I didn't know, but I found the new design attractive and tranquil. I preferred it to the former owner's gaudy decor.

The *As You Like It* theme continued in the main ballroom. Previously, it had been called the Elysian Room and the tables had been encircled by two dozen artificial palm trees; now it was the Arden Room, and the palms had been replaced by a virtual forest of trees with thick green foliage.

Just inside the double doors to the ball-room was a table with three women sitting behind it, checking guest lists.

Liddy stepped up to the nearest woman. "I'm Lydia Marshall. These are my guests, Della Carmichael and Celeste D'Martino."

"Oh, no," Celeste protested. "It's not D'Martino. I'm Celeste Fontaine."

"Fontaine?" I said.

"I use my mother's maiden name. It's less . . . *ethnic.*"

At that moment, I felt a stab in my heart for Nicholas.

Liddy picked up the little envelope of tickets that had our table number on it, and led us through the maze of tables in the ballroom to our assigned seats.

Celeste followed Liddy, and I followed Celeste, which allowed me to see how many male heads turned toward her as we passed.

We were the first to arrive at our table of eight, but the majority of members of the Hollywood Film Society were already there, milling about, looking for their seats and talking to each other.

Liddy placed Celeste between us and

began pointing out some major names in the industry. "See that man with the red hair? He's the creator-producer of *Medical Cops,* the top-rated show on CBS. The man he's talking to is the top director of sitcoms in the business."

"TV's fine, but I'm only interested in films. Who's here that does those?"

Liddy indicated a slender man with a shock of hair that stood up straight, giving him the appearance of having just suffered a powerful jolt of electricity. "That's Brian Grazer. He's produced some of the most successful movies in the last ten years. The man with him is the director Francisco Mantillo — they call him the new Fellini."

Celeste wrinkled her perfect nose in distaste. "His movies don't make much money. Anyway, he's gay."

Liddy's eyebrows rose. "You're not going to do very well in Hollywood if you don't like people who are gay."

"That's not it — half my friends in London and Vienna are gay. It's just that he stayed with us at Freddie's chateau in Gstaad last winter and wasn't interested in me at all."

Liddy asked, "You live in a chateau in Switzerland?"

"Only during the winter so we can ski."

I couldn't stop myself from asking, "Who's Freddie?"

Celeste wrinkled her nose again. "Mummy's prince." She straightened up, good posture making her even more striking. "Oh, look. There's Chad Moody!"

Currently, the world's number one movie star.

"He's one of my husband's patients. Bill aligned his teeth for him." Liddy stood. "I'll introduce you."

Celeste gripped Liddy's wrist, holding her back. "No, don't. Mummy and Freddie say that people are supposed to come to *you*."

And at that moment, someone did.

6

A man, fortyish, whose once-blond hair was streaked with silver in a way that looks better on men than it does on women, said, "Hello, Liddy. Is this your daughter?"

"Hello, Alec. No, this is my friend, Celeste." She turned toward me. "And this is Della Carmichael — you know, *In the Kitchen with Della,* on TV."

"I don't get to watch much television." He extended his hand to me. "Alec Redding."

I took it and said hello. His palm was cool and dry.

He was attractive in a kind of bland way, an older version of one of those surfer-type actors in movies from the sixties with names like Tab and Troy. His nicely chiseled face wasn't familiar, which made me wonder if he'd come to California to be an actor but it hadn't worked out and he'd become something else.

Alec Redding was staring at Celeste. "You are absolutely gorgeous. Are you a model?"

"No. I'm going to be an actress," she said politely, while still scanning the faces in the ballroom.

"I'm sure you'll make it. I have a gift for spotting future stars."

"Are you an agent?" I asked.

Redding blanched slightly, seemingly offended at my question.

Liddy jumped in. "Alec is the best, most creative portrait photographer in Hollywood," she said. "He has *exhibits.*"

Now Celeste aimed a glorious smile at Redding.

Redding warmed up again. "I haven't had time to put an exhibit together for a while." He turned his attention to Celeste. "So, who did your professional portfolio?"

"I don't have one."

"She just arrived in Los Angeles earlier this week," Liddy said.

There was an empty seat next to me. Redding indicated it and said, "Mind if I sit here until whoever comes?" Without waiting for an answer, he sat, pushed the china place setting toward the floral centerpiece, planted his elbow and forearm on the table, and leaned across me to talk to Celeste.

"Let me do a portfolio for you. As stunning as you are, you'll have to prove to the casting people that you photograph well. I know exactly what you'll need to be allowed to audition for top roles."

Celeste bubbled with excitement. "That's wonderful!"

I asked, "How much do you charge?" I realized immediately that was none of my business, but it was too late.

Redding looked annoyed. "The fee varies."

Liddy said to Celeste, "This is a great opportunity. Alec doesn't photograph just anyone."

He gave a self-satisfied chuckle. "Fortunately, I don't have to."

An angular woman with blue black hair gelled into spikes and eyes rimmed in dramatic black wings marched toward our table. She glared at Redding, her thin lips in a tight line.

"Alec, Fannie Goldberg is looking for you," she said.

Hearing the woman's voice, Redding stood up as though snapping to attention. "I'm coming, sweetheart."

"Hi, Roxanne," Liddy said, and introduced us to Redding's wife, adding, "This woman is a total genius at lighting."

"She's my assistant," Redding said. "I'd

be lost without her." He gave Liddy, Celeste, and me a sweeping smile. "Fannie Goldberg's the new chief of Trans-Global Pictures. When you're ready, you should meet her, Celeste." He reached into the pocket of his gray cashmere jacket, pulled out a business card, and handed it to her. "Call me for an appointment."

"You're heavily booked up, Alec," Roxanne Redding said.

"Darling Rox, we can always make time to launch a star of tomorrow." He made the "call me" hand gesture to Celeste and followed his wife across the crowded ballroom.

Liddy patted Celeste's hand. "Being photographed by Alec Redding is a great professional opportunity."

"And his wife works with him? That's good." What I meant was it sounded *safe.*

Celeste understood and shot me a glance of annoyance. "I can take care of myself."

I wanted to say, "Every eighteen-year-old girl thinks that," but I didn't.

"Alec is a bit full of himself," Liddy said, "but there's never been a word about his being anything less than professional when he's working with a subject. And, his wife is always right there with him. She was his protégée, and takes pictures when someone can't afford Alec."

From inside the small pouch Celeste carried as a purse, we heard her cell phone ring. She pulled it out and saw the caller ID. "Oh, God!" With a grimace, she pushed "Answer" and said, "Hello, Mummy . . ." I saw a sudden rush of color to her cheeks. "Oh, Mummy, no!"

She took a deep breath and let out a sigh. "Where are you and Freddie staying?" What Celeste heard made her cover her mouth to suppress a gasp. "Where am *I*?"

She looked around wildly. "Uhhhh . . . I'm at Disneyland! I'm losing my signal — I'll call you later." She disconnected, lowered her head, and whispered, "We've got to get out of here right now."

"Why? There are people I want you to meet," Liddy said.

I asked Celeste, "What's happened?"

"Mummy and Freddie are here. They just checked into *this hotel!*"

Three days ago, if anyone had asked me how I felt about the possibility of meeting Nicholas's ex-wife, I would have said airily that it didn't bother me in the slightest.

I would have been lying.

But now, knowing that there was a Freddie in the picture, I relaxed. A little.

I said, "If you're concerned that your mother and her friend will see us —"

58

"He's not her friend — he's her fiancé." Celeste didn't sound happy about that.

"What I was going to say is that if you don't want your mother and her fiancé to see you here, I'll take you out through the back and over to the next street. Liddy can get her car from the valet and meet us around the corner."

"Good idea," Liddy said.

Celeste nodded. "Yes. Thank you." She tried to sound calm, but as she got up to follow me, she kept her head lowered and her shoulders were still stiff with tension.

I led Celeste along the side of the room, staying close to the trees as much as possible, and into the immense, steamy kitchen. Like broken-field runners, we rushed through the maze of stoves and sinks, dodging chefs and sous-chefs, ignoring their angry shouts. Finally we were out the exit and into the alley. Celeste was in such a panic I don't think she noticed the smell of garbage arising from the trash bins. A few more yards and we'd reached the street behind the hotel, where we filled our lungs with reasonably fresh air.

Liddy's ivory Range Rover rounded the corner of Oak Drive and stopped next to us.

Climbing into the front seat, I said, "We

didn't get any lunch. I'm hungry."

"Me, too," Liddy said. "Since we're all dressed up, let's go have cheese soufflés at the Polo Lounge."

From the backseat, Celeste said with a petulant whine, "I don't want to go any-where I could be seen by Mummy and Freddie. Remember, I'm supposed to be at Disneyland."

"All right," Liddy said. "If you need to hide out until it's time to go to your father's, our house is the perfect place. My house-keeper will fix us something. It's such a nice day we can have lunch out by the pool."

"I just want some distilled water," Celeste said. "Daddy makes me eat when we're together." She shuddered. "I think food is gross."

Oh, great. I won't be able to cook my way to her heart.

But after that moment of mental sarcasm, I wondered if she had an eating disorder. While she was very slim, as far as I could tell she seemed healthy. Her color was good. She didn't look anorexic, but next time we were together at a meal, and she ate, I'd pay attention to how quickly she hurried off to the nearest bathroom. I couldn't help want-ing to protect Nicholas's daughter, even if it was from herself.

■ ■ ■ ■

Liddy and Bill Marshall's home was a stately two-story white colonial in the seven hundred block of Maple Drive, my favorite street in Beverly Hills, because it was lined on both sides with mature maple trees. It had been built in the 1960s, when houses in the area were set far enough back from the sidewalk to allow for a graceful sweep of front lawn. Many of the older homes in Beverly Hills had been torn down and replaced by huge houses that used up most of the size of their lots. When two of these monuments to excess were side by side, I was sure the residents could hear everything that was going on inside the belly of their neighbor's "whale."

Liddy, Celeste, and I were sitting under the big yellow and white striped shade umbrella on Liddy's poolside patio. Celeste sipped at her glass of distilled water while Liddy and I picked at our fruit salads. I would have liked something more substantial, and I'm sure Liddy would have, too, but that wouldn't have been polite with Celeste having only water.

While I was trying to think of a tactful

way to find out more about Freddie, Liddy just asked the question: "Who's Freddie? You called him your mother's 'prince'?"

Celeste wrinkled her nose as if a bad odor had wafted across her path. "*He* says he's a prince. I guess he is. He's got a coat of arms, and servants who call him 'your highness.' I just call him Freddie."

I wondered what her mother called him.

"I don't think I've heard of a Prince Freddie," Liddy mused. "What country?"

"One that doesn't exist anymore," Celeste said. "He says he's the grand nephew of Princess Eugenie Helene of Bavaria. I Googled her. She was the eighth child of King Maximilian. Freddie's full name is Fredric Wilhelm Karl Ludwig von Hoffner. He also told us he's a distant cousin of Queen Elizabeth. Mother joked that if the twenty-seven royals in line ahead of him all die at once he could become King of England. Freddie laughed, sort of." She stretched her mouth in imitation of a toothy grin and gave a mirthless chortle. "But I don't think he has a sense of humor about his title."

"Did your mother tell you why she's come to Los Angeles?" I asked.

"No, but I think it must be Freddie's idea. Mother always said she hates Los Angeles.

She says it's full of *pretenders*."

Liddy laughed. "It's the home of the movie business. Make-believe. Actors earn their living pretending."

"Not that kind of pretending. We like actors. They're fun to have at dinner parties. She meant that this place is full of phonies."

That was too much. I challenged her. "And Europe *isn't?*" I'd been hanging back politely, acting like the kind of careful, afraid-to-express-a-real-opinion woman that I detest.

"I didn't mean to offend you," Celeste said. The apology didn't sound sincere. "I'm sure your friends are very nice." She looked at her watch — a Rolex that cost twice as much as my Jeep. "Liddy, can you drive me to my father's place now? I'd like to take a nap before I have to call Mummy." She stood up. With a polished formality that I recognized was dismissive, she said, "I hope I see you again, Della."

"You will."

My quiet statement seemed to surprise her, then I saw the proverbial lightbulb go off in her head.

"Oh, so *you're* the one Daddy's sleeping with. I thought it was Liddy," she said.

7

I heard Liddy gasp. "Celeste, you know I'm married."

Celeste shrugged. "In Europe married people sleep with other people all the time. I'm sure they do in America, too. It's not a big deal."

"It's a very big deal!" Liddy said. "If I ever caught Bill cheating, I wouldn't divorce him, I'd kill him. And if the situation were reversed, and I did such a thing, I'd expect him to kill me, because we love each other."

She thought Nicholas was seeing Liddy because Liddy's a stunning blonde, probably like Celeste's mother.

"Well, I'm glad we cleared that up," I said lightly.

Celeste stared at me so intently I wondered if she was trying to read my thoughts.

I stared back at her. "What is it?"

Before she could reply, we heard the cell phone in her little pouch ring. When she pulled it out and saw the caller ID she pushed "Answer."

"Hi, Daddy . . . I'm at Liddy's, why?" Celeste screwed up her perfect features in a scowl. "No, I didn't know Mummy was coming. Why did she call *you?* . . . Oh. I just said Disneyland because it was the first thing that came into my head. . . . Okay . . . I'll leave now. Bye." She disconnected and looked at Liddy expectantly. "Daddy's on his way home. Can we go?"

Nicholas lived in the bottom half of a town house in the Larchmont section of Los Angeles. With its sidewalks dotted with slender trees planted in dirt that was surrounded protectively by concrete, his street was more like a little slice of New York City than a neighborhood in Southern California.

During most of the ten-minute drive from Beverly Hills, it was silent inside Liddy's Rover.

Leaving Maple Drive, Celeste told Liddy that she appreciated being taken to the luncheon. Liddy replied that she was sorry it was cut short before she could introduce Celeste to more people.

"That's all right. I found out I need to prove I'm photogenic before I can go to auditions."

I couldn't think of anything to say, and Celeste didn't say anything to me.

When we arrived, I saw that Nicholas's car wasn't in the carport beside the town house. "Would you like us to wait with you until your father comes home?" I asked Celeste.

"No, thank you. I have my key. Good-bye, Liddy. Della."

She climbed down onto the sidewalk and hurried up to Nicholas's front door. We watched until she was safely inside.

"She must take after her mother." Liddy started the car and pulled out into traffic. "I don't envy you, Del."

"There's hardly anything good in life that comes free, without some price tag."

I was thinking about Nicholas, but I was also thinking about Mack, who had been a police detective. There hadn't been a day that he left the house when I wasn't afraid something terrible would happen to him. When the phone call I dreaded finally came, it hadn't been what I'd feared; instead of being shot by some criminal, he'd had a fatal heart attack while jogging. After losing Mack, I was sure I'd never fall in love again. Then two years later I met Nicholas.

"I was in labor with the twins for twenty-one hours," Liddy said. "You remember — you were there. I was cursing at Bill, and swearing I'd never go through that again. But after a few weeks, loving those babies so much, I forgot about the pain and hoped I'd get pregnant again. Some things are just worth what you have to go through to get them."

When we arrived at my place, I saw Eileen O'Hara's little red VW in the driveway. I said good-bye to Liddy and let myself into the house. Tuffy was waiting for me, his pom-pom of a tail and his whole back end wagging an enthusiastic greeting.

"Hi, Tuff. I'm glad to see you, too. Let me put my things down and check messages and then we'll go for a long walk."

Tuffy followed me into the back of the house, where I found Eileen at the kitchen table, making notes on one of the white legal pads I use to plan the TV shows and cooking classes. Last year, shortly before she graduated from UCLA, my twenty-two-year-old honorary daughter had come up with the idea for our retail and mail-order dessert business, Della's Sweet Dreams. She had earned her partnership in the company by persuading my channel-owner boss Mickey Jordan to put up the money to launch it as a cross-promotion with the TV show. She'd since proved to be an excellent partner, handling the day-to-day business with our store manager, which left me free to create new items for us to sell.

Tall, pretty, naturally blonde of a shade between Liddy's dark honey and Celeste's pale corn silk, Eileen was athletically slim, but curvier than ultrathin Celeste. I knew she'd come from our shop this afternoon because she was wearing business clothes: a light blue cotton shirt tucked into a black A-line skirt, with her favorite navy blue blazer hung over the back of a kitchen chair.

I looked over her shoulder. "How are we doing?"

"Really well. If sales keep up, we'll be able to pay Mickey back sooner than expected. The new sugar-free line for diabetics is selling beyond projections."

"You've just given me an idea. I think I'll do a show on that subject. And a Mommy and Me class teaching that sugar-free can be delicious."

Eileen sat up straighter. Her shoulders stiffened and the smile on her face disappeared. "Speaking of 'Mommies and Mes' — what's she like?"

"Who?"

"Your future stepdaughter. We haven't had

a chance to talk since you met her at your show last night." I was surprised to hear a slight edge in Eileen's voice.

Maybe it was my imagination.

She said, "If you and Nick get married, and he moves in here, I suppose she'll have my room."

It wasn't my imagination.

I sat down opposite her and put my hand over hers. "Honey, if you want to, you can live here until you have to start dyeing your hair to cover the gray. Or until we're both old ladies with poodles and cats. Regardless of what Nicholas and I decide to do, this will be your home as long as you want it to be."

That un-stiffened her. She smiled at me and gave my fingers a gentle squeeze. "Thanks, Aunt Del. I'm so busy with the Sweet Dreams business that I don't have time to even think about moving into a place of my own right now. And I'm banking every dollar I don't have to spend so one day whether I'm alone or married I can buy a house, like you and Uncle Mack did."

I stood. "I'm going to change and take Tuffy for a walk, then I'm going to think about sugar-free recipes."

"Do you like her? Nick's daughter?"

"I don't know her very well yet. She's a

bit prickly — but it's probably been difficult for her to grow up without a father."

"Teenage girls can be the worst!" Eileen said.

"It wasn't so long ago that you were a teenager, and you weren't any trouble at all."

"Ha!" Eileen gave me a wicked little smile. "You just think that because you don't know everything I did."

It took a moment to process that statement, but then I gave her a hug. "Since you turned out so well, I thank you for keeping some things from me."

By midnight, twelve hours after he had dropped Celeste off so Liddy and I could take her to the luncheon, I hadn't heard from Nicholas. With both his daughter and now his ex-wife in town, I was beginning to think that I was never going to hear from him again. I'd gone from being annoyed at dinnertime to downright angry by the time Tuffy and I came back from our bedtime walk and there had been neither a cell phone call nor a message on my landline.

I was in bed reading *Fiddlers*, the last of Ed McBain's fifty-five 87th Precinct novels. I'd bought it several years ago, but put off reading it because the author died and there would be no more. Settled against a backrest of pillows, with Emma curled up next to my waist and Tuffy reclining at the foot of the bed, I was on chapter two when Nicholas called.

"I hoped I'd get back to the apartment in time to see you at least for a minute, when you and Liddy dropped Celeste off, but I got held up at the paper, having to add new information to my story on the Crawford murder."

"We offered to wait with Celeste until you returned, but she didn't want us to." I paused, then asked, "How are things going?"

"Good. Better than I dared hope." I heard happiness in his voice. "Honey, she's sweet and smart. Surprisingly levelheaded in her approach to wanting to become an actress. But she's not self-centered. She wants to know about me, my life here. She asked to read copies of my articles. I told her where to find them on the Internet. She has a pink laptop."

I wasn't interested in the color of her computer. Sounding carefully neutral, I asked, "Have you seen her mother yet?"

The warm tone of his voice dropped a good twenty degrees. "No, but we've talked on the phone."

"Did she tell you why she's here?"

"It seems that Celeste left Vienna while Tanis was vacationing in Rio. Vacationing from *what,* don't ask me. Tanis didn't know she was gone until she returned and found Celeste's note."

"I hope she's not going to yank her away from you again."

"No, she's not taking her back to Europe. I have a suspicion that Tanis doesn't really want her back, but she's playing the mother card."

"What do you mean?"

"She said she's come here to be sure that Celeste will be in a 'positive environment.' She actually said she wants to be sure I'll look after Celeste, keep her out of trouble."

I remembered what Eileen had said about having kept things from me when she was Celeste's age. "Teenage girls are as slippery as a ball of mercury, but if anyone can do it, you can."

"Thanks for the vote of confidence. I wish Celeste's mother had your high opinion of me."

"I have a very high opinion of you in all areas," I said softly.

I heard his throaty chuckle, and the sound of it vibrated through my body.

"Tomorrow you're teaching your class and I'm taking Celeste out to get her a car —

something safe and reliable. But tomorrow night she's having dinner with her mother. Are you free to have dinner with me? I'll take you anywhere you want to go."

"Come here," I said. "I'll make something for us. Name your favorite dish."

"You." That was what I'd hoped he'd say, and as he proceeded to elaborate on that theme, I felt a flush creeping up my cheeks.

8

Saturday evening, Tuffy and I greeted Nicholas at the front door. He arrived with a bouquet of red roses, a box of chocolate-covered strawberries, and a kiss that left me breathless. When he let me go, I took the roses and he reached down to give Tuffy a scratch on the head.

"Beautiful flowers," I said. "I'll put these in water."

"Just in the sink. I don't want you to take time arranging them."

He and Tuffy followed me into the kitchen. Tuffy trotted over to his dog bed and settled down while I filled the sink with an inch of water and propped up the roses so that their stems could drink.

Nicholas sniffed the aroma coming from the Dutch oven on the stove. "Beef Bourguignon?"

"Yes."

"Great. The longer it sits, the better it tastes."

He took me in his arms, kissed me again, and whispered, "Can we go to the bedroom?"

I liked the fact he didn't take my agreement for granted.

"Unless you'd rather make love here on the kitchen floor," I said mock-seriously.

In the bedroom, Nicholas gently slipped his hands up underneath my sweater. "I like it that you wear bras that hook in front," he whispered.

Nicholas never got to taste the Beef Bourguignon.

We made love twice — first with urgency to satisfy our hunger for each other, and then in our usual, more leisurely manner. We were lying content in each other's arms when he raised his wrist above the back of my head and looked at his watch.

"It's late." He removed his other arm from where it lay across my rib cage and sat up in bed.

I checked the red numerals on my bedside clock. "It's only nine fifteen."

He was already out of bed and reaching for his clothes. "I want to get home before Tanis brings Celeste back from their dinner together. She shouldn't be alone in an empty apartment."

"I understand," I said. And I did. I remembered all the nights I'd waited up to be sure that teenage Eileen got home safely. I joked, "Do you want some Beef Bourguignon to go?"

He looked at me, as though trying to gauge my real feelings about his hasty departure. "I'm sorry about this, honey. May I have a rain check?"

"Perhaps. The chef at this establishment is rather fond of you."

"You're wonderful," he said. "And I love you." Then he gave me a light kiss and was gone.

In the kitchen, I stuck a fork into the Beef Bourguignon to taste it. Delicious. It should have been, with all the work it took, but the multiple steps were worth it for the result. I scooped out a bowl full, gave Tuffy one of his favorite dog chew bones, and sat down to enjoy my dinner at the table I'd set for two.

Children have to come first, I told myself. In the year or so of my romance with Nicholas, I'd never stayed away overnight at his place, nor had I let him stay here all night if Eileen was home. Maybe that seemed silly — old-fashioned, even, in the second decade of the twenty-first century, but I thought it was the right way to behave. Of course Eileen assumed that I was sleeping with Nicholas, but I wasn't going to parade the fact in front of her.

The ringing of the phone on my kitchen wall interrupted my thoughts.

"Del — now don't get mad," Liddy said.

Uh-oh. "What have you done?"

"Something to help you with this Nicholas situation."

Oh, Lord.

"Maybe I should have asked you first — I mean, now I realize that I probably should have — but when the idea hit me, and Bill said it was fine with him, I was so excited I just plunged right ahead with the plans!"

"What plans?"

She took a deep breath and told me all in a rush: "Bill and I are going to give a dinner party next Friday night for Celeste and her mother and Prince Freddie. And you and Nicholas, of course — so we can all get to know each other!"

I felt the food begin to congeal in my stomach. But there was one tiny ray of hope and I clutched at it: The impression I got from Celeste's conversation at the luncheon was that Tanis — the prince catcher — was a snob and the Marshalls weren't famous.

77

"What makes you think they'll want to come to your party?"

"Oh, she already accepted," Liddy said. "I called her at the hotel a little while ago and reached her in the dining room. She said Celeste had told her about me, and that she was looking forward to meeting her daughter's new friends. She said yes to my invitation without even asking the prince if he wanted to go." Liddy chuckled. "I suspect that it's Tanis who wears the crown in that relationship."

"Well, so I guess that's all settled. Is there anything I can bring?"

"Nope. I'm going to have dinner catered. You have absolutely nothing to do."

Except figure out how to lose ten pounds before Friday night.

Nicholas called Sunday morning. Furious.

"Is Liddy out of her mind!"

"Calm down," I said. "I was shocked, too, but you know Liddy means well. No one could have a more loyal friend, so if you want to say anything negative about her you can hang up now."

He expelled a breath. When he spoke again, he was composed. "Sorry I flew off the handle. I wasn't prepared when Tanis told me about it last night."

Before I could stop myself, I said, "Tanis told you?" I resisted the temptation to ask how she looked.

"She told me about it when she brought Celeste home. I would have called you after she left, but Celeste and I stayed up until nearly three o'clock, talking." I heard warmth return to his voice.

"I'm very happy you two found each other. Girls need a father."

"It feels good," he said.

My hope was that at some point Celeste would be open to a friendship with me, or at least that she wouldn't always be hostile, but I wanted Nicholas to have a good relationship with his daughter. After their having been separated for most of the girl's life, I knew that was going to take time.

As far as Nicholas and I were concerned, I would have to be patient. I loved him. If we were meant to be together, we would be.

If not . . .

I was thankful that I had good friends and a busy professional life.

Eileen came in from her early morning run. Her face was dripping with sweat and perspiration had soaked through her tank top. She gave Tuffy a quick scratch. Taking a bottle of water out of the refrigerator, she said, "I'm so hungry I think I'd give my left

79

kidney for a piece of your stuffed French toast."

"Me, too," I said. "Except the part about the kidney. Go shower and I'll make us some."

As I took eggs and milk and blackberry preserves out of the refrigerator, I said, "Tuffy, I've decided it's impossible to try to lose ten pounds by Friday."

For the next three days, before and after taping my TV shows, Phil Logan had me giving interviews to various national TV and radio broadcasts about Operation Pie.

"The bake sale idea is really catching on," Phil said. "Your Web site is hearing from people all over the country who are starting to form up in teams. In addition to the radio and TV segments, I'm setting you up with print interviews, too. Most of them you can do by phone — I'll e-mail photos — but the *Chronicle* wants to do an in-person, and take pictures of you in your home kitchen. The reporter's Gretchen Tully. When are you available next week?"

"Today's Wednesday. . . . How about Thursday next, a week from tomorrow, if she wants to see me prepare for the live show that night."

"Good idea," Phil said. "I'll let you know

if it's good for her, but I suspect it will be. That'll really give her a look behind the scenes."

Later that afternoon, I was returning home from a long walk with Tuffy when I saw a black limousine pull up and park just ahead of the walkway leading up to my house. A uniformed chauffeur got out from behind the wheel, hurried around to open the rear door, and extended one hand to help his passenger alight.

The passenger was a very attractive woman: blonde, slender, perhaps in her forties. She wore an elegant suit that was, I guessed, the work of a name designer, and probably not an American one.

My breath caught in my throat and my mouth felt dry. I knew that this stranger had to be the former Mrs. Nicholas D'Martino. To my dismay, she was even better looking than I had imagined. Next to her, in my Tuffy-walking sweats and sneakers, I felt frumpy.

"Della Carmichael?" she said. Her voice was well modulated, her enunciation clear, her tone cold as ice. Like Celeste, she spoke with that pretentious mid-Atlantic accent.

"Yes," I said. "You must be Celeste's mother."

She turned to the chauffeur. "Leonard,

wait for me in the car."

He complied.

I said, "Won't you come inside?"

Tanis Fontaine D'Martino — the future princess of something-or-other — gave me a glare so fierce that I wondered if she was able to turn servants to stone. "I won't be here long." She nodded in Tuffy's direction. "Please put that dog in the house."

Her imperious manner made me mad, but I bit back a retort and instead forced myself to say pleasantly, "I don't want us to get off on the wrong foot —"

"There is no *right* foot after what you've done!" She indicated the thing she was carrying: a pink laptop computer.

"What have I done?"

She glanced back at the chauffeur, who was facing forward with such stiff posture that I was sure he was pretending not to listen to his employer's conversation.

Nicholas's ex-wife turned and stalked up the brick walk toward my front door. Tuffy and I followed. I unlocked the door and put Tuffy inside. "Would you like some coffee, or tea?"

"Not from you," she said.

I closed the door so Tuffy wouldn't get out. "I've had just about enough of your attitude," I said. "Because of Celeste, I was looking forward to having at least a civil meeting with you. Now, either tell me what you're upset about, or leave."

I saw a flash of surprise in her eyes. "You don't know?"

"Know what?"

"That Celeste's life is about to be ruined, as well as my marriage plans!" She opened the laptop, balanced it on one forearm, and tapped a few keys. "The photographer you introduced her to e-mailed the proofs of the pictures he took."

She turned the screen to face me. I saw three absolutely gorgeous shots of Celeste in various outfits and poses. They could have been fashion magazine covers.

"Those are very good," I said, unable to figure out what was upsetting her.

She looked at the screen and scowled. "Wrong pictures." She angrily punched another key. "Look," she commanded.

I looked. And felt my mouth drop open in shock.

On the screen was a different kind of photo of Celeste. She was holding in one hand what was unmistakably a chef's apron. It was placed against her torso strategically, but she was positioned at such an angle that the side of one hip was visible, making it obvious that she wasn't wearing anything

83

below the waist, either. Somehow her holding that apron against her front made for a more salacious picture than if she'd been standing there completely naked.

It wasn't only her posing with nothing to cover her except the chef's apron that made the picture such a shocker to me. Her left hand was raised shoulder high, palm pointed backward, like a waiter carrying a tray. Celeste was smiling at the camera — a sly smile, as though she was enjoying some private joke.

I got the joke because I was sure it was aimed at me.

Balanced on her palm was a *pie.*

9

I closed my mouth and looked away from the screen — to find Tanis whatever-her-name-was staring at me with venom in her eyes.

She said, "Do you expect me to believe that this surprises you?"

"Of course it does."

"You introduced Celeste to that man, Redding. Surely you must have known what kind of pictures he took."

I wasn't going to betray Liddy by correcting her, so I said, "All I know is that Alec Redding is reputed to be one of Hollywood's top photographers. His wife works with him — she does his lighting — so it didn't seem as though Celeste would be asked to do anything . . . inappropriate."

"Inappropriate!" Tanis snapped the laptop's lid closed. "This is a catastrophe!"

I reminded myself that this was the anger of a mother being protective of her child, so

I spoke gently. "It's a shock, I understand that, and if she were my daughter I would be as upset as you are, but nowadays many young actresses pose nude. Several even have had sex tapes pop up on the Internet. This photo isn't going to ruin Celeste's chances for a movie career."

"Celeste?" Her eyes widened, then narrowed again into a white-hot glare. "I'm not worried about Celeste's fantasy of becoming an actress. And there won't be any sex tape because I've kept her a virgin."

I wondered, silently, how many other mothers had thought that about their teenage daughters, and been wrong.

Tanis shook the pink laptop as though that would remove the offending photo.

"This is a disaster for *me*," she said. "I'm planning to marry a member of royalty. He's very conservative. His family is very conservative. If this picture gets into the press or on the Internet it will ruin everything. Not only for myself, but for the future I have planned for Celeste, once she gets this acting nonsense out of her head."

Does she intend to foist Celeste off on some "royal"? That pretty virgin Lady Diana Spencer who married Prince Charles had an unhappy life and a tragic early death.

But I didn't say that. Instead, "Of course

you're upset. Why don't you come inside and have a cup of coffee. Or tea. No bags — I brew it with leaves."

"Tea?" she said with loathing. "I drink coffee. With a sweetener. No sugar."

"Then may I offer you" — I paused, then added — "black. With a sweetener. No sugar."

Oblivious to my gentle mockery, she signed heavily, glanced at the laptop, sent a quick sideways look toward the limousine. After weighing her options, finally she said, "Yes. Coffee."

When I opened the door, Tuffy gave us his whole-body wag.

My unexpected guest looked at him in a way that suggested she regarded Tuffy as worthy of her attention. "A standard poodle," she observed. "They're actually German dogs, not French as everyone thinks."

"Not everyone," I said briskly. "Please come this way."

Tuffy preceded us down the hall. Despite my best efforts to have her go next, she gestured impatiently for me to lead off. I don't consider my back view to be my best feature. All the way to the kitchen I was very conscious that Tanis was assessing me critically.

In the kitchen, I said, "Sit down while I make the coffee. It won't take long. I have some sour cream pecan coffee cake. Would you like a piece?"

"No, thank you. I don't eat sweets."

She sat, and placed the laptop on the chair beside her. I didn't know whether she was afraid I was going to snatch it from her if she put it on the table, or if she didn't want to look at the thing. Probably some of both.

I took two china cups and saucers from the cupboard, cloth napkins from a drawer, and spoons from the chest that held the sterling silver place settings that had been a wedding gift from my parents, and put everything on a tray.

"Do you live here alone?" she asked.

"No." I spooned ground coffe into the machine. "A young woman friend lives here, too. Eileen O'Hara."

"Ah." Her tone was ambiguous. I couldn't decipher its meaning.

"Eileen is only four years older than Celeste. We're partners in a small business that she runs. Eileen and Celeste might like each other."

She ignored that and said, "I gather that you're seeing Nico."

Nico?

"Yes," I said.

"He looks wonderful. But then he always did. He's a few pounds heavier than when we were together, but Celeste tells me you cook. I didn't leave Nico because he wasn't terribly attractive and superb in bed."

Ouch. She opened that door, so I kept my voice level and asked, "Why did you leave him?"

"I wanted a different kind of life."

"But why in the world did you keep him away from his daughter all those years?"

"Frankly, *I* didn't want to see Nico and be tempted to fall into bed and return to a dull life I didn't enjoy." A brief smile curved her lips. "At least I didn't enjoy life with him when I was standing up and fully dressed." Then the smile was gone. "Looking back, I suppose that was selfish of me."

"You *suppose?* Not being able to see his daughter broke his heart," I said.

That didn't seem to faze her. She went on as though I hadn't spoken.

"I was young and I wanted excitement. Naïvely, I thought a reporter's job was glamorous, that we'd be traveling all over the world having adventures. But it wasn't like that. He wrote articles, and didn't get to go any farther away than San Francisco. I was so disillusioned that I had intended to leave him sooner, but then I found out I was pregnant. I thought perhaps motherhood would make me feel differently, but it didn't."

The coffee was ready. I brought the tray with the cups, coffee, and a little crystal bowl of artificial sweeteners to the table and sat down opposite her.

She put one packet of sweetener into her coffee. After taking a sip, she said, "I was planning to go back to Vienna tomorrow, but then I saw" — she nodded toward the pink laptop on the chair beside her — "that."

"Did Celeste show it to you?"

"No. She was out driving her new car. She'd left the computer in my suite so I could use it to send an e-mail to my houseman. Just as I was about to, I saw a message come in with the subject line 'photo proofs,' so I opened it. I was horrified. Even worse, I was afraid my fiancé, who was standing there with me, was going to have a heart attack."

Tanis put down her coffee cup. "What influence do you have with this man Redding?"

"None."

"This is really Nico's fault."

I didn't try to hide my anger. "How do you figure that?"

"He allowed her to keep her appointment with that Redding creature. Now he'll just have to get us out of this mess." She huffed in frustration. "I'm desperate for a cigarette, but my handbag's out in the car. Do you have one? I'll take any brand."

"I don't smoke."

"But don't you keep some to offer guests?"

"None of my friends smoke."

She swore softly in German.

I don't speak German, but it wasn't hard to guess the essence of what she was saying.

Tanis picked up Celeste's laptop and stood. "Thank you for the coffee. I should get back to the hotel. Freddie is terribly upset, and he's not in the best of health — he's a hemophiliac."

"I'm sorry to hear that."

"Oh, he's fine unless he accidentally cuts himself," she said in an offhand manner, "but sometimes stress makes him careless."

I saw her to the door and we exchanged polite good-byes.

Barely had the door closed behind her when my telephone rang.

It was Nicholas. "Della." His voice vibrated with anger. "Do you know what Tanis has done?"

"What?"

"She turned the perfectly good, safe

Honda I bought Celeste back to the dealer and leased her a BMW instead. She said a BMW presented a better image!"

"Nicholas, Tanis was just here."

"Where? At your house? Why?"

"*She's* upset about something. I hate to be the one to tell you this, but I think you should be prepared."

When I told him about the photo of Celeste, he exploded. In Italian. But in school I'd made "A's" in Latin so I understood almost every word.

"No, Nicholas — don't do anything foolish!"

He hung up.

I ran to the kitchen to the computer to look up Alec Redding's address. It was on his Web site. I prayed I could get there before Nicholas did.

The address of Alec Redding's photo studio was the same as his home address in Brentwood. If Nicholas had phoned me from his place in Larchmont, then being here in Santa Monica I was closer to Redding. I'd have even more time to get there if he'd called me from the *Chronicle* office in downtown Los Angeles.

Even though I'd scribbled down his phone number along with his address, I couldn't call Redding to warn him that an outraged father was on his way. Suppose he had a gun? He might think he needed to defend himself. I imagined them struggling for the weapon and Nicholas being shot.

That image was so horrible I snatched up the phone and dialed Redding's number.

The call went right to voice mail. I didn't leave a message.

Because Nicholas drove like a NASCAR champion, it would be a race to Redding's no matter where he started from. I grabbed my wallet with my driver's license and rushed out of the house without giving Tuffy a good-bye pet.

10

One-ninety Bella Vista Drive was a block and a half north of Sunset Boulevard, near the border — visible only to real estate agents and tax assessors — where upper-income Brentwood melts into upper-upper-income Bel Air.

Redding's house was a tall, two-story red brick, trimmed in white, with smooth white columns on either side of the front door and a satellite dish on the roof. The numerals "190," in black iron, were affixed to the top of the carport. One car was there: a tan Lexus. The other half of the carport was empty, but parked behind the Lexus was an older model green Buick. I heaved a huge sigh of relief that Nicholas hadn't arrived.

I parked on the street in front of the house, hurried up the walk, and pressed the little mother-of-pearl bell button. A few seconds passed, during which I anxiously scanned Bella Vista Drive while listening hard for the familiar roar of the Maserati's motor. Simultaneously with my pushing the bell again, the door was opened by a woman of sixty or so with silver hair in a braid coiled on top of her head and a light pink complexion. From her pale gray domestic's uniform I guessed this was the Reddings' housekeeper.

"Hello," I said. "I'd like to see either Mister or Missus Redding."

"They are no' at home." Her voice had the slightest trace of an Irish brogue.

"What time will they be back?"

She shook her head. "They be gone until Friday. Would ye like to leave a message?"

"No, that's all right, I'll —"

At that moment, I heard the Maserati's engine and turned to see Nicholas's car zoom up the street. It came to a screeching stop so tight behind my Jeep that if his brakes hadn't been in perfect condition he would have plowed into it.

I said a hasty "Thank you" to the woman at the door and started down the front walk. Nicholas confronted me halfway up.

"He's away until Friday," I said.

Nicholas's eyes blazed. He was angrier than I'd ever seen him. "Where did that miserable bastard go?"

"Out of town. I don't know where, but

the mood you're in I wouldn't tell you even if I did know."

His fury dropped from a boil to a simmer. "What are you doing here?"

"Don't use that tone with me. I came to stop you from doing something you'd regret."

Glancing back toward the Reddings' front door, I saw that the housekeeper was watching us curiously. As soon as she saw me looking at her, she retreated inside and closed the door.

I took Nicholas's hand. "Come on," I said. "He's not here. Do you want something to eat? Or coffee? How about a glass or two of your favorite Sicilian red wine? I still have an unopened bottle."

He removed his hand from mine. "Not now," he said, but at least he sounded calmer. "I've got to go."

"Where?"

"To talk to Tanis."

"Do you think that's a good idea?"

"I only had one good idea, but Redding's not here."

He took my arm, walked with me to my Jeep, and opened the door for me. "Go home," he said. "I'll call you later."

"All right. But take a dozen deep breaths before you talk to either Tanis or Celeste.

Acting like a maddened bull isn't going to solve anything."

His response was a grunt.

I climbed into the Jeep and watched Nicholas get behind the wheel of his car. We turned our respective vehicles around and headed south to Sunset Boulevard.

At the corner, I turned west toward Santa Monica.

Nicholas turned east, toward the Olympia Grand Hotel. And Tanis.

Nicholas didn't call me later.

He didn't call me all day Thursday, either. I had gone from being worried about him to becoming angry at being shut out. If our relationship was as serious as I had thought it was — as he had declared it was — then I deserved at least a one-minute phone call from him.

But anger wasn't a useful emotion in this situation, so I decided to concentrate on my responsibilities.

This night's show was called "Microwave Meals from Scratch," so I didn't need to prepare the finished products here at home. The three dishes I'd planned to demonstrate — Stuffed Acorn Squash, Zucchini Canoes, and Brown Rice with Raw Vegetables — could be made within the show's live hour. I didn't even need to buy the ingredients, because for the past several months a production assistant had been assigned to do that. The items would be waiting for me at the studio.

To keep from listening for the phone to ring, I busied myself baking seventy-two muffins from a homemade batter that was almost as easy to whip up as it would be to open a box mix, and it tasted a lot better. The chocolate, vanilla, and coconut muffins would be passed out to the audience to-night, with plenty left over for the Better Living Channel's staff.

It was time to drive to the studio.

No longer able to stand the suspense, I dialed Nicholas's cell phone, but after four rings, my call went to his voice mail.

"Hi. It's me," I said. "What's going on? I'm worried about you. Call me. I'll keep my cell on until the show and turn it back on again as soon as we go off the air at eight."

Disconnecting, I wished I could talk to Liddy about the trouble the racy photo Alec Redding took of Celeste had caused, my visit from Tanis, my concern about Nich-olas. But I knew I shouldn't tell anyone else — even a friend as close as Liddy was — about something that was the private busi-ness of Celeste and her parents. To take my mind off worrying about Nicholas, I wanted to talk to Liddy about silly things. She'd tell me the latest Hollywood gossip, and I'd tell her about the new supplier at Della's Sweet Dreams who misread our address and mistakenly delivered our order of superfine sugar to the muffler repair shop down the street. But Liddy was working on a movie set all this week, playing a bank robber's hostage tied up next to Bruce Willis in *Die Hard 9: Overdrawn.*

Six fifty-five PM. Five minutes to air. Still no call from Nicholas. My emotions had gone from worry to anger, but now that so many hours had passed with no word from him, my anger had been replaced by a concern so deep the feeling was almost ominous.

Instead of turning the phone off entirely, as I was supposed to while in front of the cameras, I compromised by shutting off the ringer and slipped it into the pocket of my slacks. I adjusted the earpiece concealed under my hair to make it more comfortable, and prepared to teach the studio audience and the viewers at home how to prepare delicious meals with fresh, healthy ingredients, and do it quickly by using a microwave.

I was in the middle of the broadcast's second segment, slicing zucchinis lengthwise to show the audience how to make what I called "Zucchini Canoes," when I felt my cell phone vibrate. It was frustrating, but I had to continue talking to the camera and to the studio audience while I chopped the veggie mixture that would fill the canoes.

As soon as the red light over the camera lens went off and we were into another commercial break, I hurried behind the set to pull the phone of my pocket.

I was sure it had been Nicholas who tried to reach me, and the number on the incoming call record confirmed that. But he hadn't left a message.

"Ten seconds, Della," the director's voice said in my ear.

Back behind the preparation counter, I was smiling at the audience when the red light over Camera One came on and I began to talk and demonstrate again.

The show continued without a problem, and without another call. The Stuffed Acorn Squash, Zucchini Canoes, and Brown Rice with Chopped Raw Vegetables — a dish I could, and *have,* I told them, made a meal of all by itself — came out of the microwave on time, and perfectly cooked. After wrapping up the show with another announcement about our national bake sale for charity, I displayed the muffins and summoned interns Cliff and Jerry to distribute them.

The studio audience applauded as the trays of muffins were passed around, and again when I told them that tonight's microwave recipes, and also those easy-to-make-from-scratch muffins, were on my Web site. When we went off the air, even my TV director, a woman hardly ever given to compliments, said that this show had been one of our best.

Ironic, considering the drama that was going on in my private life.

As soon as the audience filed out, I untied my chef's apron — an object I had a hard time looking at without thinking of that deliberately salacious seminude photo of Celeste — said quick good-byes to the crew, and hurried outside to my Jeep.

I hadn't lingered back at the studio, but still it was nearly eight forty-five by the time I'd turned off Lankershim Boulevard and onto Ventura Boulevard. The night was clear and cool and traffic was light. There were about a quarter of the number of vehicles that would be on the roads in twelve hours, during the morning rush. Most of those who worked days were at home by now, and people on night shifts were at their jobs.

Usually when I'm on my way home taking my normal route to Santa Monica via Beverly Glen Canyon, I passed the corner of Coldwater Canyon and Ventura Boulevard with barely a glance sideways.

But not tonight.

Without a previous conscious thought, instead of going straight ahead to Beverly Glen, I made a left turn onto Coldwater. I was a hundred yards into one of the three canyons that connected the San Fernando Valley to Los Angeles before I realized what I had done.

What's the matter with me?

Going across "the hill" via Beverly Glen Canyon would take me closer to Santa Monica.

Taking Coldwater Canyon into Beverly Hills meant that I would have to pass Brentwood on the way home.

Once my Jeep was accelerating through the narrow, twisting canyon there was no turning back.

By fifteen minutes after nine I'd reached Sunset Boulevard and turned west. Within a few more minutes I saw the corner of Sunset and Bella Vista up ahead. I knew I should have ignored that intersection. I should have turned south to Montana Avenue and gone straight to my home on

Eleventh Street.

But something made me rotate the steering wheel to the right, onto Bella Vista, at twenty minutes after nine.

In the second block, I felt my heart lurch in my chest and my hands go damp and cold.

A different car was in the carport: a big black SUV. The Lexus I'd seen yesterday was gone. So was the older model Buick that had been in the driveway behind the Lexus.

In its place was Nicholas D'Martino's silver Maserati.

That black SUV must belong to Alec Redding. Either the housekeeper lied about how long he'd be gone, or he came back early.

My heart pounding, I cut the motor and sprinted up the walk.

The light in the carriage lamp above the front door was on. I reached out to press the bell, but my hand stopped inches short of the button because I saw that the front door was standing open a few inches.

Automatically, perhaps a muscle-memory from my years as a police detective's wife, I used my shoulder to push the door open far enough for me to step across the threshold.

I called, "Hello?"

Silence.

Brass wall sconces provided dim illumination, but stronger light poured into the hall from an archway about twenty feet ahead of me on the left.

I took a few steps toward it, when suddenly I realized that I was about to become one of those stupid women in novels or TV shows who go alone into strange houses and through doors that shouldn't be open. Those scenes made me slam a book closed or turn off the TV. Instead of continuing that stupidity, I grabbed my cell phone and spun around to leave. I was a foot from the front door and two numerals into punching nine-one-one when behind me I heard, "Della!"

I turned again and saw Nicholas emerging through the lighted archway.

"Del, get out of here!"

I couldn't move. A fresh surge of fear momentarily paralyzed me.

"Get out, now!"

"No," I said. The same instinct that had led me to this address dissolved my paralysis and compelled me toward the archway.

Nicholas stepped into the middle of the hall, blocking my path. He half whispered, "Don't go in there."

I pushed past him.

And I was immediately sorry that I hadn't

turned and run.

The archway led into a high-ceiled room that had been turned into an elaborate photo studio. Blackout drapes covered the windows. Three rolls of heavy background paper, each three feet wide, in white, in light blue, and in darker blue, hung from the ceiling. Lights on stands faced a roll of white paper that had been unfurled so that it covered not just the wall, but provided an unbroken line on the floor.

Before I could have articulated what I saw, my mind took a flash picture of the scene.

A man lay facedown on the white paper. Blood covered the back of his head and had pooled onto the paper. Vivid red against stark white. An overturned white wooden stool, an edge of the seat stained dark red, lay near the body.

The wound in the man's skull was so deep I didn't need the expertise of a medical examiner to know that Alec Redding was dead.

I was transfixed by the sight in front of me. Then I felt Nicholas's hand on my arm.

"What happened?" I whispered.

"I don't know. I just got here and —" He turned me around to face him. "You don't think *I* did this!"

I wanted to say "No, of course not," but

105

my mouth had gone so dry the words wouldn't come out.

Nicholas let me go and looked at me with pain in his eyes. "Jesus H. Christ. You don't believe me."

"Yes, I do," I said, recovering my senses. "Who else is here in the house?"

"I don't know. This room is the only place I've been."

"How did you get in?" I asked.

"The front door was open."

"Have you called the police?"

"Not yet. I was about to when you came in."

"We've got to call them now."

"I will," he said. "You get out of here."

"I'm not going to leave you," I said emphatically, handing him my cell phone.

But it seemed that someone had already phoned for the police. In the distance, we heard the unmistakable siren of a patrol car.

I knew what was going to happen within the next hour.

A pair of uniformed officers would be first to arrive on the scene. They would see the body. One would secure the area, while the other asked for our identifications, questioned us briefly, and contacted their headquarters — the West Bureau office which had been Mack's base — to request that a medical examiner, SID techs, and homicide detectives be sent to this crime scene.

I hoped that when the detectives in plain clothes arrived, one of them would *not* be Eileen's father, John O'Hara.

The first responders were patrol car officers Downey and Willis. Downey, in his twenties, blond, blue-eyed, and stocky, looked more like a corn-fed Iowa farm boy than he did an urban cop. Willis was black, a few years older than Downey, with a body taut as wire. The expression in his dark eyes suggested automatic skepticism. While Downey, with his easygoing lope of a walk, seemed like a big kid in an LAPD costume, Willis inhabited his uniform as though it were a suit of armor. His default expression appeared to be skepticism. The two went through their routine, and asked the predictable questions.

Officer Willis nodded toward us and said to Downey, "Stay with them. I'll check the grounds."

Willis was still outside when an unmarked LAPD car carrying two West Bureau homicide detectives pulled up in front of the house. Watching from just inside the front door, where Officer Downey had told us to stand, I saw the first detective step out of the vehicle.

It was Lieutenant "Big John" O'Hara.

Nicholas grunted. "Things aren't bad enough. Now the only person who hates me more than my ex-wife does is going to investigate the murder where I'm bound to be a suspect."

11

"Big John" O'Hara earned his soubriquet because he's six feet five and built like a pro ball player. At age fifty, he's still in starting lineup shape. He was halfway up the front walk by the time his partner, Detective Hugh Weaver, seven inches shorter and three years older, maneuvered himself out from behind the steering wheel. Weaver, who I knew had quit smoking a few weeks ago, had put on considerable weight since the last time I saw him.

When John was working a case, he had a classic poker face. That's what Mack had told me about him when they were partners, and there had been a few times since Mack's death when I had seen it for myself. No matter what John found at a crime scene, or what someone told him, on the job his stony expression seldom changed. According to Mack, John's rigid jaw and piercing eyes had caused more than one felon to confess before they began interrogating him. Mack had said, "John never hit anyone in custody; it was the look on his face that made some of them wet their pants and start babbling."

But when he saw me inside that doorway on Bella Vista, his eyebrows shot up in surprise. He wasn't playing poker now. I saw concern in his eyes. "Della — are you all right?"

Then he spotted Nicholas standing behind me. The eyebrows came down and his eyes narrowed. Big John O'Hara was back on the job.

Hugh Weaver, puffing his way up the path, saw me in the group at the front door and gaped. "What the hell's going on?"

Before I could say anything, Officer Downey, who was guarding the entrance, identified himself to John and Weaver.

I saw a light go on across the street. Second floor. A man and a woman came to the window and peered at us. The front door of the next house opened a crack. Someone was there and stared out at the activity in front of number 190 Bella Vista.

While keeping me in his peripheral vision, John asked Downey, "What have we got?"

"Victim's an adult white male. Looks like he died from a blow to the back of his skull, but we didn't roll him over, so I don't know if he has any other wounds. According to these two" — Downey indicated Nicholas and me — "his name is Alec Redding and this is his house. I found them inside when I got here." Downey consulted his notebook. "Their names are —"

"I know their names," John said curtly. "Who else is here?"

"My partner, Officer Willis, searched the house, and didn't find anybody. He's checking the property out back."

A silent signal passed between John and Weaver.

Weaver responded by addressing Officer Downey. "Show me the vic."

"Sure. This way, Detective."

Weaver followed Downey inside the house. He gave me a quizzical look as he went past, but shot Nicholas the hostile glower he usually aimed at members of the press.

As soon as they were out of earshot John said, "Tell me."

I resisted the urge to glance at Nicholas. I was going to tell John the truth, but only as much of it as I had to. Nicholas was right — he was likely to be a suspect — but I didn't believe he had killed Redding and I didn't want to make his situation worse.

"The front door was standing open," I said. "We came in and found Redding on the floor in his studio. We were about to phone the police, but before we could dial nine-one-one we heard a siren and Officer Downey and his partner arrived. Obviously, for the police to be called, someone had to have been in the house with Redding before we got here."

"Not necessarily. A neighbor might have spotted the open door and become alarmed."

"Did you hear the nine-one-one tape? Do you know if it was a man or a woman?" I said.

"I'll ask the questions," John said curtly. He nodded toward the driveway and street. "I see both your cars. Who got here first?"

"I did," Nicholas said. "And Redding was dead when I found him." His voice was strangely without inflection. I looked at Nicholas, but he didn't look at me.

"How did you know he was dead?" John asked.

"I felt his neck for a pulse, but that was just automatic. As soon as I saw him, I knew he was gone." There was no emotion in Nicholas's voice; his tone was the same as though he was answering a stranger who had asked him what time it was.

"What else did you do, D'Martino?"

"Nothing else," Nicholas said.

I stared at him, willing him to show some emotion. He was behaving as though he wasn't really present in this scene.

John turned his attention to me. "What time did you get here?"

"About twenty after nine. Maybe a couple of minutes later."

"You said the front door was open when you arrived?"

"Yes." I realized what question was coming next and I braced for it.

"You're smart enough to know it's not a good sign when somebody's door is standing open. Why did you go in the house instead of locking yourself in your car and calling nine-one-one?"

Because I knew Nicholas was here and knew he was angry and I wanted to stop him from doing something rash.

Of course, I didn't say that. I used the old "exigent circumstances" excuse that allows police to enter a building without a warrant. "I thought I heard a cry — I was afraid someone inside needed help."

Nicholas said softly, "That's not true. Della came in because she saw my car outside."

"And why were *you* here?"

"I wanted to talk to Redding," Nicholas said.

John again turned his focus on me. "It's Thursday night. You usually go right home after the live show. Why did you come here instead?"

"I . . . wanted to talk to Nicholas."

"Don't you both have phones?"

"Mine was off," Nicholas said.

"Della, how did you know D'Martino would be here?"

Nicholas stiffened and shot a pleading look at me. I guessed he was afraid of what I was going to say. I would have preferred that he trusted me to protect him as best I could, but at least I saw life in his eyes again.

"Della, I asked how you knew D'Martino would be here?"

I was saved from answering that loaded question by the sound of another siren. Flashing red and blue lights were racing toward us from Sunset Boulevard.

More of Redding's neighbors were turning on lights and stepping out onto their front walks, watching as an official LAPD van — the medical examiner's — double-parked beside my Jeep.

Just a few yards behind came an SID vehicle that would be carrying the Scientific Investigation techs. That van double-parked behind the ME's.

The medical examiner, Dr. Sydney

Carver, stepped down onto the sidewalk, followed by a young male assistant with a platinum buzz cut. Both carried medical bags.

Behind the two of them, three SID criminalists wearing identifying jackets opened the back of their van and began unloading the paraphernalia they would use to document the murder scene.

As she came closer, I noticed that Sydney Carver had dyed her hair auburn since the last time I'd seen her. Also, she had let it grow out from cropped at the ears to a well-shaped style that touched her chin. With the pewter gray color banished and the longer length, she looked younger than the "I'm-fifty-and-mind-your-own-business" she admitted to. Nothing else about her had changed. Her walk was still brisk, and her strides as long those of a man who was six feet tall. Her face was set in a serious expression, but she was a decidedly more attractive woman now than when she'd been hired as the new ME a year ago.

Nicholas let out a low, appreciative whistle. "Looking good, Sydney."

"Against all odds, I got myself a personal life," she said. Glancing from Nicholas to John, she added in a sardonic tone, "Cops and reporters — natural enemies. I thought next time I saw you two together at a fresh crime scene, one of you would be sprawled inside the chalk lines."

"Maybe next time," John said.

"You wish," Nicholas said.

"Boys, boys, stop the pissing contest," she said. "Big John, what have you got for me tonight?"

Just as the SID techs were coming up the walk with their cameras and their equipment cases, Officer Downey and Hugh Weaver came out of the photo studio and joined us in the crowded doorway. John gestured for Nicholas and me to step back against the wall as he told Downey, "Take Dr. Carver and SID inside."

"Yes, sir."

As Dr. Carver moved past him, John said, "As soon as you can, I need a TOD."

"When I know, you'll know," she said brusquely.

Weaver aimed a thumb over his shoulder toward the back of the house. "I've been outside with Willis. The gate to the alley doesn't have a lock on it — just a latch with a pull cord that lets you open it from either side."

"That must be how the killer got away," I said.

Weaver gave Nicholas a skeptical stare. "*If*

the killer got away," he said.

I was about to protest that, when we heard the sound of a racing motor speeding up the street toward us and looked outside. The new arrival was driving the tan Lexus that I had seen in the carport on Wednesday. It came to a brake-slamming stop at the mouth of the driveway. A woman whose bony arms and legs made her somewhat resemble a marionette leapt out of the car and bolted toward us. Her black hair was still gelled into spikes and her eyes were still heavily outlined in that extreme Cleopatra-style. I wondered if she ever allowed herself to look natural.

"That's Roxanne Redding," I said. "Alec Redding's wife." *Now his widow.*

"What's going on?" she demanded. "What are you people doing in my house?"

John showed her his detective's shield, and introduced only himself and his partner. "Are you Mrs. Redding?"

"Yes." Her eyes were wide with apprehension. "What's happened? Was there a robbery?"

"We don't know yet if anything's been taken. You can help us with that."

"Where's Alec? He was home —"

"I'm sorry, Mrs. Redding. I have some bad news."

An agonized moan arose from her throat. "No! No! Not Alec!" Both hands flew to her mouth, fingers pressed against her lips as though to suppress a scream.

"Is there someone we can call for you, Mrs. Redding? A friend, or a relative who can come over to be with you?"

"No . . . I don't know. . . . Maybe. Wha– what hap–happened?"

"That's not entirely clear yet," John said carefully. "Mrs. Redding, we're going to need you to make an identification." He told Weaver, "Take Mrs. Redding inside. I'm going to put Della and D'Martino into the cars. Her in ours and him in the black-and-white. Tell Willis or Downey to come out here and keep an eye on them. I don't want them talking to each other until we've had a chance to take their statements. Separately."

Weaver nodded, put his hand on Roxanne Redding's arm, and said, "Come with me, ma'am."

She shook off Weaver's hand. "Wait a minute!" She squinted at me. "I recognize you. You were at the luncheon."

"What luncheon?" John asked, but immediately changed course. "Never mind. Save it until I get your story."

Roxanne Redding demanded of John, "Why is this woman here? Has Alec been

118

hurt? I want to see him!"

Weaver took Mrs. Redding's arm again. "Let's go inside."

She gave me a puzzled look, but she didn't say anything more as she allowed Weaver to guide her down the hallway.

Procedure dictated that she identify the body of the man lying on the sheet of background paper. I had recognized the victim as Alec Redding, but a formal identification had to be made, if possible by the next of kin.

"John, I need to phone Eileen and ask her to walk Tuffy," I said. "I don't know how long it will be before I get home tonight."

"I'll do it for you. Give me your cell phone. Phones — both of you. I don't want either of you making any calls until I've had a chance to take your statements."

I was about to protest, but then I saw Nicholas take his cell out of his jacket pocket and hand it to John.

To someone who didn't know Nicholas, it probably seemed that his face was as expressionless as was John's, but I knew better. I saw resignation in his eyes. He was acting like a robot again.

Did he kill Redding?

But my flash of doubt was gone in a moment. I refused to believe that Nicholas had murdered Redding, no matter how angry he was, or how atypically he was behaving right now.

"Della?" John was staring at me, his hand outstretched. I reached into the pocket of my slacks to give him my phone.

"Don't forget to call Eileen for me," I said.

"I won't." John cupped his hand under my elbow and gestured for Nicholas to walk ahead of us down the path.

From inside the house we heard a shriek.

"It sounds like Mrs. Redding identified the body," Nicholas said.

"I don't think this is the best time for sarcasm," I told him.

Officer Downey joined us at the sidewalk. He took the keys to the patrol car out of his pocket and unlocked the rear door.

John said to Nicholas, "Inside."

Nicholas started to follow John's order, but then turned to face him. "I want to hear my Miranda rights."

"I'm *requesting* your compliance," John said. "You're not under arrest."

"I expect to be because I don't intend to tell you one damn thing. As soon as we get to West Bureau I'm going to invoke my right to call an attorney."

I said, "Nicholas, stop it. You didn't kill Redding."

Nicholas's eyes were cold and distant. "How do you know I didn't? You weren't there."

"You want to play hardball, fine," John said. "Nicholas D'Martino, you have the right to remain silent. Anything you say can and will be used against you in a court of law. . . ."

"John, please don't do this," I said.

John ignored me and continued. "You have the right to an attorney. If you cannot afford an attorney, one will be provided for you. . . ."

As I stood on the sidewalk watching John finish his legal speech and Nicholas climb into the backseat of the patrol car, my heart ached.

Nicholas had deliberately provoked John, forcing him to treat Nicholas like a criminal. He was acting guilty, but nothing short of his looking me in the eyes and confessing would convince me that Nicholas had killed Alec Redding.

I believed I knew what he was doing.

And for whom he was doing it.

"Della?" John's voice broke into my thoughts. "Get into my car. Please." He glanced back at Redding's house. "I don't know how much time we have to be alone but I want you to tell me everything you know."

He opened the passenger door for me.

I got in, while desperately trying to decide how much of the truth I could tell John. Certainly the things that he would easily discover on his own, but I would try to omit the one detail that might convince John of Nicholas's guilt and keep him from widening his investigation.

When Eileen was a teenager and left something out of an explanation she was giving me, I called that "telling the truth, but with an asterisk."

I wasn't proud of what I was about to do.

12

John got in behind the wheel and said, "How well did you know Alec Redding?"

"I didn't know him. I met him for the first and only time last Friday at the Hollywood Film Society luncheon."

"How well did D'Martino know him?"

"I'm sure they never met."

"Then what was he doing in Redding's house, and why did you come looking for him here?"

"Redding is a well-known portrait photographer," I said. "He shot a portfolio for Nicholas's daughter, who wants to be an actress. Maybe —"

"D'Martino has a daughter?"

"Yes. She's eighteen, a beautiful girl. Maybe Nicholas came here tonight to pay him for the photographs." That sounded lame, even to me, but John didn't show any reaction.

"Did you know he had a teenage daughter?"

"Not until recently." I related to John what Nicholas had told me about his long-ago divorce, and that the girl had been living in Europe with her mother, but had decided to come to Los Angeles to get to know her father.

"And to be an actress." I heard cynicism in John's tone. "Did Redding come on to the girl, or force himself on her?"

John had lasered in on the one area I wanted to get him away from: photographs.

"I doubt there was anything like that," I said. "The man's wife works with him. Liddy says she does the lighting for his portraits."

"Liddy knows them?"

"Casually," I said. "I think he took Liddy's professional photos. Anyway, she introduced Nicholas's daughter, Celeste, to both the Reddings when we were all at the Hollywood Film Society luncheon last week."

Before John could pursue the subject of Celeste any further, I said, "Look, John, unless Redding's death turns out to be the result of a burglary that went bad, the answer is bound to be somewhere in Redding's relationships. I don't know anything about his personal life, and I can't imagine that Nicholas does either, but think about this: Maybe his wife hated him and her grief tonight is an act. You know how often the killer is the victim's spouse. That's the first person every detective looks at, and for good reason. But if it wasn't his wife, maybe he owed money to mobsters and couldn't pay."

"Oh, come on now. That's a pretty long reach."

"Don't be so dismissive. Think about it. Unless somebody's killed by a stranger, statistically, aren't the four main motives for murder love, money, a crime cover-up, or revenge?"

"What are you doing, taking night school courses in detecting?"

"I'll ignore that crack. Think about this: Redding might have been having an affair with a married woman. Her husband could have found out about it and killed him in a jealous rage. Unless Dr. Carver finds another cause of death, from what Officer Downey said it seems as though Redding was killed by being struck on the back of his head with a stool. That doesn't sound premeditated, does it? More like a jealous rage, someone lashing out in the heat of the moment. I can't imagine that whoever killed

Redding brought the stool in with him — or her — intending to use it as a murder weapon. You should start digging deeply into Alec Redding's personal life."

John's poker face was back in place.

"You're talking too much, and not enough," he said quietly.

Okay, you're playing poker, so I'm going to bluff.

I manufactured a tone of righteous anger. "Is anything I've said illogical? You know the world is full of unhappy wives and jealous husbands and people who gamble more than they can afford to lose. You've got a lot of investigating to do!"

John was about to reply when movement behind me caught his eye. I turned to see Sydney Carver coming toward us, removing her latex gloves.

John immediately opened his car door and got out to meet her. I followed him.

"What do you know?" he asked the ME.

"My TOD guesstimate — based on his liver temp and postmortem lividity and the fact that he's just now going into rigor — is that your vic was killed close to nine o'clock tonight. I can't be sure until I do the autopsy, but those are pretty reliable signs."

"And cause of death?"

"Again, this is preliminary, but it appears

to be blunt force trauma to the back of the head. I won't swear to it until I can take a look inside, and get the results of a tox screen, but you can get started on that assumption. According to the wife he didn't have any medical problems and wasn't on medication. Not even Viagra. I didn't take her word for it, so I looked. The only pills in their medicine cabinets were hers, for birth control."

"Thanks, Syd."

She nodded and started toward the ME van. I watched her assistant wheel a gurney down the driveway. On it was a black body bag.

John turned to me. "Time of death rules you out."

"Thanks a lot," I said dryly.

His jaw stayed firm, but I saw a hint of softness in his eyes. "I didn't mean that the way it sounded. But since you were on the scene, I'll need your statement. I have to stay here and talk to Mrs. Redding, if she's up to it. Will you go over to Butler Avenue and write the statement?"

The West Bureau station on Butler.

"And be careful what you put in it," John added. I didn't miss the warning in his words.

"I'll go as soon as the ME van moves. It's

blocking my Jeep. What about Nicholas?"

"I'll have a uniform drive him over. I'm serious about not wanting you to talk to each other before I have your sworn statements."

"All right. Did you reach Eileen?"

"Yeah. She's at your house and said not to worry. She'll take care of Tuff."

"That's a relief. I see the ME's van is moving, so I'll get going. May I have my phone back?"

John shook his head. "Sorry. Not until the techs go through your call log, and D'Martino's."

"We have nothing to hide," I said.

John started up the front walk. "If that's true, then you're the only two people in the world who don't," he said.

The medical examiner's van made a U-turn and headed down Bella Vista toward Sunset Boulevard. I walked toward my newly accessible Jeep, but looked over at the patrol car. All I could see was the back of Nicholas's head leaning against the rear seat. Officer Downey stood guard on the sidewalk.

As I made my own U-turn, I saw that Redding's neighbors — one or two in front of nearly every house on the block, with a few peering out through windows — were giving what they could see of the proceedings their rapt attention.

Most of the houses had satellite dishes on their roofs — metal disks that brought much of the world right into their homes. But in spite of having more than 150 channels to choose from, they seemed to prefer the real reality of neighborhood drama to the fake "reality" that came through their receivers.

I felt the same kind of contempt for them that I feel for people who slow their cars in order to rubberneck at crash scenes. Years ago I was the car just behind a fatal collision: a convertible T-boned by an SUV that ran a red light. So much blood . . . I never wanted to see carnage like that again.

Half a block above Sunset Boulevard I saw a dark van with antenna rigging on top turn up Bella Vista. On the side, in bright yellow letters against dark blue, it said "Channel 4."

The first of what was certain to be a parade of TV cameras had come to join the watchers.

As I turned east onto Sunset Boulevard, the direction that would ultimately take me to the West Bureau Station on Butler Avenue, I forgot about nosy neighbors and TV news and began looking for a restaurant.

I wasn't hungry.

Restaurants had working pay telephones. It had been a long time since I'd seen a public phone on the street that hadn't been destroyed by vandals, and I needed to make a call before I got to the cop shop.

13

There were no restaurants on Sunset Boulevard near Bella Vista, so I had to go down into Westwood Village. From a wall phone at the first restaurant I saw, I dialed the office of criminal defense attorney Olivia Wayne and reached the answering service. I gave the operator my name, and said it was an emergency. In less than twenty seconds the operator connected me to Olivia.

As was her usual practice of eschewing small talk, her first words were, "What kind of trouble are you in?"

"Not me. It's Nicholas D'Martino. He may be charged with murder, but he didn't do it."

"First, give me the bottom line. Details later."

"Nicholas and I went, separately, to the home of photographer Alec Redding and found him dead. Murdered. Before we could call nine-one-one, we heard a police siren and two uniformed officers arrived."

"So someone else called it in." She was quiet for a moment. "You said *Nick* is under suspicion. If you both were there, why not you, too?"

"The preliminary time of death rules me out. I was doing a live TV show and couldn't have got there in time to kill him, even if I'd had a motive, which I don't. Nicholas arrived at Redding's house before I did, and he's refusing to cooperate with the police. He insisted John O'Hara — he and his partner are the homicide detectives on the case — read him the Miranda warning."

I heard a grunt of disgust on her end of the line. Then: "Do you remember a few months ago when you gave me a one-dollar retainer?"

"Yes, of course."

"You haven't dismissed me as your attorney, so our relationship is still in place. Anything you tell me is confidential. We won't discuss it in this call, but I got it when you said that *you* have no motive. Where are you and Nick right now?"

"I'm at a pay phone on Westwood Boulevard. When I left Redding's a few minutes ago, Nicholas was sitting in the back of a patrol car. John O'Hara told me to go to the Butler Avenue station to write my statement. An officer is going to drive Nicholas there. Listen, Olivia, I know in my heart that Nicholas didn't do it."

"That's sweet as sugar," she said in a tone laden with sarcasm, "but I can't put your heart on the witness stand. I'll meet you at Butler as quick as I can." As usual, dispensing with pleasantries, she hung up.

I've always thought that the building housing the West Los Angeles police station at 1663 Butler Avenue, just south of Santa Monica Boulevard, had an oddly tropical look, that it should be surrounded by swaying palm trees with leafy fronds fluttering in the breeze. It's painted in beige and cream, with its entrance framed in red tiles as bright as hibiscus blossoms, which is a color scheme that strikes me as more appropriate to Hawaii than to this gray green and brown section of West Los Angeles.

The facade of the police station may have suggested fruit drinks with paper umbrellas stuck in them, but none of the two- and three-story apartment houses in the neighborhood looked festive. The general atmosphere was one of younger tenants on their way up, or older ones whose dreams hadn't been realized.

Law enforcement had two parking lots on

Butler, one next to the station house, but that was closed off with an iron gate. In the lot across the street, that also contained the division's private gas pump, I spotted three or four empty patrol cars. The rest of the fleet was probably out on the streets, cruising for criminals.

I drove a few yards past the station's entrance, turned right at the corner, and found a parking place on Iowa Avenue.

In the time since I had been here last, the department had installed an ATM machine inside the building. The big sign out front advertising its location was impossible to miss. I've never used an ATM because of the general lack of security around them, but I was pretty sure that this ATM was the safest one in California, if not the entire country.

Tom Leland, the silver-haired desk sergeant on duty, was a man I'd known for years, all the time I was Mack's wife. After his initial expression of surprise at seeing me in front of him, and at night, he said, "Hey, Della, what brings you here? Everything okay?"

"I stumbled onto a crime scene. John O'Hara asked me to come by and write a statement."

He gestured toward the detectives' squad

room. "You know the way. Take any empty desk. Come ask if you need anything."

"Thanks. And, Tom, someone's coming here to meet me. Her name is Olivia Wayne and she's —"

"I know who she is." His warm smile vanished. "I'll send her in."

After eleven o'clock at night the detectives' squad room was nearly deserted. A boyish man in his early thirties, unshaven, wearing a sleeveless sweatshirt and a shoulder holster, sat typing at a computer in a far corner of the room. He didn't look up when I came in.

A man and a woman at facing desks against the wall and nearest the table with the coffeemaker on it had their heads bent over stacks of file folders. The man appeared to be in his sixties, and looked vaguely familiar. Then I realized I'd met him five years ago, when Mack and I gave a Christmas party at our house for his detective colleagues. He shot me a quizzical look, gave a quick nod of recognition, and went back to concentrating on the files. I'd never seen the woman before. She seemed young enough to be his daughter, but judging from the holstered weapon hanging over the dark jacket on the back of her chair she must be his partner. She gave me a brief glance, didn't seem to find anything about me of interest, and returned to reading a file. I had the thought that when I was a bride, most of the police officers and detectives I met were older than I. Now half of them looked too young to carry a badge.

The pair of desks against the wall on the opposite side of the room had been John and Mack's. John still sat there because I could see the framed photo of his wife, Shannon, and their daughter, Eileen. I supposed that Hugh Weaver had the facing desk, but there were no pictures on it. I'd heard Weaver had been married and divorced more than once, but I knew him to be essentially a loner. John was probably his closest friend. Maybe his only one. In spite of Weaver's dyspeptic personality and his former habit of grinding out his cigarette butts in the grass on my front lawn, I'd become fond of him. No one would ever describe Weaver as charming, but in his work he was smart and, whatever his personal feelings about a suspect, he could be fair.

I chose an empty desk in the center of the room, and settled in the chair that faced the entrance.

It didn't take long to write my statement because I kept it strictly to the immediate facts: I'd arrived at Redding's door at approximately nine twenty PM, found it open, went inside, and discovered Redding lying facedown on the floor of his photographic studio with blood on the back of his head and an overturned stool nearby with what looked like bloodstains on its edge. Nicholas D'Martino had arrived shortly before I did. Nicholas checked for a pulse to be sure that Alec Redding was dead, but neither of us touched anything else in the room and backed out of it immediately. I added that we were about to dial nine-one-one when we heard a patrol car's siren. Officers Downey and Willis arrived. We gave them our names and contact information and told them how we happened to discover the body.

The statement was true, as far as it went.

The only possible wobbler was my saying Nicholas had arrived "shortly" before me. Had he got there one minute earlier? Or ten? Or . . . ? To myself, I had to admit that I didn't know. But however much longer he was there in the house, I refused to believe he had killed Redding. I wished I'd thought to feel the hood of his car when I arrived. If it had still been warm . . . But I'd been in too much of a hurry to think to do that.

I'd just finished reading the statement

over, dating it, and signing my name at the bottom of the page, when I heard footsteps and looked up to see Olivia Wayne coming into the squad room. A head-turning blonde with long legs, she may have been good-looking enough to be on the cover of a *Sports Illustrated* swimsuit issue, but she radiated an attitude so intimidating that I would have bet muggers crossed the street to avoid her. Nicholas had referred to her once as "Xena, the warrior princess." Except that she didn't have dark hair, didn't wear leather and metal, and didn't brandish a sword, I thought it was a pretty accurate comparison.

Olivia closed the distance between us in a few strides, pulled a chair from the nearest empty desk, and sat down close to me.

Indicating the sheet of paper in my hand, she said, "Your statement?"

"Yes."

Olivia took it, read it, folded it into quarters, and slipped the page into her handbag.

"No statement until I hear everything. Start with how well you and Nick knew Alec Redding, and why you went to his house tonight."

I glanced about and saw that the unshaven young man at the computer was still typing, but the man and woman were watching us.

"Forget them," Olivia said. "Give me the story, but keep your voice down."

I started by telling her that Nicholas had an eighteen-year-old daughter.

Her eyebrows rose and a slight smile flickered at the corner of her lips. "That studly Sicilian is full of surprises."

I repeated what Nicholas had told me about his divorce, and told her about my meeting Celeste, Celeste's later meeting Alec Redding, his offering to shoot photos of her for her acting portfolio, and the resulting seminude shot with the pie that had enraged her mother and Nicholas.

"How do you know the mother?"

"She came to my house and accused me of being responsible for Celeste meeting Redding, when actually Celeste and I met Redding at the same time — at the Film Society luncheon."

"Was she mad enough to commit murder?"

"I can't give you an opinion on that because I've only met her once. She was upset because she thinks that picture of Celeste, if it gets into print or on the Internet, will harm her plan to marry a man with a title and a conservative family."

"What kind of title? CEO or Duke of

Windsor?"

"Prince. According to Celeste, he's descended from a princess of Bavaria."

Olivia shrugged dismissively. "Sounds like Eurotrash. So, O'Hara thinks Nick killed Redding to get the picture of his daughter?"

I shook my head. "John doesn't know about the photo. I didn't tell him, and Nicholas certainly won't. If John has interviewed the wife — Roxanne Redding — she might have told him about it, but she was so upset, or seemed to be, that John wasn't sure he'd be able to talk to her tonight."

"Do you think Nick is acting like he is, deliberately throwing suspicion on himself, in order to protect his ex?"

"No, I think it's to protect Celeste. He might be afraid that Celeste killed Redding."

"Why?"

"I don't know. From the expression on her face in that picture she certainly wasn't posing for it reluctantly. And, I think the way she posed, with a chef's apron barely covering her, and holding a pie — of all things — that she was mocking *me.*"

"Because you're Daddy's main squeeze?"

"I sure I'm his *only* squeeze," I said.

"Don't get prickly, Della. Since he's been with you, he seems to have lost his playboy ways. The first time I met you, I saw something nice in his eyes I'd never seen before, so whatever you're doing, you're doing it best."

At that moment, a man appeared at the entrance to the squad room and came toward us. He was alone.

I whispered, "That's John O'Hara." I felt my stomach muscles clench with apprehension. *Where's Nicholas?*

Olivia and I stood up to face John. She handed him her card. "I'm Olivia Wayne, representing Nicholas D'Martino. Where is my client?"

14

"How did you get here so fast?" John asked.

"On the wings of justice," Olivia Wayne said.

John ignored that and focused on me. "Did you finish your statement?"

Olivia said, "Della's my client, too. No statements until I've been allowed to confer with both of my clients."

"Look, Ms. Wayne. I'm investigating a murder —"

"And I'm sure you're doing it brilliantly," she said. "Have you booked D'Martino?"

"Not yet. Depending on the case we put together, it's possible he could soon be charged with murder, but right now he's been brought in for questioning. Unless he starts cooperating, we'll put him under arrest for obstruction of justice. At the moment he's even refusing to confirm his name and tell us his address."

"And you couldn't beat it out of him? A

great big, strong man like you?"

"Cut the crap! We don't do that." I saw the effort John was making to control his temper.

"Of course you don't." She softened her tone. "Look, Detective O'Hara, it's late and I interrupted a very pleasant evening to come rushing down here. When I've had the opportunity to speak to my clients, I'm sure we can find a way to protect their rights and also be helpful to your investigation. So, let's play nice, shall we? Let me talk to D'Martino alone first, and then we'll have a conference. Deal?"

At ten minutes to midnight, the detective partners had reduced the pile of files they were going over by two-thirds, and the young man who had been typing at the computer had finished whatever he was doing and departed.

While I was alert for John and Olivia to come through the door, I'd read every one of the "Wanted" circulars tacked up on the big cork Announcements Board between the front windows, had gone through a two-page recruiting flyer, and was now trying to concentrate on a slickly printed brochure about joint community and police department activities and opportunities for volunteerism.

Just as I was on the last page, reading the name of the printing company that had produced the pamphlet, John came to the entrance to the squad room and gestured for me to follow him.

Escorting me down a hallway, John said, "Liddy called you."

"Here?"

"On your cell. I answered. She'd heard about Redding on the eleven o'clock news. I asked her why she was calling you about it. She told me she took you and D'Martino's daughter to a Hollywood luncheon where you two met Redding. Apparently she doesn't know anything else."

"Didn't she ask why you were answering my phone?"

"That was the first thing out of her mouth when she heard my voice. She wanted to know if you were all right. I told her you were, that you were giving me some background information. I said you'd call her tomorrow."

"Did your tech person look through my phone log?"

"I did. I saw your calls to D'Martino. And you got a call from his cell at seven forty-one tonight. No message."

"I was on the air."

"Yesterday afternoon you dialed Alec Redding's number. The duration was too short for you to have talked to him, or left a message. Why did you call him?"

I felt my cheeks grow hot and hoped that John couldn't see that in the ugly fluorescent lighting in the hallway. "I was thinking about having some professional pictures taken," I said. "Now, may I have my phone back?"

He looked at me thoughtfully for a moment. I was sure he knew I wasn't telling the truth. He didn't say anything, but until the murder of Alec Redding was solved, my fib was going to lie between us like an unexploded bomb.

John fished my cell phone out of his jacket pocket and handed it to me.

Hoping to distract him by going on the offensive, I said, "You could have asked me for it, instead of demanding I turn it over."

"Would you have given it to me?" he asked.

"Certainly."

"Would D'Martino have?"

I couldn't answer that. And I didn't have to because we'd reached the first of the interrogation rooms. He opened the door and ushered me inside.

Nicholas was sitting at a rectangular wooden table that would have been no thing of beauty when it was new several decades ago, and had since aged badly.

Olivia and Nicholas sat together on one long side, with Hugh Weaver at the far end, next to Nicholas. I was relieved to see that Nicholas wasn't handcuffed.

John indicated that I sit opposite Weaver, and near Olivia. He placed himself across from Nicholas and Olivia.

My chair was hard and uncomfortable, and I felt a sharp splinter stabbing the back of my right knee. I reached down, broke it off, and placed it on the tabletop.

Indicating the splinter, I said, "I'm going to report this seating to Amnesty International."

Silence greeted my attempt at humor.

I smiled at Nicholas, who nodded in response. He looked tired.

In front of Olivia was a sheet of paper with handwriting on it. Next to that sheet was the page she had taken from me. I recognized it immediately because of the creases where she had folded it into quarters.

"Your two statements match," Olivia said. "At least from the time you discovered Redding's body."

Weaver said, "D'Martino says he got to the vic's house two minutes before you came in. Prior to that, he claims he was at

146

home with his daughter. We haven't been able to reach the daughter for confirmation." Weaver's tone dripped with sarcasm.

"She's eighteen, probably out with her friends," Olivia said lightly. "You can ask her tomorrow, in my presence."

"Eighteen's old enough she doesn't need a babysitter to talk to us," Weaver said.

"She will be discussing my client. You interview her with me, or we'll let a judge decide, and that will likely delay your interview by several days. That's my offer."

Scowling, John said, "I want her here at nine AM."

"You're not going to question her *here* at all," Olivia said. "I'm not going to subject an innocent young girl to the intimidation of being questioned in a police station. You can talk to her tomorrow, in my office. Noon. The address is on the card I gave you, Detective O'Hara."

"To make sure he doesn't coach the girl, D'Martino can stay here tonight, as the guest of the city of Los Angeles," John said.

"No way, Jose. My client is not under arrest."

"That can change," Weaver said.

I felt like a spectator at a tennis match, my attention swinging from one speaker to the other. But I kept silent in order to remain in the room.

Olivia ignored Weaver's implied threat and spoke directly to John. "I have another arrangement in mind. My client can stay in my guest room tonight. I will guarantee that he has no contact with his daughter, or with anyone except myself, before you talk to the girl tomorrow."

Nicholas sat up straight, his face animated for the first time since I'd come into the room. "No," he said. "If I don't come home Celeste will wonder about what's happened to me. And I don't want her staying in the apartment alone."

"She can stay with me," I said.

"No!" John and Weaver barked at me simultaneously.

"Come on, fellas," Olivia said. "She's old enough to vote, join the army, get married without parental consent, so she's old enough to stay by herself tonight. I will phone her later, introduce myself, and make arrangements to pick her up tomorrow. You have my guarantee as an officer of the court that I won't tell her what D'Martino said, and father and daughter will not have a private conversation before you interview her. Good enough?"

In the end, they agreed that it had to be good enough. John didn't look happy about it, and I saw Weaver patting his jacket pockets for the cigarettes he no longer carried.

A few minutes later I climbed into my Jeep and fired up the motor. With Eileen looking after Tuffy and Emma, I knew I didn't have to go home immediately.

I drove to the next block and then worked my way north to Wilshire Boulevard. At Wilshire, I turned east, toward the Olympia Grand Hotel.

Where Nicholas's ex-wife and her hemophiliac prince were staying.

And where, I suspected, I would find Celeste.

15

Guessing that she probably called herself by
her maiden name, Tanis Fontaine, I gave
the clerk at the reception desk my name and
asked him to connect me to her suite. At
first, he balked, citing the late hour. I assured him it was important. He looked
doubtful, but phoned upstairs, apologized,
and recited what I had told him. Presumably he was granted permission because I
was put through.

The voice that answered on the first ring
was male.

"And vat does your call at this hour concern?"

His voice was light — pale, if I were to as-
sign a shade to it — and with a slight German accent.

Aware that the reception clerk was trying
to listen, I moved as far away as the telephone cord would allow, turned my back
on him, and kept my voice low.

"I am sorry to have disturbed you tonight —"

"To be precise, it is now morning."

I visualized a man in a gray military uniform asking for my "papers," but pushed the image aside. "*Last* night now, a photographer named Alec Redding was killed."

"Ah." Then silence.

"I believe it would be helpful to Ms. Fontaine, her daughter, and perhaps yourself if I could speak to you before you're questioned by the police."

Another silence, but a brief one.

"Come up. The Presidential Suite. Take the private elevator."

"Yes, I will."

I remembered where the private elevator was: on the far side of the public elevators, separated from them by a potted tree. When the hotel's previous owner lived here, it was the way up to his apartment. I guessed that the space had been renamed "The Presidential Suite."

The inside of the elevator was as I remembered it: polished brass, a mirrored back wall, and a bench padded in dark red velvet for anyone who needed to sit down during the fifteen-floor ride.

When the elevator stopped, it opened onto a corridor painted in a shade I would call

151

Pippin apple green and lighted with a succession of small brass and crystal chandeliers. Across the hallway, directly facing the elevator, were a pair of polished oak double doors with "Presidential Suite" in brass letters affixed to them. To my left, perhaps fifty feet down the corridor, I saw another pair of double doors. Probably another suite, but before I had time to speculate further, a door to the Presidential Suite opened.

I was greeted by a man in his sixties, with close-cropped silver hair, gray eyebrows over dark eyes, and a soft pink complexion. He was incongruously — for the late hour — dressed in a black frock coat and gray trousers. The prince was considerably older than I had imagined.

Then the man spoke.

"This way, madame."

The accent was British. I realized my mistake. I had been admitted by a butler, not a prince. Mickey Jordan, owner of the Better Living Channel, has an English butler at his house in Beverly Hills: Maurice, pronounced "Morris." I should have registered the similar manner of dress. Over time, Maurice had begun to smile when he saw me at the Jordans' front door. I doubted that I would know this man long enough for that congeniality.

While the interior of the private elevator had remained the same, the suite had been redecorated. In keeping with the Forest of Arden theme below, the walls were hung with hunting tapestries and the electric wall sconces were carved to look like tree branches. The public rooms of the suite now resembled the interior of an English castle — or one of the sets from that old musical, *Camelot.*

I followed the butler deeper into the suite and saw a slender man rise from a green couch. Narrow face. Almost colorless blond hair, thinning, cut into a fringe above a high forehead. Intense — no, more like *steely* — pale blue eyes set in a pasty white complexion. He appeared to be in his mid- to late thirties, which would make him about ten years younger than Tanis. In spite of his less-than-robust appearance, he was an attractive man with fine features.

He extended his hand to me. "Frau Carmichael. I am Fredric von Hoffner. Here in America, ve can ignore titles."

I took his hand. His skin was soft — he had probably never done anything remotely resembling manual labor in his life — but his grip was surprisingly firm.

"How do you do," I said. "I was hoping to find Tanis and Celeste here."

"They are in their bedrooms, asleep for some time. I prefer not to disturb them."

His accent was definitely German, but it wasn't heavy. I guessed that he had been educated in England.

Fredric von Hoffner — *a prince by any other name* — gestured for me to take a gilt-framed straight-back chair opposite the couch.

"May I offer you something to drink? Perhaps a port? Or tea?"

"Nothing, thank you."

"Port for me, Mordue."

With barely a nod, the butler went to a wet bar on the back wall of the room. I saw two doors in the far wall, perhaps leading to bedrooms, and a third door next to the bar. All were closed.

"You said you came to discuss something about the man who vas killed?" Von Hoffner's manner toward me was cordial, but guarded, his features composed in a bland expression.

"The man was a photographer named Alec Redding." I wasn't sure how much he knew. Tanis had said he was a hemophiliac and that she was concerned about the effect of stress on him, implying that his health was fragile. I chose my words carefully.

"Redding took the portfolio pictures of Celeste."

He produced a short grunt of disgust. "You are referring to that ridiculous picture vit a pie? Children can be most foolish. Vy do you bring this up?"

Mordue carried a silver tray with a small crystal glass of port on it and placed the glass in front of his employer. "Your highness."

"The police are certain to find out about that photograph," I said. "And when they do, they may think of it as a possible motive for Redding's murder."

Von Hoffner took a sip of the ruby red port and shrugged. "Vy are you telling me this?"

"Where were you and Tanis this evening around nine o'clock? And Celeste? Where was she?"

"Ah, so that is vat you think?" His lips curved into a smile, but there was no sign of amusement in his eyes. He said, "Mordue."

"Yes, your highness?"

"My fiancée, her daughter, and I were here all evening, playing cards, ya?"

"Yes, your highness." There was not a flicker of expression on the butler's face.

"So, you see, Frau Carmichael, this matter is no concern of ours." He stood. "Now, if you vill not think me rude, ve shall say good night, ya?"

"You were all here, together?"

"Just so. Mordue, ring for the elevator for my guest."

I kept my face as devoid of expression as was that butler's. I did not believe "his highness," nor his robotic servant.

"Good night," I said. "Perhaps we'll see each other again while you're in Los Angeles."

"Ah, I regret, no. Ve vill be leaving tonight for Vienna."

As I went down in the private elevator, my heart was pounding. If von Hoffner, Tanis, and Celeste — backed up by the butler — presented a united alibi, it would be terrible for Nicholas, who had said that Celeste was with *him.*

There was not the slightest doubt in my mind that von Hoffner was lying to me. But I was sure Nicholas had lied, too.

Where *were* they all last night when Redding was murdered?

Had Tanis, Celeste, and the prince been together in the suite? I doubted it.

Maybe all three of them were innocent of murder, but for Nicholas's sake, I had to find a way to keep them from leaving the

country until the truth of their whereabouts
was known.

16

I paid the valet parking fee, my Jeep was brought to the hotel's front entrance, and I swung out of the long, curving driveway and onto Wilshire Boulevard. It took only a few minutes to find a parking space on Wilshire near a streetlight where I felt it was safe to stop and make a call from my cell phone.

Unfortunately, I hadn't thought to ask Olivia for her home number, so again I had to go through the routine with her answering service, give my name, and wait to be put through.

When Olivia came on the line, it was clear she was irritated. "Della, if you're calling to say good night to Nick, I can't let you do that. I can't have the slightest whiff of collusion —"

"Oh, *please,* Olivia. This isn't high school. I have information you need to know, something that could be bad for Nicholas."

"What is it?" Her tone was professional now.

"Nicholas isn't allowed to talk to Celeste," I said, "but I wasn't forbidden to do it. I had a hunch that she hadn't gone home to his place, but was probably at the Olympia Grand Hotel with her mother and the mother's fiancé. I was right."

"What did she have to say?"

"I didn't get to talk to her. Prince Fredric von Hoffner, her mother's fiancé, told me that mother and daughter were asleep. When I brought up the death of Alec Redding and asked him where Tanis and Celeste were last night around nine o'clock, he immediately said the three of them spent the evening together, in the suite playing cards."

"The three-way alibi? How convenient," Olivia said dryly.

"The English butler, Mordue, confirmed it. But then, he would."

"What's Mordue's full name?"

"I don't know. But the three of them, and I'm sure Mordue, plan to fly back to Vienna tonight. You've got to stop them, Olivia."

"I can't, but O'Hara could. He'll have to convince the DA's office to find a judge who'll issue an order preventing them from leaving the country, at least for a few days. Before our government starts slugging it out

159

with his consulate. What's his home country?"

"Austria, I think; they live in Vienna. But he also has a chateau in Gstaad, Switzerland. Celeste says he presents himself as a prince from a royal line in old Bavaria. So he's probably a citizen of Austria, Switzerland, or Germany."

"I'll call O'Hara as soon as we're off the line."

"In case he's left the West LA station, I'll give you his cell and his home number. Don't tell him how you found out about their plans to leave the US."

Olivia snorted a laugh. "So you don't want O'Hara to know you slipped the leash and went detecting?"

"I'd rather not. He'll think I'm just trying to help Nicholas, and he may not move quickly enough."

"Good point. We can do the full-disclosure bit after we've ruined their plans for leaving the country."

I gave her John's numbers. She said she'd get right on it, and disconnected.

When I finally made it home, only Tuffy was at the door to greet me, with a full-body wag. There is nothing in the world that makes me feel better after a long, stress-filled day or night than the unconditional love of a pet. I scratched beneath his ears, and stroked his silky face and head.

Straightening up, I saw Eileen had left a note for me on the hall table. She said she'd gone to bed because she had to get up to be at our retail shop early to interview a new supplier and she added, "Aunt Liddy called and Mother called. They'll both phone you again tomorrow."

As it turned out, my two closest female friends didn't call in the morning; they appeared. I opened the front door to Liddy wearing navy blue slacks and a white knit fisherman's sweater, and carrying a garment bag, and Shannon in an emerald green blouse and a black pantsuit.

Although we'd talked on the phone, I hadn't seen Shannon O'Hara for almost a month, and it was wonderful to see how good she looked. The psychotropic medications she was taking had kept her stable for nearly a year. One of the side effects of the pills was that she had gained some weight, but not enough to ruin her Pre-Raphaelite beauty. She'd always reminded me of a painting by Rossetti, specifically *Fazio's Mistress,* the portrait of the redheaded woman at the mirror, braiding her wet hair so that it would dry into a crimped halo around her face. Shannon's resemblance to the famous painting was even more pronounced this morning with her mass of bright copper hair hanging loose around her shoulders.

I'd only had a few hours sleep, but I was awake early enough to shower, dress, take Tuffy for a walk, and have some breakfast. I was about to have a third mug of coffee when Liddy and Shannon arrived. Tuffy greeted them enthusiastically, and after the ritual of petting, like the old friends they were, they settled themselves in the kitchen. I poured coffee and moved the half-and-half and a bowl of sweeteners to the center of the table.

Liddy hung her garment bag on the wall hook that also held Tuffy's leash. "Are you going to an audition?" I asked.

"No. It's a skirt suit and heels, and some accessories, in case I have to look more businesslike."

"For what?"

"Investigating," Shannon said. "But don't tell Johnny I'm in this with you."

"Wait a minute, you two —"

"I heard about Alec's murder on TV last night and called you right away," Liddy said. "John answered your phone, so I figured it was something serious. I called Shannon to find out if she knew anything."

"I didn't — not then. But later, Johnny had hardly come in the door when he got a call from somebody named Wayne —"

"Olivia Wayne," I said. "She's the criminal lawyer who's representing Nicholas."

"Johnny was really angry," Shannon said. "I practically saw steam coming out of his ears. He barked into the phone that he didn't want anyone interfering in his case, and he mumbled something about Nicholas D'Martino. Naturally, I couldn't stop listening *then.* When he got off the phone he was red in the face. All he would tell me is that your Nick is 'a person of interest' — that ridiculous phrase! — in the new murder he's investigating. He told me to go to bed, that he'd be up soon, but he had to make some phone calls first. I asked, 'Who are you going to phone at this hour?' He said it was police business. I shouldn't worry about it. Hell, he was treating me so cautiously you would have thought I was still nuts."

I winced. "Shannon, you're not —"

"Hey, let the mental patient make fun of herself. It's healthy. But thanks for sticking up for me, even to *me.*" She squeezed my hand with affection. "Anyway, as soon as Johnny shut himself up in the den, I called Liddy."

"We decided that if Nick is in trouble then

we're here for you," Liddy said. "Shannon phoned this morning as soon as John left, so the minute Bill was out the door, I left to pick her up."

"Bring us up-to-date," Shannon said.

Liddy added, "And tell us what can we do to help."

17

"You can help me, and I want to tell you everything that happened. But there's one thing I don't want John to know about, at least not yet, because it might make him focus more rigidly on Nicholas." I looked at Shannon. "Are you willing to keep something from him for now?"

"You really believe that Nick isn't guilty?" Shannon asked.

"Nick is *not* guilty. There's a possible motive John is sure to discover, but I hope it will be after he starts investigating other people. He won't be happy until he's caught the real killer."

"Since it's for John's good, too" — she made a zipping motion across her lips — "I promise."

Liddy said, "You have my promise, too, even though the only things Bill investigates are dental cavities and gum disease."

I picked up the story, detailing Tanis

Fontaine's arrival at my house, enraged by a picture of Celeste posed nearly nude with just a chef's apron and a pie.

Shannon's green eyes were wide. "A *pie?*"

"Isn't that a modern twist on the old pie-in-your-face stunt?" Liddy said, grinning.

"Oh, I get it," Shannon said. "Because your show — the one Nick brought her to see — was all about pies. I know, I watched it. Yikes. That does sound like she was giving you the single-digit salute."

Liddy propped her elbow on the table, cupped her chin in her hand, and nodded knowingly. "I told you that girl was going to be trouble."

"I could ignore the whole thing, because eventually Celeste is going to recognize that we aren't competing for her father's love. But Tanis saw *her* future threatened. She aims to marry a prince of European nobility — maybe! — so the woman blames me for introducing Celeste to Redding."

Liddy said, "Didn't you tell her *I* introduced them?"

"Of course not. No way was I getting you mixed up in this mess. Whoever Celeste went to for photos, I think it's more than likely one pose would have been the pie shot."

They were silent as I told them about last

166

night — finding Redding's body, and how Nicholas was already there.

"Redding was supposed to be out of town. I never intended to go into his house, or even talk to him that night. I just swung by on my way home from the studio. But then I saw Nicholas's car there."

"You went to Redding's because you were afraid of what Nicholas might do," Shannon said quietly.

"It doesn't look good, Nick being there alone with the body before you arrived," Liddy said. "I can understand why John might think he did it."

I stated with emphasis: "But *we* don't think Nicholas is guilty, *do* we?"

Almost simultaneously, Shannon and Liddy answered that no, they didn't think he'd committed the murder. I ignored the fact that their tone was just a little less firm than mine.

I went on. " 'John, you should investigate the wife,' I said. 'You know how often the killer is the victim's nearest and dearest.' And I urged him to take a serious look into Redding's personal life for someone who had a grievance against him."

"Last night Johnny told me, and I quote, 'D'Martino looks guilty as hell,' " Shannon said.

"I can't blame him for thinking that. Nicholas is refusing to cooperate — deliberately acting guilty. He's afraid his daughter's involved," I said. "I don't want to believe she is — and I don't, not really — but I wanted to establish where she was last night. That's when I met her mother's prince."

I described going to the hotel, the conversation with von Hoffner, and his claim that he, Tanis, and Celeste were together in the suite all evening, playing cards. "He has a butler who backs him up, but I think if von Hoffner had said that they were all together on a magic carpet circling over Paris the butler would have confirmed it."

Liddy sat up straight, smiling brightly. "So we have to crack that alibi wide open."

"That's my thought," I said. "I considered going back to the hotel, but now that you two are here I have a better plan."

Shannon pushed aside her mug of coffee. "What do you want us to do?"

"When Eugene Long sold the hotel, his apartment was turned into the Presidential Suite. He had the whole floor, and he also used it for his corporate offices, so I'm guessing there must be another large suite or two on that floor." I smiled at my friends. "It's a lot to ask, but I'd like you to go there

168

and talk to the hotel's manager. Say you're working with a major international star. You can't name him just yet, but he's considering renting the Presidential Suite for a month, or longer. You want to know when it will be available and — most important — you want to know if there is a private way off that floor that will keep him safe from the prying eyes of the paparazzi."

Shannon grinned enthusiastically. "A back exit, or a private elevator to the underground garage?"

"That's it," I said. "Ask about servants' quarters, too. Find out where your star's personal assistant would sleep, and if there's a 'discreet exit' from those rooms. The prince told me they're planning to leave for Vienna tonight — unless John can stop them — so the Presidential Suite is occupied. You won't be able to get into it to look around, but if any other suite or room on that floor is available, check it out."

"Find out how similar it is to the Presidential Suite," Shannon said.

"Exactly." I turned to Liddy. "Watch out for Celeste. She's the only one who could recognize you and ruin your cover story."

"I'll look before I leap," Liddy said. She went over to my computer and turned it on.

"What are you doing?" I asked.

"Detecting isn't the same as snooping for personal reasons. What's the name of that prince?"

"Fredric von Hoffner. According to Celeste, he claims to be descended from the royal family of Bavaria and calls himself a prince."

As she logged onto the Internet, Liddy told Shannon, "Del wouldn't let me try to find out what I could about Nick's ex, but this is different."

Shannon and I moved over to watch the monitor as Liddy began her search.

"Ah! Here it is!" By typing in Freddie's name and "Bavaria," she'd found a recent photograph of von Hoffner at some gala in Vienna.

"That's Tanis," I said, pointing. "The blonde on his right."

"Bingo," Liddy said. "We got 'em both."

She copied and pasted the picture into e-mail, edited out the other people in the shot, enlarged the figures of Tanis and her prince, and printed three copies of the page.

"Don't delete that picture of the two of them," I said. "Let's send it to Nicholas's lawyer. I'll call her office to get her e-mail."

"While you're doing that," Liddy said, "I'll put on my private-eye outfit." She took her garment bag and went into my bedroom to change.

Shortly after I'd sent the picture of von Hoffner and Tanis to Olivia, Liddy returned to the kitchen. She, indeed, looked "businesslike" in an attractive dark gray skirt suit with a cream silk blouse and black pumps with two-inch heels.

"You're the star's representative," Shannon told Liddy. "Make a point of not introducing me." She gave her luxuriant hair a fluff. "Let the hotel manager think I'm the star's 'bit on the side.'"

"We're off, Della," Liddy said. "What are you going to do?"

"Focus, no pun intended, on Roxanne Redding." I believed I had come up with the perfect cover story excuse to spend some time with her.

18

It appeared I wasn't going to see Roxanne Redding after all. At least not this morning.

From the street corner stop sign a few doors down from 190 Bella Vista Drive, I spotted an SID van and an LAPD Crown Victoria parked in front of the Redding house. The Crown Vic was the unmarked car used by John O'Hara and Hugh Weaver while they were on duty. It was easy to recognize, even if it had been in the middle of a dozen similar Crown Vics, because I had been on the scene the afternoon a few months ago when Weaver pressed a "Ban Politicians, Not Guns" banner to the rear chrome bumper. One corner had been scraped off, but the glue must be super-strong because the message was still clear.

The front door had yellow crime-scene tape hanging from the far side of the entrance. I presumed it had been put up after I left last night, and taken partway down with the arrival of SID techs this morning.

I was in the middle of a U-turn to go back to Sunset when in my rearview mirror I saw the Reddings' front door open and Hugh Weaver come outside.

Before he saw me, I completed the U-turn, but instead of fleeing down to Sunset, I steered my Jeep into the street between the boulevard and the Redding house. I was looking for . . .

And there it was: the trash pickup alley that ran behind all of the houses on the Reddings' side of the street, as well as behind the houses that faced out onto the next block.

I pulled to a stop just short of the back gate of 190. It was crisscrossed with more yellow crime-scene tape. Clearly, I wasn't going to be able to visit Roxanne Redding until the techs had finished their work. I gave a silent prayer that they would find evidence implicating someone other than Nicholas.

I backed up, turned around, and returned to the mouth of the alley. Concerned that some householder, nervous because there had been a murder in their neighborhood last night, would see me parked and call the police, I took the *Thomas Guide* out of my glove compartment, and pretended to be looking up a location.

With the thick, spiral-bound book of street maps propped in front of me on the steering wheel, I bent my head over it, but kept Bella Vista in my peripheral vision. In less than a minute, I saw the Crown Victoria heading south toward Sunset.

Hugh Weaver was alone in the car.

Where is John?

Another question occurred to me: Where was Roxanne Redding? If the techs were still going over her home, perhaps she hadn't stayed there last night.

I dug into my handbag for the piece of paper on which I'd scribbled Alec Redding's phone number and address, found it, and dialed it from my cell.

What I got was a mechanical voice telling me that calls were being forwarded to another number. I heard a few rings, and then a woman answered.

"Hello. Who's calling?"

The voice sounded subdued, but I recognized it.

"Mrs. Redding? I'm so sorry to bother you during this difficult time, but I have one quick business question to ask. May I?"

"What is it?" She sounded curious, and a little less subdued.

She was on my line, so to speak; now I

hoped she would swallow the hook I was about to bait.

I said, "I had been planning to make an appointment for photographs with your husband, but now . . ." Faking embarrassment, I said, "I feel terrible about asking you this, but it is a professional emergency. Could you tell me who you might recommend as a photographer?"

"I do portrait sittings," she said.

I knew that because Liddy had told me, but I pretended to be surprised. "You do?"

"I'm a photographer, too. My husband was the celebrity, but my work is the equal of his. He often said so, bless him. I'll be happy to show you a sample portfolio."

"No, that won't be necessary, Mrs. Redding. I'm sure your work is excellent. I'd be delighted to have you take my photographs." I heard the Call Waiting signal in my ear. "Someone's trying to reach me. May I contact you later, to make an appointment?"

"Yes. I'll have some time next week."

"I'll call you."

"Fine. Oh, what is your name?"

Instead of answering her then and giving her time to find an excuse not to see me, I disconnected, and pressed the "Answer" button.

"This is awful!" It was Shannon, sound-

175

ing frantic. "I'm at the hotel. Johnny caught me!"

"Oh, Lord — I'm so sorry, Shan! Where are you now?"

"In the restroom. He told me to go home. I didn't tell him that I can't because I came with Liddy. He doesn't know Liddy's here, too."

"Where is Liddy?"

"Still in the Queen's Suite with the manager, I think. Unless he found her, too." She took a deep breath. When she started to speak again, she sounded calmer. "I was going down to check out the underground parking garage when that private elevator door opened and — *whoosh!* There was Johnny!"

"What did you tell him?"

She chuckled. "I'm kind of proud of this. I said I was looking for a special suite we could rent for a night to celebrate our anniversary next month."

"Did he believe you?"

"I don't know. Johnny had his poker face on. He didn't challenge me about it, but maybe that was because he was with a young man who looked like a lawyer. You know the type: suit, tie, briefcase, doesn't look like he's out in the sun much. Running into Johnny like that made for a pretty

176

awkward moment, but he recovered quicker than I did. He introduced me to the guy with him. Name is Leary, or Cleary, or maybe Drury. I was so shocked I'm not sure I heard it right."

"Currie? Could it have been Stan Currie?"

"Yes . . . that was it. Currie. Do you know him?"

"Only slightly. He's an assistant district attorney. If he's there with John, it may be to stop that quartet in the Presidential Suite from leaving the country tonight."

"Let's hope," Shannon said.

"Do you want me to come and pick you up?"

"Liddy and I made plans to meet at her car after she finished looking around upstairs and I scoped out the garage. Which I'm going to do right now. Della, I have to tell you, this little adventure is making me feel more alive than I've felt in months."

"I'm glad, but are you sure you want to check out the garage today? What if John goes down there, too, and sees you again?"

I heard her chuckle again. "What can he do? Arrest me?"

After we ended the conversation, I looked at my watch and saw it was twenty minutes before twelve.

It wouldn't be long before John and Weaver arrived at Olivia Wayne's office for their noon interview with Celeste.

Nicholas had said that he and Celeste were together at his place last night until just before he arrived at Redding's. I'm sure he said that only to protect Celeste.

Later, Prince Freddie told me that he, Tanis, and Celeste were together in the Presidential Suite playing cards all evening. I didn't believe him, either — or his butler — but I had no idea whom he might be trying to protect by lying.

Shortly, Celeste would be giving her statement to the police. I had no idea what she was going to say, but I was sure that it wasn't going to be good for Nicholas.

There was no time to think about that now. I had to get back to my house. Phil Logan had me scheduled to do radio phone-in interviews from home with stations around the country from twelve thirty until two PM. I'd be talking to the various hosts about the national bake sales for charity that I was encouraging. Radio technology was so good that it sounded as though the show guest was right there in the studio with the host.

I had to stop thinking about murder and plan how to promote our bake sale contest.

19

Before I went to bed last night I'd gone on the computer with the list of cities I'd be speaking to, learned something significant about each of them, and made notes. While waiting for the first call to come in — from a station in Chicago — I reviewed them, and put the pages in order.

When the phone rang a few minutes before I was to go on the air, I was ready.

Not so the producer on the other end of the line.

"What are you going to be talking to Chet about?" he asked.

Chet? That's not the name of the host on my list.

I said, "I thought I was supposed to talk to Bob Roman."

"The Big BR's out sick. Chet is subbing today. He's our sports guy." I heard the producer mumbling to someone in the background. When he spoke to me again, he said, "You're up right after this commercial break. Stand by."

While a man's voice urged listeners to "start looking like one of life's winners by purchasing a pre-owned Mercedes," I tried to figure out what I would talk to a sports guy about.

Commercial over, the producer came back on the line. "You're up next, Delta."

"It's Della," I said.

The producer said, "Huh. Are you sure? It says here on my sheet —"

He was interrupted by a burst of lively music. In a few seconds, I heard a hearty male voice.

"Hi, there, folks. Welcome back to the dugout. You'll know you're listening to live radio because we've got a guest on our inside line, but there seems to be some dispute about her name. Hello, mystery guest. Am I talking to the actress Delta Burke?"

"No, I'm Della Carmichael."

"Who?"

"I do the TV cooking show *In the Kitchen with Della* on the Better Living Channel."

"Hey, pretty good! You got the plug in smooth as a thirty-foot outsider in the last five seconds of the fourth quarter. What sport do you want to talk about, Miss D on the BLC?"

"Baking."

"When did baking become a sport?"

"Just recently. Since my network and I proposed national bake sales to raise money for charity. *In the Kitchen with Della* is sponsoring a *competition* for *teams* of four to see which team can raise the most money for their charity. Competitive baking is an *indoor sport,* with the *finals* played outdoors when it's time to sell the baked goodies. Your listeners can find the rules on the Better Living Channel's Web site."

"Cute," he said, chuckling. "I never thought of baking as a team game, but then I didn't predict synchronized swimming would come to the Olympics, either. Well, why not? All we sports people like to raise money for good causes. Give us the stats again, Miss D. You got twenty seconds before the buzzer. Go!"

I went. Watching the second hand on my kitchen wall clock, I repeated information about the bake sales, and stressed that to win, a team had to produce a valid receipt as to how much money was turned over to their charity. I finished my spiel in exactly twenty seconds. It wasn't hard, because I was used to timing things down to the second for the TV shows.

The host said, "While you were talking I looked you up. You're the cooking babe who brained Dodger pitcher Tony Cuervo last year!"

He must have Googled or Binged me and found out about one of Phil Logan's early publicity stunts where he had me suited up like a Los Angeles Dodger so his photographer could take a picture of me holding a baseball bat. My unexpectedly connecting bat to ball resulted in my picture on sports pages around the country. Some headlines read: "Cook Creams Cuervo."

"I only hit Tony Cuervo on the ankle during batting practice, and he wasn't hurt, just surprised."

"Well, it's been fun having you on the show, Miss D from the BLC. Time now for the latest news. This is Chet Wall filling in for Bob Roman, the Big BR, who should be back in this oversize chair tomorrow."

A woman's voice came on with news headlines, the line disconnected, and my first radio phone-in of the day was over. After making a note of the name of the substitute host so that I could e-mail a "thank you" note to him, as I would to the other interviewers, I poured myself a glass of water and reached down to pet Tuffy. While I waited for the call from the next radio show, I couldn't help wondering what was going on in Olivia Wayne's office, where John and his partner were interviewing Celeste.

What was she saying?

While I was talking to a show host in Boston — my final interview of the day — my cell phone vibrated in my pocket. I had to ignore it then, but the moment my interview was over, I accessed the message and listened while I made a fresh pot of coffee.

Liddy had called. She sounded breathless with excitement.

"I didn't get to see inside the Presidential Suite," she said, "but the Queen's Suite, which I did tour thoroughly, is laid out exactly the same, according to the manager. Living room, guest bath, kitchen, butler's pantry, dining room, three bedrooms, each with a bathroom. Del, there *is* a back entrance. It's a rear elevator that goes right down to the underground garage without stopping on any other floor! *Zip, zoom, and out.* Even though there's one private elevator that goes to the fifteenth floor, there's a separate back elevator for each of the two suites! The manager described that as 'a little amenity' for famous or important guests who need to bypass crowds in the lobby or outside the hotel's entrance."

My spirits soared. What Liddy had learned shot the prince's alibi full of back-elevator-size holes.

Liddy took a breath and continued. "At the west end of the corridor there's also an elevator that's used by the kitchen and housekeeping staffs for transporting meal tables and laundry and cleaning carts. But that elevator stops on every floor, and it goes down only as far as the ground floor kitchen. There are kitchen workers on duty twenty-four hours a day, so that's not a secure escape route. Bottom line of this report is that any one of them — Tanis, Celeste, the prince, or the butler — could have left the hotel without being seen. This is Agent 003 — licensed to snoop — signing off. Let me know what my next assignment is."

End of message.

"Good job, Liddy," I said to the dead phone in my hand.

I wonder if Shannon was able to find a walk-out exit in the hotel's basement garage. For reasons of employee safety, there must be one.

Before I had a chance to call Liddy back, someone at my front door was ringing the bell with an insistent series of sharp jabs.

I wasn't expecting anyone.
My heart lurched with anxiety.
What now?

20

I looked through the front window to see who was treating my doorbell like a punching bag for the index finger. I'd been afraid that it was John, furious because he'd discovered that I'd been investigating his murder case, so it was with a combination of relief and puzzlement that I discovered my visitor was female, and a stranger.

She appeared to be in her early twenties, with the muscular build of an athlete. Her brown hair was cut short and feathered into wisps framing a round face devoid of makeup. She was neatly dressed in a chocolate brown skirt and a pumpkin-colored jacket. While her right hand stabbed my doorbell, her left clutched a bulky leather shoulder bag. I thought she might be one of Eileen's friends, another recent graduate of UCLA.

I opened the door and said, "Yes?"

"You're Della Carmichael." It was a statement, not a question.

"Yes. And you are . . . ?"

She pulled a slim wallet out of her bag, and opened it to flash a *Los Angeles Chronicle* press card. "I'm Gretchen Tully. Phil Logan arranged for me to interview you."

Like the great Yogi Berra had said, it was déjà vu all over again. I met Nicholas when he came to interview me in his capacity as a crime reporter because a woman had been murdered during the first broadcast of my television show. He had arrived two hours early, and found me scrubbing the kitchen floor. I looked awful.

He admitted that he had deliberately shown up at ten in the morning instead of noon, to catch me off guard, because he wanted to meet "the real" me. I told him that I was also "the real me" after I'd had a shower, and when wearing clean clothes.

Nicholas's early arrival had been annoying, but Gretchen Tully's surprise visit was worse because I wanted to talk to Liddy and Shannon, to get details of what they'd learned at the hotel and to plan what I was going to do next. I couldn't do that with a reporter here.

I made an effort to sound pleasant as I said, "Our appointment was scheduled for next Thursday. You're six days early."

If she'd sensed my irritation, she was unfazed by it, and unapologetic. "I had some time today, so I thought I'd take a chance. If you're busy right now I'll just sit down and wait until you finish what you're doing. But I'd love to observe you in action. May I come in?"

Trapped. It seemed unlikely that I could get rid of her without turning her into an enemy. Because Phil Logan had arranged the interview, albeit not for today, and because I know it's important to keep good relations with the press, I decided to make the best of this situation. Also, she worked for the same paper that Nicholas did and they might be friends. "All right," I said.

I opened the door wider and moved aside to let her enter, but she'd taken only the first step when she gasped and pulled her shoulder bag tight against her chest. She was staring at Tuffy, who stood just behind me.

"That's a big dog! Does he bite?"

Only people who arrive at my house a week early. That's what I wanted to say, but I restrained myself. "Give me your hand," I said.

I could see she didn't want to, but she did. I gave her points for grit.

"Hey, Tuffy," I said. "This is Gretchen. She's a nice person." That statement was more a matter of hope than knowledge, but I guided her fingers close to Tuffy's nose so he could sniff her. She either passed the Tuffy test, or he took the warm tone of my voice to mean that she wasn't a threat. He wagged his rear end and I let go of her hand.

"Come in, Ms. Tully," I said.

"Call me Gretchen."

"Gretchen. Would you like some coffee? Or tea?"

"Coffee, thanks. Do you have anything to munch? I missed lunch. I know that's a nervy request . . ."

"It's not a problem. I'd rather you told me than have you be uncomfortable. Now that you mention it, I realize I haven't had any, either. I've been doing phone interviews with radio shows. Come back to the kitchen."

As we passed through the living room, she stopped. "Oh, wait. Is that a picture of your husband on the mantel?"

"Yes, is it. His name was Mack. Why?"

"No reason, really. I just heard you were the widow of a policeman."

Even though I don't have any embarrassing secrets, it always made me a little uncomfortable when I learned that people were talking about my personal life. But I supposed it was natural for Gretchen Tully to find out what she could about my background before she interviewed me about the show and our bake sales for charity promotion.

In the kitchen, Tuffy trotted over to his bed. I invited her to sit at the table.

"Let me see what I can put together."

"I'm a vegetarian, so any kind of salad would be great."

"You're an easy guest. Just this morning I picked some tomatoes and fresh basil from the little garden I put in out back." I opened the refrigerator door. Surveying the contents, I saw a few items that gave me an idea. "Are you willing to try a vegetarian dish I've never made before?"

"I'm game," she said. "Can we talk while you do whatever you're going to do?"

By "talk," I knew she meant "interview."

I put a mug in front of her, along with sugar, sweeteners, and a small pitcher of half-and-half. "The coffee's right over there," I said, indicating the Mr. Coffee machine. "It's fresh. Please help yourself."

She did. I'd washed the tomatoes and basil leaves right after I picked them this morning, so I put a handful of basil and three tomatoes on my workspace, took three red potatoes from the vegetable bin, washed them, cut them in half so they'd cook faster, put them in a pot, covered them with salted water, and turned the flame to boil.

Gretchen Tully brought her mug of coffee over to watch me.

During the few minutes it would take for the potatoes to become fork-tender, I seeded the tomatoes, cut them into chunks, tore the basil leaves into pieces, chopped up some black olives and flat-leaf Italian parsley, sliced half a red onion, cut half a loaf of French bread into cubes, and put it all together in a wooden salad bowl.

"That looks good already. I love the smell of fresh tomatoes. What are you making?"

"Tomato-Potato Panzanella. It's a vegetable bread salad. Why don't you ask your questions while I work?"

She went back to the table and pulled a small recorder from her handbag.

"Do you mind if I record our interview?"

"Not at all. But wait a minute." I dried my hands on a paper towel, opened my "catchall" drawer and took out an old microcassette recorder of my own. "We'll both record it," I said.

She frowned. "Are you going to tell me that you're doing this in case my recorder breaks down?"

I smiled. "It's because this way we'll both have a record of what I said. Not that I expect you to misquote me. The *Chronicle* has a reputation for accuracy in its reporting."

"With so many papers cutting staff, I'm lucky they hired me, but I had good clips and they're moving toward a younger perspective."

What does that mean? And is it going to be bad for Nicholas?

"Did you always want to be a journalist?" I asked.

She shook her head. "My original plan was to join the FBI, but that didn't work out."

"What happened?"

"Too many layers of bureaucracy. Too long before I'd be assigned any cases." She sipped some coffee, gazing into the mug.

With the potatoes bubbling on the stove behind me, I began whisking together extra virgin olive oil and red wine vinegar with a clove of minced garlic, a little salt, and some black pepper.

"I read your bio. We can skip over the fact that your dad was a veterinarian, your mom and two sisters are accountants in San Francisco, you run a cooking school in Santa Monica, and that a year ago you were hired, without any TV experience, to host a cable show that's become very popular. Unless any of that isn't true."

"It's all accurate," I said.

"How did you get your TV break?"

"One of my cooking school students, Iva Jordan, was the wife — I mean, she still *is* the wife — of Mickey Jordan, the man who owns the Better Living Channel. When he decided to replace the previous cooking show host, Iva recommended me. I auditioned and got the job. It was good luck for me, because they needed someone right away, and my years of teaching made talking to the cameras easy. I just imagined I was explaining cooking techniques and recipe tricks to a room full of students."

The potatoes were done. I was carrying the pot to the sink to drain them when Gretchen Tully abruptly changed course.

"Everybody at the paper knows you and Nick D'Martino have a *thing* going on. You know him so well, why do you think he killed Alec Redding?"

I set the pot down so hard that if my sink hadn't been stainless steel I would have chipped the enamel. *"What?"*

"I asked, Why —"

"I heard the question. My answer is that I do *not* believe for one minute that he had

anything at all to do with Redding's death."
I gestured to our recorders. "You have that statement on tape. Now tell me why you're so quick to condemn him? He's not some stranger — he's your colleague."

"If by colleague you mean 'fellow reporter,' he's not anymore. He's been put on the rewrite desk. The boss doesn't want anybody else in the media getting to him, at least not until after he's arrested. When he's in police custody we won't be able to keep him to ourselves anymore."

I took a deep breath to control my anger and said calmly, "He's not going to be arrested because he's innocent."

"You can repeat it like a mantra, swear it on a Bible, but the truth is that D'Martino was in the house alone when you came and found the man's body," she said. "He's the cops' primo person of interest."

"Who told you that?"

She puffed out her chest. "I can't reveal my source."

She said "source." Singular. I couldn't believe it was either John or Weaver. Maybe Officer Downey or Willis?

I wanted to know who was leaking information, but for Nicholas's sake, I couldn't afford to make an enemy of Gretchen Tully. Somehow, I had to turn her into an ally. I put a friendly smile on my face.

"You're right. Of course you shouldn't reveal a source. Besides, I thought you were here to write about my TV show's national bake sales project. What would you like to know about that?"

"Nothing." She grimaced with distaste. "Your big bake whatever was the subject *before* this murder, when I was stuck in the Home and Family ghetto. But with the staff cuts and now that D'Martino's sidelined, I'm getting my shot at crime reporting."

You have a lot to learn, Ms. Tully, about getting people to reveal information. Don't use an ax to open a bottle of milk.

I composed my face into an expression of sympathy. "This is an important opportunity for you, I understand, and I feel bad because you're not exploiting it to the fullest."

"What do you mean?"

"You're locking yourself into only one theory of the crime. What happens if evidence surfaces that exonerates Nicholas D'Martino? If you're concentrating only on him you'll miss getting a great scoop because you weren't looking for the real killer."

Her forehead creased in thought.

The red potatoes were cool enough to handle. I cut them into chunks, added them to the bowl with the other ingredients, and tossed the vegetables with the simple vinaigrette dressing I'd made.

She said speculatively, "If D'Martino didn't kill Redding . . ."

"Then somebody else did. That's your real story."

I dished the Tomato-Potato Panzanella salad into two pasta bowls and set them on our place mats. I put out the cutlery and gestured for her to sit.

"You wanted to join the FBI, so you must have an urge to investigate," I said. "Use it. Think what a coup it will be if *you* solve the murder before the police do."

I saw her eyes begin to glow with excitement.

I said, "As soon as you've had something to eat, to get your brain cells in gear, why not start digging into Alec Redding's life and find out who might have wanted him dead?"

After saying that my Tomato-Potato Panzanella "rocked," Gretchen Tully left the house full of an investigator's zeal. I felt a stab of apprehension. I had set her on a path that I hoped would help clear Nicholas of suspicion, but what if the information she turned up made his situation worse?

John O'Hara's voice echoed in my head: *Stay out of police business.*

Tuffy nudged me for an ear scratch.

"I can't stay out of this case," I whispered.

Tuffy must have caught the tone of worry in my voice, because he leaned against me and nuzzled his silky face into the palm of my hand.

21

It was four o'clock in the afternoon, a little less than an hour after Gretchen Tully left my house, and the time that Olivia Wayne had said she could spare a few minutes to talk to me. She told me to meet her at Moonstone's, a café on Century Park East in Century City, a block south of her law office.

I got there a little early, took one of the two booths in the rear, and positioned myself so that I faced the door. Moonstone's was small and clean, with a counter to the left of the entrance, tables at the front window and along the right side. The space was anchored in the back by the pair of booths. The decor was glass and chrome, with black Formica tabletops, black vinyl chair backs and banquettes. Framed black-and-white photos lined the walls: stills from old movies starring Fred Astaire and Ginger Rogers, dancing in art deco splendor.

The café was nearly deserted. A young couple, a man and a woman, occupied seats at the counter, drinking coffee and talking softly with their heads close together. An older man sat alone at a table near the front, reading the *New York Times*. He had a half-eaten sandwich in front of him.

I had just ordered a cup of coffee when I saw Olivia Wayne enter.

Saw her? She was impossible to miss.

Hurricane Olivia swept through the heavy glass and chrome front door with the authority of a gale force wind. From the smiles and waves with which the counterman and the waitress greeted her, it wasn't hard to guess that she was a regular here, and that she probably tipped well.

Olivia returned their smiles as she headed toward me. Just as she slid onto the opposite banquette, the waitress appeared with pad in hand.

"Hi, there. What can I get for you today?"

Olivia ignored the plastic-covered menu in a metal holder between the salt and pepper shakers and the bowl of artificial sweeteners.

"Bacon cheeseburger with avocado and tomato, no onion, no pickle. And coffee," she said.

"Fries?"

"Of course."

"You got it." The waitress turned to me. "Are you ready to order yet?"

"Just this coffee."

"I'm ravenous," Olivia said as the waitress hurried to the kitchen. "No lunch, and probably no dinner."

She put her black leather handbag on the seat next to her and shrugged out of her dark blue Armani suit jacket, revealing a pale blue silk shell underneath. Her only jewelry was a strand of what were unmistakably real pearls. No earrings. No rings on her long fingers, nails perfectly manicured and finished with colorless polish. Her watch had a black leather band. Its large face was turned to the inside of her wrist, allowing her to check the time without being obvious about it.

"What did you learn from Celeste?" I asked.

"I'll get to that. First the crime-scene news: Nick's prints are not on the stool that was used to bash in Redding's skull. Nobody's were."

"Somebody wiped it clean." I was immediately embarrassed that I'd stated the obvious. Before she could say "Duh" or something equally as derisive, I said, "No prints on the murder weapon means that

200

the only thing tying Nicholas to the crime is his finding the body. That's good."

She grimaced. "Did the Pollyanna-bug bite you in your cradle?"

I snapped back at her. "Being nasty is not a good use of your valuable time."

"You're right." She expelled a breath. "My disposition is rotten when I go too long without eating."

"I accept your apology," I said.

A corner of her lips lifted in a hint of a smile. "You're tougher than you look."

" 'Look like the innocent flower, but be the serpent under it,' " I quoted.

"Fortune cookie?"

"Shakespeare. When I was in the public school system I used to try to teach Shakespeare, as well as good grammar, to pre-felons."

"Nick told me you stopped being the pretty little schoolmarm when some hard case took a shot at you."

"Not every career path runs smoothly," I said. "Now, *please,* tell me about the police interview with Celeste."

She shook her head. "Not good." But before she could elaborate, the waitress returned with her order. She put the large plate down, and filled Olivia's coffee cup and refilled mine from the pot she carried in her other hand.

Olivia lifted the top part of the bun, added a few shakes of salt and a squirt of catsup, then picked up the burger and took a bite. She closed her eyes and made an *mmmm* sound that comes from happy dining, or good sex.

I watched, fascinated. It was a big, juicy burger. I expected that at any moment her silk shell was going to acquire some serious staining. But she ate a full third of the burger before putting it down, and without getting even the tiniest spot on her blouse.

How did she manage it? If I ate that wearing good clothes, I'd look like a Jackson Pollock drip canvas.

Olivia blotted her lips, picked up a French fry, and took a bite. "Bad news from the police interrogation of Celeste. She said she hadn't seen her father all evening. Worse, she said she went to the hotel to stay with her mother because she was afraid Nick was angry with her."

I felt a cold lump of dread form in my stomach. "Naturally, John asked her why . . ."

"And she said it was because of 'the picture.' O'Hara jumped on that like a hungry cat on a fat, sleepy mouse. Celeste started to cry. Frankly, I think it was an act, but she managed to produce real tears. She described the picture she'd posed for — the one you told me about, nearly naked with a pie — and sniffled that she'd meant it as a joke, but now everybody was *so upset.* Boo hoo."

"She said 'everybody.' Meaning that her mother, and maybe even the prince, were angry at Redding?"

"That was my argument, but O'Hara and Weaver didn't see it that way. They want to question Nick again. I agreed that I'd have him back at the West LA station at six o'clock tonight. That's why I'm sure I'm not going to get any dinner." She started in on the burger again. "By the way, that party of four in the Presidential Suite has been ordered to stay in town for at least the next five days. Thanks for the tip that they were planning to fly away."

"Here's another one. There's a back elevator in the Presidential Suite that goes straight down to the underground garage. Any one of them — Celeste, Tanis, or Prince Freddie — could have left the hotel the night of Redding's murder without being seen."

"It's our good luck that nobody in this case so far has a solid alibi." She smiled at me, and I saw to my dismay that not only hadn't she stained her blouse, but she managed to eat a big, sloppy burger without getting food stuck in her teeth.

Well, Olivia Wayne may be able to eat with gusto and leave no trace, but I have Nicholas.

I think.

I hope.

He hadn't called since we'd said good-bye last night at the police station. My feelings were a tangled mix of sympathy for what he was going through and anger that our relationship might not be important enough for him to reach out to me.

I resolved to sort through my emotions later.

Whether Nicholas D'Martino and I would remain a couple was immaterial. Right now, I had to do whatever I could to save him from being arrested for murder.

22

As soon as I got back to my Jeep, I called Liddy and Shannon and asked each if they could meet me at my house this evening to compare notes and plan our next steps. I told Shannon that John would be away from home because he'd begin questioning Nicholas again at six o'clock tonight at the station house.

She agreed immediately. "He'll probably get home late, but in case he comes in before I do, I'll leave a note saying we're having a girls' night out and that there's a plate of cold cuts and potato salad for him in the refrigerator."

Liddy was just as eager for us to get together.

"I'll have the housekeeper make dinner for Bill, and a giant bowl of popcorn," she said. "We were just going to watch the latest *Iron Man* movie on DVD. I usually fall asleep during those big action pictures, so he won't even miss me."

I prepared the world's quickest dinner for Liddy and Shannon and myself. It also happened to be one of our favorites: linguine with my homemade meat sauce. Because I'd defrosted a quart of the sauce that I'd had in the freezer, all I had to do was cook the pasta. When I make that meat sauce, I always double the amount so I can store enough extra to have for an impromptu meal.

During the nine minutes it took for the linguine to reach al dente, I put together a mixed green salad and dressed it with the leftover vinaigrette from the panzanella I'd made for Gretchen Tully earlier.

Liddy and Shannon set the table while they reviewed for me what they'd learned of the layout at the Olympia Grand.

"Just as I'd guessed, there was a pedestrian exit in the garage," Shannon said.

"Four concrete steps up to a plain metal door that leads out to the alley."

I asked, "Does it lock?"

"Automatically, from the inside, but all anybody going out that way would have to do is wedge a piece of paper in there so the door wouldn't really lock when it was closed. I tried that and it worked."

Liddy said, "When I went down to the

garage in the private elevator with the manager, he pointed that door out to me and said that all my 'principal' would have to do to avoid crowds in the lobby or outside the hotel's entrance would be to have a car meet him in the alley and 'his privacy would be preserved.' That's how he put it. I acted pleased and told him that he'd be hearing from me about booking one of the suites."

"That's great work, you two."

As we ate the pasta and salad, I filled them in on my unexpected visit from Gretchen Tully, and my later conversation with Olivia Wayne.

Liddy frowned and shook her head in sympathy. "Things don't look good for Nick."

"I know Johnny doesn't like your Sicilian stallion, but he wouldn't let anybody be railroaded." Shannon's tone was defensive.

"Of course not," I said quickly. "What worries me is that with the focus on Nicholas, John and Weaver won't be able to look in other directions immediately. John would never intentionally arrest an innocent person, but time is critical in a murder investigation."

Liddy asked eagerly, "What's our next assignment?"

"Roxanne Redding. I'll be through teaching my cooking classes tomorrow at three o'clock. I'm going to try to persuade her to take publicity photos of me after that. If she agrees, I'd like you two to come with me."

"We need cover stories," Liddy said. "I'll do your makeup. Shan, you can bring extra outfits for Della to wear."

"Okay. That's how we get in, but what do we do when we're there?" Shannon asked.

"I'll keep her busy taking my pictures. One at a time, you two will ask to use the bathroom. Once you're out of the studio, I want you to find out where the Reddings keep their bills and the checkbooks."

"We keep ours in the desk in the den," Liddy said.

"Eileen takes care of our bills twice a month," Shannon said. "We've got a file box for that stuff in the kitchen."

I indicated the little desk against the wall. "That's where I do mine. Everything's in the drawer underneath the computer."

"What do you want us to look for?" Liddy asked.

I had to admit that I didn't know precisely. "Anything that seems unusual. Large cash deposits or withdrawals from banks or broker accounts. And I'd like to know who Redding photographed in the last six months. Also, look for their phone bills. How many phone numbers do they have, note the numbers, and see if you spot anything odd when you scan the charges."

"Letters!" Shannon said. "I'll look for hidden letters."

"I don't know anybody who writes letters anymore," Liddy said. "People e-mail or text. But, hey, maybe they keep copies."

"We've got to be methodical and not be discouraged if we don't find something that solves the case immediately," I said. "What John does, what Mack used to do, was go places, talk to people, check alibis, listen to gossip. If investigators do enough looking and asking and listening, sometimes they find the one significant piece of the puzzle in the middle of" — I lifted a forkful of pasta — "the bowl of linguine that most cases start out being."

Shannon said, "I was sick and out of my head for so many years I hardly ever got to hear Johnny talk about his work. How do you know what piece of information is useful?"

"It's *all* useful," I said, "in the sense that at least it allows you to rule some things out. If you can eliminate one or two pieces of information from the picture, suddenly something else might look more important."

"A few years ago I took a sculpting class," Liddy said. "It turned out I couldn't even make an abstract that wasn't hopeless, but I remember something the instructor told us. 'Look at a block of marble,' he said. 'Somewhere inside is the statue of David. Pick up your chisels and keep chipping away until you find him.'"

"I never heard a better description of detective work," I said.

"When the twins were babies, a lot of the time Bill and I were too exhausted for sex, so we used to do picture puzzles while we listened for one or both of them to start crying. We wouldn't look at the photo on the box after we opened it up. Trying to fit pieces together without seeing the overall design, we got a lot of them wrong, but then one part would fit into another, and little by little we began to see what the thing was supposed to look like."

We'd finished dinner. As we were clearing the table, I asked my friends, "If I can get Roxanne Redding to photograph me tomorrow afternoon, or even on Sunday, can the two of you get away to come with me?"

"No problem. Bill's playing golf all weekend," Liddy said.

"I'll tell Johnny I'm helping you with your publicity pictures. He'll be happy that I'm keeping busy." She chuckled. "We just can't let him know what I'll really be doing."

I said, "If either of you finds anything that looks as though it could help Nicholas by pointing toward somebody else, you have to leave whatever it is right where you saw it. I'll tell Olivia about it and she'll have to convince John, or someone, to get a search warrant so the police will find the information legally."

Liddy said to Shannon, "There's a spy shop in Beverly Hills. Tomorrow morning I'll go get us a couple of tiny cameras."

I went to the wall phone to call Roxanne Redding.

23

I spent a restless night, worried about Nicholas, but annoyed that I hadn't heard from him. I tried to watch a movie on TV, but there was nothing that engaged my interest for more than a few minutes. Several times before eleven o'clock, I started to dial Nicholas's number, but put the phone down each time before I'd completed more than four digits. I didn't want to invade his privacy, but I was disturbed that he wasn't reaching out to me when he was in trouble. I hadn't thought we'd been having a "fair weather" romance, but I knew that I didn't want one.

My marriage to Mack had lasted for nearly twenty years, in sickness and in health, and only death had parted us. When Nicholas was out of danger, I decided that we were going to have a talk about what each of us wanted in a relationship. I wasn't young enough to be insecure, and I would never be so old that I'd settle for less than a total emotional partnership.

I went to bed at eleven thirty, dozed, and woke up. At midnight, I decided to iron one of the blouses I'd wear at my four PM photo shoot with Roxanne Redding. Afterward, I slept for a while, but awoke again at two AM. I put a load of linens into the washing machine. While waiting the half hour before I could transfer them to the dryer, I gave myself a fresh manicure.

Tuffy and Emma, unaccustomed to my restlessness, and perhaps worried about it, snuggled closer than usual to me. The second time I got up, after lifting Emma from where she was curled up beside my neck to the pillow on the other side of the bed, the two of them jumped down and followed me from room to room. Looking at them watching me warily made me feel so guilty that after doing my nails I went back to bed and determined to stay there for the rest of the night.

The rest of the night didn't last all that long.

At a quarter to five Saturday morning I awoke again, and decided to get up for good. I showered, gave Tuffy and Emma fresh food and water, and took Tuffy for a walk. To my surprise, even though I had slept little, I wasn't tired. I was too on edge to feel fatigue, too eager to find out who killed Alec Redding so that Nicholas would be cleared. Then we would see what a normal life was going to look like.

I was tempted to call him. I was tempted to jump in the Jeep and go over to his place, ring the bell, and knock on the door until either he opened it, or I was satisfied that he wasn't there.

Why didn't I?

"Pride," I said, surprising myself that I'd spoken aloud. But the words I heard jolted me.

"That's positively antediluvian," I said. We were only a few yards from my driveway and I had the keys in my pocket. "Come on, Tuffy."

With Tuffy in his safety harness in the backseat, I put the key in the ignition and backed out onto Eleventh Street. Because it was so early, barely dawn, I started out at a fast clip, but then made myself slow down when I realized that while I had my keys, that was all I had with me. No wallet with my driver's license in it. This was no time in my life to be stopped by the police.

Nicholas wasn't home. His car wasn't in the carport. Nevertheless, I climbed the few steps to his front door and rang the bell. Rang it repeatedly. His doorbell sounded in chimes. I could hear them inside, but, as in that famous poem "A Visit from St. Nicholas," "Not a creature was stirring, not even a mouse."

Where would he be at six o'clock in the morning?

"You looking for Nick?"

It was a male voice, coming from the sidewalk below me. I turned to see a man with a shock of white hair, clearly well north of seventy, a little stooped, with a small dog on a leash. It looked like a terrier mix.

"Yes, I was."

"He drove out 'bout ten o'clock." He gestured toward his dog. "Ruby an' I were just coming back from our bedtime walk. Doesn't look like Nick's been home all night."

"Did he mention where he was going?"

"Oh, we didn't talk. I waved at him, but I don't think he saw me. If you want to leave him a note, he's got a mail slot in the door."

I came back down the steps. "Maybe I'll call him later."

The man was peering though the Jeep's window at Tuffy. "That's a fine-looking dog you've got there."

"Yes, he is."

"Man's best friend," he said.

"Woman's, too," I said, climbing into the Jeep.

As I drove away, my confusion at not having heard from Nicholas fought with my concern for him. Where was he? What was he doing? If we were meant to have a future together, he would have to understand I would not accept being shut out.

My impulsive trip didn't accomplish what I'd hoped, but at least Tuffy enjoyed the ride.

Home again, I washed my hands and went into the kitchen to make the low-calorie Strawberry Cloud Pie that I planned to demonstrate at the Mommy and Me class at ten o'clock. We would have time to prepare it, and other dishes, during this session featuring low-calorie meals, but the Strawberry Cloud Pie had to be chilled for at least two hours before the moms and children could eat it, so I would bring the finished product with me for them to taste.

As I was packing the items I'd need to teach both the Mommy and Me class, and the cooking class for adults from one to three PM, Eileen came into the kitchen. Grinning.

"I just got an e-mail from your friend Carole Adams."

I looked up from packing the Strawberry Cloud Pie in a cooler lined with plastic bags full of ice cubes.

Carole, a friend I'd known since high school, who now lived in Delaware with her husband and two beautiful Korat cats, had created the best fudge — Chocolate Nut Butter — I'd ever eaten. She had given me the recipe. It was the first item that Eileen and I began to sell in our little mail-order and retail dessert business. A few months later, Carole turned her fudge recipe into Chocolate Nut Butter pudding. It's so delicious we're selling pots of that, too, along with our line of cakes, cookies, and brownies.

"You'll never guess what she's done now," Eileen said.

"I can't imagine."

"First thing, she wants me to tell you she's formed a team to compete in the bake sales for charity contest. She said she looked up the rules on the channel's Web site and it's okay that you two are friends because you don't have anything to do with choosing the winner. It's all a matter of which team donates the most money to their cause."

"Carole has so much energy she might raise enough to win the trip to Hollywood. I'd love to see her again."

"But that's not what I'm so excited about," Eileen said. "She's been experimenting, testing versions on her husband and neighbors, and now she's turned her fudge and pudding recipes into a three-layer pie version. She's come up with a chocolate nut butter cookie crust on the bottom, then a layer of the fudge, then a layer of pudding on top. She calls it 'Carole's Deadly Chocolate Nut Butter Pie à la Mode.' I think I gained five pounds just reading the recipe she sent us. She warned that it's addicting."

"Sounds as though it should come with a surgeon general's warning on the plate," I said.

"I'm going to the shop to make one this afternoon. While I'm doing it, I'll cost out the ingredients to see if we can sell it for an affordable price without cutting quality."

"Great idea."

"Come over after class to taste test."

"Can't," I said. "I've got an appointment this afternoon for some new professional photos."

That surprised her. "You hate having still pictures taken."

"Unfortunately, I need them. My hair is longer now than when I started on the show. Bring a piece of Carole's 'Deadly' pie home for me."

"If there's any left. Our employees are all sugar junkies."

Gesturing to the cooler and my tote bag, she asked, "Do you want help loading up for class?"

"No, thanks. I put the rest of what I'll need in the Jeep earlier, along with my outfits for the photos."

"If you've got it covered, I'm going to make myself a quick breakfast and get to the shop." Her tone was full of affection as she added, "Aunt Del, I know you'd rather have a tooth filled than sit for publicity shots, but don't freeze up in front of the camera. Just be yourself, like on TV."

"All right. I promise."

Saying that I was going to be photographed this afternoon was true as far as it went, but my lie of omission made me remember the discussion we'd had a few days ago. What I had just told Eileen was another example of "truth with an asterisk."

After securing all the food items I'd need in the back of the Jeep, I climbed into the driver's seat. Before I turned on the ignition, I dialed Nicholas's numbers.

No answer on his home phone. No answer on his cell.

I didn't leave a message on either of his numbers.

24

My little cooking school, The Happy Table, is located in the rear of a home appliance store on Montana Avenue and Seventeenth Street in Santa Monica. A very nice, elderly Vietnamese couple, Mr. and Mrs. Luc Tran, own the store and allow me to rent what had formerly been a large storage room, where they had lived when they first went into business. As the enterprise became successful, they moved into the apartment upstairs. My good luck was finding that a bathroom and running water were already in the space when I was looking for a location for the school.

The Trans, refugees from South Vietnam, had spent years either trapped in war or waiting in camps for their turn to emigrate to the US. In spite of the horrors they must have endured, Mrs. Tran's demeanor was always sunny. Mr. Tran, frail from what she had told me were his several years of imprisonment in North Vietnam, spoke little, but his eyes were warm and kind. I liked them, and admired them. Over the years, when I faced some inconvenience, rather than let it upset me, I reminded myself of the Trans and what they had gone through. It snapped me right out of any trace of self-pity.

My arrangement with the Trans was that they supplied the six freestanding working stoves on which my students would cook and bake. In addition to the rent I paid, having my school in the rear of the store was to their advantage because it meant that anyone coming to The Happy Table had to reach it by walking a winding path through artful displays of their wares. My students not only bought their merchandise, but often returned with friends to shop for more items for their homes.

That Saturday, I managed to put worry about Nicholas out of my mind during the classes I taught, and found pleasure in the people who enjoyed learning new things about cooking. It was special fun to watch the children, who were excited to be creating good things to eat with their mothers. Part of the Mommy and Me class was encouraging the "mes" to help their "mommies" neaten up after the cooking and the subsequent eating.

My class for adults was composed mostly of widowed men who wanted to learn to cook for themselves, and three widows and a divorcée who said they'd enrolled to expand their food knowledge. I suspected that the women were more interested in meeting single men. There was also a young couple who planned to share kitchen duties, and wanted to learn how to make meals that tasted as good as what they'd order in restaurants but cost a lot less.

The student who always arrived first and left last was a silver-haired man who dressed like a Broadway dandy from a 1940s movie musical: freshly barbered and shaved, with an ascot around his neck and a white carnation in his lapel. His name was Harmon Dubois, and he must have been close to eighty years old, but walked with the quick steps of a man half his age.

Eileen jokingly referred to him as "the suck-up" because on the second week of class he brought me a bouquet of pink roses he said he'd handpicked from his garden, and on the third week presented me with his self-published book of poetry titled *Dark-Haired Goddesses*. When I opened the slim volume to the page where he'd placed a bookmark, I saw he had autographed it to me as his "muse." He said he'd been inspired to write it when he saw my television show. He and his late wife — who, like me, had dark hair, he said — watched every episode during her final illness. Those months had compelled him to begin writing poetry, and to learn to cook.

In class, Harmon made a habit of walking behind me, wiping off countertops, and generally helping to clean up. I usually found his extreme attentiveness a little much and tried to discourage it, but today I was thankful he was there because I needed to leave class as quickly as possible after three o'clock to meet Liddy and Shannon for our trip to Roxanne Redding's home studio. His help with straightening up and taking out the trash would save me a precious fifteen minutes.

The big hit of today's session in my adults' class was a new creation by my producer friend, Fred Caruso. Fred was a terrific Italian cook with a sense of humor. He had dubbed his new main dish "Don't Be a Fool, Eat Fred's Pasta Fazool."

As usual, when I asked for comments, Harmon spoke up first, declaring the pasta to be "worthy of the lovely lady who just taught us how to make it."

Our plan was that Shannon and I would meet at my house at three thirty and go together to Roxanne Redding's home and studio in Brentwood. Liddy lived in Beverly Hills, which was on the other side of Brentwood, so she was going to catch up with us there.

Thanks to Harmon Dubois's after-class help, I got home at three twenty. I thought I'd be ten minutes ahead of Shannon, but she was already there, sitting on the front stoop with Tuffy, who started wagging his back end when he saw me.

Shannon said, "I got here at three so I could take Tuffy for a walk in case you were late. I hope you don't mind."

"Of course not, but how did you get in? Eileen's at our store."

"I remembered where you hid your spare key." She gestured toward the ceramic statue of a black poodle that stood next to a pot of red geraniums beside the stoop. "I put it back under your little replica of Big Tuff."

While greeting Tuffy with a vigorous two-handed petting, I said, "Remind me to give you a key for emergencies. Liddy has one. In fact" — I lifted up the poodle figure and removed the key Shannon had used — "take this one. I shouldn't keep it here. It's the first place a burglar is likely to look."

Shannon slipped the key into one of the

pockets in her cargo pants.

Cargo pants?

I had been so surprised to see her outside with Tuffy when I came home that I hadn't immediately noticed what she was wearing: olive green cargo pants and a matching safari jacket. It was an unusual look for Shannon, who had always chosen clothes that were closer-fitting, to make herself look slimmer. I asked, "Is that a new outfit?"

"From this morning. I went shopping with Liddy because I wanted to get something so I could conceal . . . this." She pulled an object out of her jacket pocket that fit into the palm of her hand. It took me a moment to realize it was a small camera.

Shannon beamed. "It's digital. The latest thing from that spy shop we went to. Takes a hundred pictures before you have to put in a new *whatchamacallit* — the brain card. Liddy got one, too. We practiced for an hour and now we can work 'em just with our fingers, without even looking. Honey, we are *set* to investigate."

"Thank you."

I hugged her for her loyalty, and because I was so happy to see her well. She — not to mention John and Eileen — had suffered through her long, dark years of psychotic breakdowns and hospitalizations, until finally the right doctor and the right combination of medications had given her back her life.

When I'd phoned Roxanne Redding the day before, I was prepared to have a difficult time getting her to agree to photograph me, considering that we'd last seen each other the night of her husband's murder. But she hadn't been as hard to persuade as I'd feared, even after she remembered who I was. Not that she was eager to do it, but she admitted that she could use the distraction of work. She quoted a price of eight hundred dollars for the session, for which I would receive two finished prints of my choosing. Additional prints could be purchased separately. There would be an extra charge for anything more than minimal retouching.

"I hope I won't need more than minimal. I want to look like myself — just a little bit better," I'd said.

"And I prefer to photograph people as they really are, but good lighting can disguise a multitude of sins." She added that any use of her work for publicity purposes must carry her photo credit.

I told her those terms were acceptable and we made the date.

When I repeated Roxanne Redding's fee

to Liddy, she was amazed.

"Alec charged three thousand dollars for a sitting. If she just shoots you in focus, you're getting a bargain."

Bargain or not, eight hundred dollars was twice what I'd hoped she would charge, and more than I could really afford, but for Nicholas's sake I needed to talk to her, and to give Liddy and Shannon the opportunity to search the house for clues to the identity of Alec Redding's killer. I knew the risks we were taking, but I couldn't think of any other way to get us into 190 Bella Vista Drive.

At ten minutes before four Saturday afternoon, I brought my Jeep to a stop in front of the Reddings' house. Before Shannon and I could climb out, Liddy pulled up behind us. She got out of her Range Rover carrying her makeup case. If our mission to find information helpful to Nicholas hadn't been so acute, I would have laughed when I saw what Liddy was wearing. It was a new outfit almost identical to Shannon's, except that Liddy's cargo pants and safari jacket were tan.

Shannon and I divided the six outfits I'd put together to keep Roxanne busy taking pictures. The three of us, carrying our assorted burdens, went up the walk to the entrance.

The crime-scene tape was gone and the two-story redbrick house would have looked exactly as it had when I'd come here before, except for the black funeral wreath on the front door, stark and dramatic against the white paint.

"I hope the housekeeper I told you about doesn't work on weekends," I said.

"Don't worry," Liddy said. "If she does, we'll take turns keeping her occupied while the other looks for clues."

I shifted the outfits I carried onto my left arm, pressed the bell button, and waited.

A minute passed. No response.

"Maybe she's not home," Liddy said.

"I'm sure she is. The tan Lexus she drove Thursday night is in the carport."

Beside it was the big black Mercedes SUV that must have belonged to Alec Redding. I was glad to see that the car I had guessed might belong to the housekeeper was not in the driveway today.

I rang the bell again. This time I leaned close to the door and heard the faint ringing inside.

Then I heard footsteps coming to the door.

25

Roxanne Redding opened the door. She was all in black: turtleneck sweater, jeans, running shoes. Her short black hair, which had been gelled into spikes the two times I had seen her before, wasn't gelled today. It lay in a flat, boyish no-style cut around her narrow, pale face.

When I met her at the Hollywood Film Society luncheon, I had thought of her frame as angular and athletic, but now she seemed thin and soft. Her eyes, without the dramatic eye makeup, showed dark rings of sleeplessness. And grief. I recognized the grief; I had seen it in my own eyes for months after Mack died, every time I caught a glimpse of my reflection.

"Hello, Mrs. Redding. Thank you for letting me come for a sitting. I wouldn't have asked if I didn't have a serious time problem."

"It's all right," she said. "It's better for me

to keep busy."

"I think you know Liddy," I said.

"Yes. Hello."

"She's going to do my makeup. And this is my friend, Shannon, who's going to help with the clothes. I brought a selection for you to look over and choose the ones you'd like me to wear."

"Fine." She acknowledged Shannon with a nod and stepped back to allow us to enter.

When I was inside Thursday night I was too worried about Nicholas, and then shocked at the sight of Redding's body lying in his photo studio, to notice anything else about the house. Now, as we followed Roxanne down the hallway, I saw that the floor was dark wood, protected by a wool runner in a burgundy and black floral pattern. The stark white walls were an effective background for a dozen black-framed Picasso drawings that I recognized as replicas from the artist's erotic one-hundred-print Vollard Suite. To anyone who had seen the entire collection, as Mack and I had ten years earlier during one of the rare occasions when it had been on public exhibition, the work was unforgettable. The prints in the Reddings' hallway were part of the sequence that showed "life" in Picasso's studio, featuring idealized portraits of the artist reclining with nude models and various pieces of his art. I wondered what this choice said about Alec Redding. I didn't have to know his wife to feel that those prints weren't what a woman would have selected.

I've always been fascinated by what kind of art people choose in decorating their homes. Except for an oil portrait of Liddy and Bill and their then five-year-old twin boys above the living room fireplace, the Marshalls' home is otherwise filled with paintings and prints of flowers, reflecting their sunny personalities.

John and Shannon O'Hara have pictures of Eileen at every stage of her life all over the house, along with Shannon's needle-point pillows and John's collection of old magnifying glasses. Mack wasn't into collecting anything except books by Joe Wambaugh, but I loved finding beautiful crystal bowls and interesting dishes at yard sales for bargain prices. Nicholas has the most unusual collection I've ever seen: license plates. Each one is connected in some way to the crime stories he's been covering for twenty years.

Roxanne Redding paused for perhaps a second at the archway leading to the photo studio. It was no more than a hitch in her step, and I probably wouldn't have noticed if I hadn't known that we were going to the site of her husband's murder. After that fleeting moment, Roxanne proceeded into the studio with a determined stride.

"There's a dressing room on the other side of that curtain," she said, gesturing to a partitioned-off space on the far left side of the studio. "There's a makeup table and chair, too. Also a rack for the clothes."

"I'll go hang them up so they don't get wrinkled," Shannon said, taking my load and adding it to hers.

As Shannon hurried to the dressing area, I noticed for the first time the wall opposite the lights. It was a gallery of eleven-by-fourteen-inch dry-mounted portraits of famous faces. "What marvelous photos. Were they taken by your husband?"

Previously, the only examples I had seen of Alec Redding's work were a quick glance at the modeling shots of Celeste, and then a much closer look at that pie photo. Even as I was shocked by the obvious intent of her props and the pose, another part of my brain was registering the high quality of the photographer's work.

Roxanne nodded, and swallowed. I saw a glint of moisture in her eyes, but she was apparently strong-willed enough to keep back tears. "He was an absolute genius," she said softly. "It was my incredible luck to have worked with him." Then she added, almost shyly, "Would you like to see some of my photos?"

"Absolutely," I said. Liddy and Shannon, who had returned from the dressing room, concurred with enthusiasm.

Roxanne led us past the living room and a formal dining room across the hall from the studio to a small den next to a swinging door that I guessed led into the kitchen. Like the other rooms on this ground floor, except for the kitchen, it was entered through an archway instead of a door.

She turned on the overhead light. "Those are mine."

There were six photographs, also eleven-by-fourteen inches and dry-mounted on the wall behind the couch. Portraits, too, but not of the famous. An elderly couple holding hands; a boy in a field of flowers; a little girl peeking out at the camera from behind a tree trunk, her smooth face in contrast to the rough bark; a red tree kangaroo sitting on a limb with a kangaroo baby peering out of her pouch; a chimpanzee washing his hands in a basin of water; a father holding his son close against his chest.

"These are beautiful," I said.

Roxanne Redding was a different kind of photographer than her husband had been. His work was bold and dynamic, celebrating his famous subjects in flattering shafts of light and softening shadows. Her photographs showed a gentleness and sensitivity that were at odds with the image she'd presented of herself, with the spiked hair and heavy eye makeup.

"Alec taught me photography." Her smile was wistful. "I've been nursing this fantasy that one day we would be hailed as the twenty-first century's Edward Weston and Tina Modotti."

"Who were they?" Shannon asked.

"He was one of the most famous photographers of the early twentieth century," Roxanne said. "She was a pretty Italian immigrant who'd acted in a couple of silent films. They met at a party. She became his lover, his model, and then his protégée. He was the famous artist; she was the heart." Roxanne sighed. "Their story didn't end very happily, either. I never thought about that until now."

"Was he killed?" Liddy asked.

"No. She was. She went to Spain and died in the revolution. I don't want to talk about it anymore."

To lighten the mood in the room, I said,

"I'm delighted that you're going to photograph me."

"You need pictures. I need the work." She switched off the overhead light and her tone became all business. "We'd better get to it. Let me see what you brought to wear."

Roxanne Redding examined my six outfits and immediately eliminated two of them. "In a photo, this one will add twenty pounds, and this one positively screams *this year.*"

"It's my newest dress," I admitted.

"Which would be fine if we were selling the dress, but we're supposed to be selling *you.*" She shoved it down the rack next to the first one she had purged from consideration. She came to my red skirt suit. "Definitely not."

"That's my favorite outfit."

"Della looks really good in it," Shannon said.

Roxanne Redding shook her head. "Wear it out in the world as much as you like, but the color's too strong for your purposes. If you wore that in a photo, people would see the color first, and then maybe look at your face."

Liddy nodded agreement. "That's the difference between a modeling shot and publicity pictures."

Roxanne held up my black pantsuit with the sapphire blue sweater. "Lose the jacket. This sweater's perfect."

"I think my hips will look too big without the jacket," I said.

"Don't worry about it. I'll be shooting you from the waist up. This blue is a great shade for you, with your dark hair and blue eyes."

The next garment she approved was my long-sleeved beige silk shirt. And, finally, my pale gray wool dress. "Perfect," she said. "Jewel neckline to show off your face, long sleeves to hide the arms."

That hurt. For a moment I forgot why I was really in the studio. "There's nothing wrong with my arms."

"Not to the naked eye," she said. "Cameras have X-ray vision. The skin on your arms isn't loose yet, but if you don't start exercising them — like by dawn tomorrow — you'll start flapping in a few months."

Silently vowing that I was not going to let myself "flap," I asked, "What do you want me to put on first?"

She took the gray dress off the rack and handed it to me. "Do you have a piece of signature jewelry?"

"Just this." I fingered my silver pendant watch. It had been Mack's last Christmas present to me. "I can only wear a pendant watch because I do so much cooking and washing my hands I'd ruin one on my wrist."

"Then that's your signature accessory. Get dressed and I'll set up."

When I emerged from the dressing area, wearing the gray dress and after receiving Liddy's makeup expertise, I saw Roxanne positioning a white enamel two-step kitchen stool in front of a roll of sky blue background paper. The white background paper on which Alec Redding had lain was gone, as was the painted white stool that appeared to have been the murder weapon. Both, I thought, must be at the police forensics lab.

Gesturing to the kitchen stool, Roxanne said, "Sit."

I sat.

"Put both hands flat on the seat of the stool, then turn your face and torso toward me."

I did.

While she was positioning me, I saw Liddy and Shannon slip out of the studio.

Roxanne raised one of the several cameras that rested on a small worktable next to her, looked through the lens, adjusted the focus, and fired off a few shots.

"Now, without moving your body, take your hands off the seat and let them lie relaxed in your lap," she said. "Stomach in. Chest out. Don't slouch."

When she was satisfied with my posture, she moved around me, a few inches at a time, snapping different angles, stopping sometimes to make a minute alteration to one of the standing lights.

When she paused to change cameras, I said, "Will you be going into business for yourself?"

She examined a lens. "I have to earn a living. It's going to be hard. Alec was the celebrity. The big clients never knew how much of the work I did. Sometimes his only act was to press the button after I'd set the lights." She said that matter-of-factly, with sadness, and without any trace of resentment.

"That must have been painful for you sometimes, not to get the credit you deserved."

"No, not at all. He was a genius. I just take pictures. I loved him so much." She made a sweeping gesture at the studio. "We were a team, but I'm not going to be able to keep this house without his income."

"I'm sorry," I said. "Isn't there life insurance?"

She shook her head. "We thought we were too young for that — and we don't have children to educate. Because this is *Hollywood*" — she scowled on that word — "we had to keep up a front, go to all the big-ticket events, be seen everywhere, drive the best cars, have this great house. . . ."

Her voice trailed off, then she straightened her shoulders. "We lived the good life, spending, spending — like squirrels who don't save any acorns to eat during the winter."

I thought this was my opportunity. "Have you thought about who had a grudge against your husband?"

She looked up at me, frowning. "Don't they have the person who killed Alec?"

"There's no real evidence against him." I tried to sound casual. "Do you have any idea who the police should talk to?"

"Everyone loved Alec. If one of us was going to be murdered, it should have been *me*. Alec was my best friend — I don't have anybody else."

I saw her eyes fill with tears. She took a tissue from her pocket, turned away, and blew her nose. After a moment, she said, "Sorry. Allergies."

I knew it wasn't allergies, and I suddenly felt as though my visit was not just a pretext to investigate, but a cruel hoax. I wanted to tell her how sorry I was that I had invaded her grief, but I couldn't do that, so I said gently, "My husband died. I know how you feel."

Roxanne froze. "Do you? You've got a career of your own. Alec was my whole world." She tossed the crumpled tissue into the wastebasket below the worktable and said briskly, "Go put on that beige silk blouse."

It was almost two hours into the photo session and I was wearing the third outfit that Roxanne had approved as camera-worthy, the blue sweater and black slacks.

Liddy and Shannon had come in and out of the studio several times. Whenever one of them returned I tried to read her face, but if they had found anything, they were keeping it to themselves.

Shannon had said she needed to make some phone calls and she was going outside so she wouldn't disturb us.

Roxanne, intent on photographing me, waved one hand in assent. This time Shannon had been gone for half an hour.

Liddy's new pretext for leaving the studio was to ask if Roxanne would like something to drink.

"No," she said, without looking at Liddy. "We're almost finished. If you're thirsty, the refrigerator in the kitchen is full of soft drinks. Help yourself."

Liddy thanked her and left the studio again.

Roxanne Redding hadn't seemed to have noticed their coming and going. As a photographer, she was meticulous, completely into her work. I doubted that she would have noticed an earthquake if one hit the area while she was concentrating on taking a picture.

But it wasn't an earthquake that interrupted us. It was the ringing of the doorbell.

At first, she didn't appear to have heard it. But the third time the person outside pressed the bell, long and insistently, she looked up from the camera lens and cursed.

Liddy appeared at the entrance to the studio. "Do you want me to answer the door?"

"All right. But don't let anybody in. I'm busy."

I heard Liddy going down the hallway, her steps light and quick, the sound of the front door opening.

Then I heard her gasp.

Heavy footsteps pounded toward us.

Roxanne Redding lowered her camera and I half rose from the stool just as a large male figure appeared at the entrance to the studio.

"What the hell is going on here?" demanded John O'Hara.

26

John wasn't alone. Close behind him was Hugh Weaver. When Weaver saw me, his eyebrows shot up toward his receding hairline.

Liddy, the tail on their kite, stopped behind them and pressed her back against the archway's curve. She looked as guilty as I felt, but John and Weaver weren't staring at her.

I decided to brazen it out. "John, hello."

"What do you think you're doing?"

"Having my picture taken."

Weaver's brows came down and met in a glower of skepticism. *"Here?"*

I considered pretending to be offended at his implied accusation, but decided to play bland innocence. "I need new photos, and Mrs. Redding is a wonderful photographer."

John turned his laser gaze on Liddy. "And what's your part in this?"

"I . . . we . . ."

"Liddy's helping me," I said.

"Helping you to do *what?*"

At that moment, Shannon came into the room. The bright smile on her face died when she saw John. "Oh, dear."

John was as shocked as she. "Shan?"

Shannon moved to Liddy's side, clutched her hand, and said in a small voice, "Hi, honey."

Roxanne Redding put down the camera she'd been using and stepped toward John. "Detective . . . O'Hara? That's your name — O'Hara? You know these women?"

Weaver gave a snort. "Oh, we know 'em all right."

John glared at him.

Liddy said, "Los Angeles is actually a small town."

At some five hundred square miles, Los Angeles is far from a small town, but no one paid attention to her facile comment.

Making my tone casual, I told Roxanne, "We do know each other. John O'Hara and my late husband were detective partners. By coincidence, we're all social friends."

"*Is* this a coincidence?" Her voice was heavy with suspicion. "Is something going on here?"

Okay, time to leave.

I said, "Mrs. Redding, I appreciate you

244

taking the photos I need. Will you let me know when I can see them?"

"Yes, but —"

"I don't want to interfere with whatever John and Detective Weaver came to see you about, so we'll just clear out of your way."

"We'll get the rest of your clothes," Shannon said.

Shannon and Liddy snapped out of their rigid positions and headed for the curtained-off dressing room.

John gave Weaver a silent signal. Weaver lumbered over to Roxanne, took out his little notebook, and said, "Sorry to interrupt, but we wondered if you could fill us in on a few details."

John clamped one hand on my arm and drew me off to the side. "What are you doing here?"

I pulled my arm from his grip. "Don't *do* that. I was having my picture taken. Liddy and Shannon came along to help with clothes and makeup." That was my story and I was going to stick to it.

Shannon and Liddy emerged through the curtain, laden with my other outfits and Liddy's makeup case.

John growled to me, "Later. And I want the truth."

Shannon blew John a kiss. "See you at

home, Johnny."

He managed a smile for her, but I knew he was angry with me.

The three of us hurried out of the studio and down the pathway to my Jeep and Liddy's Rover.

"I found out something," Liddy whispered.

"Maybe I did, too," Shannon said, "but I don't know what it means."

I heaved the armful of clothes into the back of the Jeep. "My house. So we can talk freely."

Back in my kitchen, with Tuffy on his bed by the refrigerator and Emma curled up at the base of the computer monitor on the desk, I put my pantsuit jacket over the back of one of the kitchen chairs and we sat down to compare notes.

Liddy, grinning, took her spy camera out of her pocket and put it on the table. "I found the folder with their income tax returns for last year and photographed all the pages. I didn't get a chance to study their expenses for more than a few seconds, but I found out that they have five phones: two landlines at the house, and three cell phones."

"They're two people. Why do you suppose

they need three cell phones?" Shannon asked.

I speculated, "For private calls? Maybe private from the other spouse?"

"Could be," Liddy said. "The bills for one of those cell phones are addressed directly to a business manager, Birnam Woods, instead of going to the house like their other bills do. I recognized the name of the management firm because it's the same one that handles our money."

"If they have a business manager, why do any bills go to their home?" Shannon asked.

"Maybe they do what we do," Liddy said. "I go over all the monthlies that come in to make sure they're accurate, and then send them over to the business manager for him to pay out of whichever account is appropriate, household or business. That way, by tax time, they already know what we can deduct and what we can't. I also found out the Reddings have a huge mortgage, pay big property taxes, and have a lot of credit-card debt."

"That substantiates Roxanne's fear that she may not be able to keep the house without her husband's earnings. She also told me they didn't have life insurance policies." I turned to Shannon. "Did you have any luck?"

"I found out their housekeeper doesn't vacuum under the bed. That's probably why Roxanne has a box of pictures there — under her side. I could tell whose side was whose because she has a picture of him on her bedside table, plus harlequin reading glasses that no man would ever wear." She took her spy camera out of one of her pockets and put it on the table next to Liddy's. "They photographed each other *nude!*"

I felt my eyes widening in surprise. "Both of them nude?"

Shannon gestured to her camera. "I took some pictures of the pictures. Whoever photographed him — I suppose it must have been her — took pictures of his assorted body parts."

"Which body parts?" Liddy wanted to know.

"Not *those* parts," Shannon said with a giggle. "There's a picture of his naked leg, and his upper back, his wrist, and one hand. Very artsy stuff. His hand is resting on a wrinkled sheet. I swear, it just reeks of sex."

"Any pictures of his face?"

"No. I just assumed it was Alec Redding," Shannon said. "I never met the man. Anyway, the pictures of Roxanne are different."

"How?" I asked.

"Full-length shots of her, starkers. Front,

248

back, sideways, standing, leaning, curled up with her knees touching her forehead. I have to say she looks a lot better without clothes than you'd think to see her dressed. Oh, and she's a secret eater. She's got a Ziploc bag full of Oreo cookies hidden on the top shelf of her closet, behind her handbags." Shannon sighed. "Up until I found the cookies, I thought of what we were doing as a mission to help your Nick, but I felt a little dirty when I found her stash. Strangers shouldn't know something like that about a person."

I reached across the table and squeezed Shannon's hand with affection. "I'm sorry I put you in that position."

Suddenly I heard the sound of Tuffy's toenails on the kitchen floor and a low whine deep in his throat. I turned to see him standing up. Alert.

Then someone rang my doorbell.

27

Tuffy was staring toward the front door, but he wasn't barking.

He knows who's there.

I was afraid that I did, too.

So did Shannon. "Oh, Lord. I bet it's Johnny."

"We can't panic," I said.

"Who can't? Those orange prison jumpsuits make everyone look fat," Liddy said.

The doorbell rang again.

I took a deep breath, squared my shoulders, and went to answer it. Tuffy trotted behind me.

I opened it and said with a pleasant smile, "Hello, John."

John leaned forward and gave Tuffy a quick pat. "I saw all your cars outside," he said.

John's tone wasn't warm, but at least he wasn't wearing his designed-to-intimidate face.

"Come in," I said. "I was about to make some fresh coffee."

When I returned to the kitchen with John, Liddy and Shannon gave him cheerful greetings. If they were nervous, they hid it well.

John said quietly, "Hello. Again."

Liddy stood. "Well, this has been fun, but I've got to go. Bill will be getting home from his golf game any minute."

"Do you have your makeup case?" I asked.

"It's in my car."

"Thanks for getting me camera ready," I said.

"Anytime."

Shannon got up. "I should go, too, Del." She smiled at her husband. "What time do you want dinner, hon? I'm going to make shepherd's pie."

"Sounds good," John said. "Figure I'll be home by eight."

Shannon gave her husband a quick kiss on the cheek before she and Liddy made their hasty departure.

John and I looked at each other as we listened to the front door open and close.

To break the awkward silence, I said, "How about that coffee?"

"No." He gestured toward the chairs just vacated by Liddy and Shannon.

That's when I noticed the two spy cameras that had been on the table were gone.

"Della, sit. I'm too tired to have this conversation standing up."

I sat, and he took the seat across the table. For a moment, he just gazed at me, which made me very uncomfortable. It was worse than if he'd started shouting. What was most disturbing was that he looked sad. John O'Hara was one of the dearest people in the world to me. I didn't want my trying to help Nicholas to ruin my close friendship with John. I decided to face the problem head-on.

"Are you angry with me?" I asked.

He shook his head. "I was before, but I'm not anymore. I'm seriously worried that you're going to get hurt."

"What do you mean?"

"You're so convinced your . . . D'Martino . . . didn't kill Redding. You won't even consider that you're backing the wrong horse. It's going to be devastating if you find out you're wrong about him."

He'd hit a nerve, and it stung, but I didn't want to admit it. "I believe Nicholas is innocent, but I want to know the truth. Whatever that is."

"I guess you think you're helping me investigate."

"I know I am," I said with heat. "Mack used to tell me that even simple investigations were a group effort."

"He probably said 'collective' or 'team,'" he said in a sardonic tone.

"Yes, you're right; he did say 'collective.' So many times I heard you two talk about gathering information, collecting enough facts to make sense out of a case. You said that the tiniest bit, even if it didn't look like anything much at first, sometimes turned out to be just what you needed to break the case."

John's smile was rueful. "I didn't know you were paying attention."

"Surprise," I joked.

"Let's get serious. You kept telling me how often a victim's spouse is the killer, so you went to see Roxanne Redding. That's interfering with a police investigation."

"Not really. I didn't ask her, 'Where were you around nine o'clock Thursday night?' That's your job. What I did do was persuade her to take new publicity pictures for me — which I need — so I'd have an excuse to talk to her in a casual way. Woman to woman."

"Fine, but why involve Shan and Liddy?"

"They wanted to help." Now came the hardest part of this conversation, but I had to tell him. "And while I kept Roxanne busy, they looked around the house."

"Damn it, Della!" He smacked his hand on the table so hard the salt and pepper shakers jumped.

"Don't go ballistic on me, please. I only want to help," I said sincerely. "Could you have gotten a warrant to search the Redding house?"

"We didn't need one. Redding's photo studio was the scene of the crime. The SID techs went through the rest of the place to check for blood, or signs of a struggle, but the only blood was in the studio. The widow said she didn't think anything was missing. The expensive cameras were all there. We asked her to check her jewelry box, and his, and she said nothing had been taken. She was getting hysterical, so I asked the name of her doctor. It's a woman. I called her and she came over to stay the night. She told me she and Mrs. Redding went to college together."

"When you went through the house, you were only supposed to look for things out in plain sight. You didn't have probable cause to search through their files, or their closets," I said.

John carefully aligned the salt and pepper

shakers against the rack of napkins. "Go on."

"Shannon and Liddy left everything exactly as they found it. But we learned some things that might help you."

He grunted. "Nancy Drew and her two girlfriends."

"Why don't you take out your notebook? In case you want to write anything down."

John gave me a look that was somewhere between amused and surprised, but he did take out his investigator's book and opened it to a fresh page. That was progress.

I recounted my conversations with Roxanne, before and during the photo session, relating her fear that she'd lose the house without Redding's income, and that they had no life insurance policies on each other.

"But you can check that out, John. Maybe they didn't have life, but it could be they had mortgage insurance."

I added that according to the records Liddy found, they were living very high and in debt.

"Liddy discovered Redding has the same business manager that she and Bill have, a firm called Birnam Woods. And that they have two landlines and three cell phones. I don't know what it means, but the bills for one of the cells go directly to the business manager and not to the house. You can get the phone dumps. It would be interesting to know who they called."

"Weaver's already on that," John said.

"Sorry. I didn't mean to tell you your job."

He raised an eyebrow at me and said dryly, "Thanks."

"Shannon discovered a box of nude photographs under their bed. Pictures of Roxanne, that he probably took, and shots of a naked man — or at least of his arms and legs and hands. Shannon described them as art studies. Roxanne probably took those. I told you she's a talented photographer."

"Any indication who the man is?"

"We guessed it must be Redding, but what if it isn't? Can't the medical examiner take measurements of Alec Redding's limbs and hands and compare them to the photos?"

"I don't know why I had to spend all that time in the academy, and then the years in uniform, before I got my gold shield." In spite of his sarcasm, he made another note, then sat back in his chair and looked at me. "I'd like to have your impression of the widow."

"Friends again?"

"We'll always be friends," he said. "No matter what."

Until that moment, I hadn't fully realized

how worried I had been about that. "That's a relief. Okay, Roxanne Redding . . . I think she really loved her husband. She said he was her 'world.' But people have killed the ones they love before. Does she have an alibi?"

"She said she was down in Little Tokyo, at a Japanese movie house showing *Seven Samurai*. She opened the purse she carried that night and found her ticket stub. I put it in an evidence bag to give to Forensics tomorrow. Not that I expect we'll learn anything useful."

"I saw *Seven Samurai* on TV a couple of years ago," I said. "It's a long movie, but it has magnificent black-and-white photography."

"Speaking of photography, she showed me the picture Redding took of D'Martino's daughter, the one with the smirk on her face and the pie in her hand. If a jury saw that photograph, they'd think it could have made D'Martino mad enough to kill Redding to get it."

I said, "First of all, if it ever came to a trial, I'm sure Olivia Wayne would get that picture suppressed as prejudicial. Second, if Roxanne showed you the photo, then it's still in the studio, so whoever killed Redding didn't take it."

"He couldn't have. It's on a digital smart card, stored with others in their temperature-controlled wine cellar."

"Clever. I thought most people kept their valuables in safes concealed behind paintings."

"Old school," John said. "Movies and TV made that the first place a thief would check." He gazed at me with concern. "According to the widow, the last picture that girl, Celeste, posed for was her idea. Celeste brought the apron and the pie to the photo shoot with her. Said she wanted Redding to take the picture as a joke. Mrs. Redding said Celeste didn't tell them what the joke was, but I got it. She was making fun of *you,* wasn't she, Del?"

"That was my guess," I said.

"And my guess is she's not happy about your . . . relationship . . . with her father."

"Oh, John, she looks sophisticated and she has an arrogant manner, but she's just a young girl who was kept away from her father for most of her life. Now that she's finally getting to know him, it's only natural that she would be possessive, and hostile to whatever woman he liked."

"Must be pretty tough on you," he said.

It was, but I didn't want to admit it to

John. "I'm the grown-up. I'll try to be patient."

"Have you seen D'Martino, or talked to him since we were all together at the station Thursday night?"

"No." I wanted to get away from that subject, so I pointed to his notebook and asked, "Are you going to follow up on the information I gave you?"

"It isn't much, but, yes, I will. And I'm developing some other avenues of exploration. In spite of what you seem to think, I'm investigating this murder with an open mind."

I felt a surge of hope. "What have you found out?"

He tucked the little book into his jacket pocket and shook his head. "You should know I can't share information with a civilian."

"That's ridiculous! I'm not some stranger."

"You're not on the job, either." He stood. "I'm letting you off the hook for what you did today, but I don't want any more interfering."

"There's one thing you can tell me," I said.

John rolled his eyes and sighed loudly.

Grinning, I said, "Just one more thing. Promise."

"That is . . . ?"

"What Celeste said when you interviewed her. Did she claim she was with her mother and the prince in their suite all evening?"

"No comment."

"Oh, John, don't be so stubborn. Olivia will tell me. I'm still her client, too, from that situation we had a few months ago. You remember."

"I remember," he said grimly. "You almost got yourself killed."

"Since she's going to tell me anyway, why not just save me the time?"

He gave an exasperated sigh. "Celeste said she and her mother were out driving in Celeste's new car all evening, that her mother wanted a tour of the city she'd left a long time ago. They got back to the hotel at ten thirty. Garage attendant confirmed. That blows her father's alibi right out of the water."

"What it means is that none of them have an alibi."

"But so far D'Martino's the one with the motive."

"There was a time when the police thought that about *you*," I said softly. Without thinking, I reached out to take his hand, but he stepped away quickly.

"Take care of yourself," he said, and left

without another word. A moment later I heard the front door close.

I exchanged my slacks for a pair of sweatpants, and the high heels I had worn for the photo shoot for a pair of running shoes, hooked Tuffy's leash to his collar, and took him for a walk. We were well into the second block when I realized that John had gone without asking me to give him my word that I'd stay out of police business.

Had he forgotten? Or didn't he ask because he knew I wouldn't promise and he didn't want to fight?

By the time Tuffy and I had strolled the neighborhood for a good half hour, I had decided on my next move. It didn't involve investigating; this was personal. Inside the house, I shoved my driver's license, some cash, and my keys into a pocket of the sweats, and gave Tuffy and Emma good-bye strokes. Climbing into the Jeep, I drove down to the Santa Monica Pier where I planned to spend as long as I could manage working out on their climbing wall. That exercise was not only good for strengthening my legs and tightening my waist, but it was going to keep my upper arms from the dreaded "flapping" that Roxanne Redding had predicted.

■ ■ ■ ■

I got home two hours later, my hair damp with sweat and every muscle in my body aching.

In the kitchen, intending to find something to have for dinner after I showered, I noticed that I'd left my black suit jacket on the back of a chair instead of hanging it up in the closet with the matching slacks.

When I picked the jacket up by the collar I got a surprise. It was heavier than it should have been. Looking closer, I saw a bulge in one of the pockets. When I slipped my hand inside, I pulled out the two little spy cameras that had disappeared from the table.

Liddy or Shannon must have put them there when they heard John at the front door.

I had no idea what I would find, but after taking a shower and having something to eat, I planned to carefully go through the pictures they had snapped.

It was a place to start.

28

After showering and taking Tuffy for his final evening walk, I lay down. I told myself that I just needed a few minutes to rest my eyes before beginning to examine the spy photos, but I fell asleep in my clothes with the light on and didn't wake up until a few minutes before five next morning.

Tuffy was lying on the foot of the bed, snoring softly, and Emma was curled up on what I called "the guest pillow" beside me. "Guest pillow" was a term Liddy had coined a year after Mack died, when she told me it was time I started to date and "to live again." It took another year before I could even think about romance. Since then, the only human head that had rested on that pillow was Nicholas's.

I thought about Roxanne Redding. Was she lying in the bed she had shared with her husband? Was she sleeping? It was Sunday, the beginning of her fourth day of widow-hood.

When Mack died, I'd lain on his side of the bed for several nights, as though that could somehow reverse time, flip the calendar backward to an hour before his heart attack, when I'd be able to think of something that would have kept him from going out on the jog that killed him. Part of me knew that nothing I did could change what happened, but I wasn't being rational. The pain of his loss was deeper than I could have ever imagined. I thought I'd never be able to breathe normally again.

There's a cliché that claims "time heals all wounds." Many clichés are rooted in truth, but not that one. Yes, pain fades with time. Even the memory of pain fades, but there are some wounds that become part of who we are. As horrible as it was to lose Mack, it made me stronger. Not tough, but tougher. Short of losing a child, the worst had happened to me, and I survived.

My faith holds that I'm still here, alive, for a reason. Nobody can tell me what that reason is, but, to me, "faith" means believing what you cannot see.

I believe Nicholas is innocent of Alec Redding's murder.

At the moment, I'd like to thump him over

the head with a sauté pan for shutting me out of whatever he's doing, or feeling. But the reality is that I've never hit anyone who wasn't trying to kill me, so I'll have to exorcise my frustration about Nicholas by trying to solve a murder.

John O'Hara made it clear he doesn't want my help.

Too bad, John; you're going to get it anyway.

Another shower. Put on clean clothes. Clean Emma's box. Take Tuffy for a walk, and serve breakfast and fresh water to my friends in fur. Feeding them, I realized that I was ravenous; I'd fallen asleep last night without having dinner.

Passing Eileen's bedroom door, I heard the sound of her shower running.

She's up. Good. I have an excuse to make pancakes.

I heard her turn off the water, and tapped on the door.

She called out, "Yes?"

"Pancakes in ten minutes?"

"I'll be there," she said.

While Eileen and I were eating, I told her that I wanted to view some pictures from a digital camera on the computer monitor, but I didn't know how.

"It's easy. People have been doing it for years."

"I haven't. Basically, I use my computer like a typewriter."

"You've got a USB port," she said. "All you need to do is attach a cable from the camera to the computer. I know you have a cable." She gestured toward the desk on which the computer sat. "I saw one in the junk drawer over there."

"Oh, right. I've got a collection of mystery cables and electronic gizmos."

With teasing good humor, Eileen rolled her eyes at me. "Aunt Del, you're one step away from being a Luddite." She took our empty plates to the sink to rinse them off and put them into the dishwasher. "Give me the digital camera and I'll set it up for you."

When I returned to the kitchen with the little cameras, Eileen examined them closely. "Where did you get these? Have you been moonlighting with the CIA?"

"Liddy bought them at a spy shop in Beverly Hills. She and your mother helped me do some investigating yesterday afternoon at Roxanne Redding's. Your dad arrived and wasn't too pleased to find us there."

"That's a safe bet. I can just hear him."

She lowered her voice and frowned with ferocity. " 'Della, this is police business. Go home and cook something.' "

It was a pretty good imitation of John O'Hara and made me laugh.

Eileen connected the cable she found in the drawer to the first camera, then to the computer's USB port. "This is all you do." She turned on the monitor and we saw a panel made up of a dozen postage stamp–size photos. From what I could make out, this camera held Liddy's photos of the Reddings' financial records, but they were too small for me to read the information.

"Enlarge whatever you want by choosing the image, and . . ." Eileen moved the cursor to the first of the little images and clicked the mouse. "There."

The first page of a tax return materialized almost life-size on the screen.

"Looks like dull stuff," Eileen said, scanning it.

"Your tax returns and mine are dull," I said, "but I'm hoping this one has a useful secret somewhere in here."

"What are you looking for?"

"I don't know. Something unusual, that doesn't seem to fit with the total picture." I admitted that I was on a fishing expedition, and the chances were that it would be a waste of time as far as finding a clue to Redding's killer. "But I have to try."

Eileen said, "Dad calls working a murder case a matter of wearing out the shoe leather."

I gestured to my chair. "Or wearing a shine in the seat of the pants."

"Good luck," she said. "I'm off to do a little investigating of my own."

That yanked my attention away from the computer. I turned to look at her. "What do you mean?"

"Not *your* kind," she said with a smile. "I'm going to meet a man for coffee, see if I like him enough to try having a whole meal with him sometime."

I saw that her cheeks were coloring.

"Tell me about him."

Eileen straddled one of the kitchen chairs and propped her elbows on the back of it. "He came into the shop yesterday to order a box of cupcakes to take to his parents. He's a lawyer. Seems nice. He asked me out, but all I agreed to was Sunday morning coffee at that place on Montana and Fifth. After coffee, I'm going to take Mother out to lunch. Daddy's working today."

"Tell your mom from me that she's been a terrific help."

Eileen stood and put the chair back in its

place at the kitchen table. "Listen, I know you and Daddy are on opposite sides of the fence about this, but I'm really hoping you, or somebody, can prove Nick didn't kill that man."

"I appreciate that. I know you're not crazy about Nicholas."

"He makes you happy, so I've learned to like him. More important, his daughter needs a father."

"I love you, honey," I said.

"I know. You're the best second mother and business partner anybody could have. Happy detecting."

She gave me a quick hug and was gone.

I went back to examining the pages and pages of financial information that Liddy had copied. An hour into the tedious work of studying the couple's financial life line-by-line, I saw an item in their list of deductible expenses that snagged my attention. Roxanne claimed $3,000 for "continuing education," but there was no explanation as to what that meant. Probably nothing, but . . .

I advanced the frames, hoping that Liddy had photographed their cancelled checks. She had. I went through them quickly, looking for the name of a class or a school. Nothing. But I did find two checks made out to "cash" for $1,500 each. But what kind of "continuing education" had she paid for in cash?

Eileen had called me a Luddite, and she was partly right. I did prefer some things as they used to be done, such as getting one's cancelled checks back from the bank instead of just a sheet of tiny replicas. By turning over cancelled checks, one could find out who cashed them.

"Wait. My bank also sends sheets duplicating the backs of my checks. They don't use the same bank, but maybe . . ." I made a note of the two check numbers.

I didn't realize I'd spoken aloud until Tuffy got up from his bed and came over to look at me curiously.

"Good boy. Did I wake you? I'm sorry." I reached down and gave him strokes with my left hand while with my right I kept advancing though the photos.

Yes! There were pages showing the backs of the checks. I skimmed through them until I found the back of the first check number I'd copied. It had been endorsed by a man whose name was vaguely familiar, but I couldn't remember where I'd heard it.

The second check for $1,500 had been endorsed by the same man: Galen Light.

Galen Light? Where have I heard that name?

"Liddy," I said to Tuffy. "I think Liddy knows him, or at least has mentioned him."

I got up from the computer, reached for my wall phone, and dialed the number I knew as well as my own.

29

"Galen Light is famous," Liddy said. "He's been on all the daytime talk shows."

"I don't have time to watch. What does he do?"

"He's the best known life coach in Los Angeles."

I suppose it was too much to hope for that she'd tell me he was a contract hit man.

I said, "You mean he just tells people how to live?"

"He does a little more than that. Gives business advice, too. Why are you asking?"

"Roxanne paid him three thousand dollars and deducted the money as 'continuing education.' "

"I'm not sure that deduction would stand up if they get audited, but maybe it would — after all, this is California, the fountain of crazy ideas."

"I wonder why she didn't just make out the checks to him instead of to 'cash.' I know he got the money because he endorsed the checks."

"Maybe she didn't want Alec to know she'd gone to him," Liddy said. "When Alec did my new pictures a couple of years ago, he said something about not bothering to look at his tax returns, that Roxanne took care of all that. I remember because he said it dismissively, not as though it was a compliment to his wife's ability. I didn't like to hear her diminished."

"Maybe it's Roxanne who's using that second cell phone, the one where the bills go to the management company," I said.

"Are you thinking Roxanne might be keeping secrets from her husband?"

"It's possible. Do you know anyone at Birnam Woods who could tell you which of them has a second cell?"

"I'm afraid not," Liddy said. "That firm is so protective of its clients you practically have to show photo ID if you want to go to their office to pick up any of your own records."

Galen Light didn't advertise in the yellow pages, at least not as a life coach. However, while looking, I did find five companies that offered Lie Detector and Polygraph Services. I had thought those two things were the same, but I didn't have time to ponder technical semantics.

I didn't find Galen Light listed in the white pages, either, but I found several articles about him on the Internet. There wasn't much about his personal life: divorced, no children, born in either Montana or Hawaii, depending upon the story. The one thing all the articles mentioned was Light's "gift" for helping people find their "bliss." Each article included one or two celebrity endorsements of Light.

There wasn't much specific biographical information about Light; he claimed he "preferred to remain a blank page so as to keep the focus on my clients."

One thing I did learn was that Light had a publicist. I thought that seemed to be at odds with his wanting attention focused on his "clients," but the information was useful to me. I was about to phone Phil Logan to ask him to call Light's publicist to find out how to reach the life coach, when I found an article that included a phone number for prospective clients to call. His area code was 310, which meant that he "coached lives" in one of the higher-end sections of Los Angeles.

I noted the number and reached for the phone again.

Galen Light agreed to see me at four

o'clock that afternoon.

"I don't usually make appointments on Sundays, but I've seen you on television, so I realize that your work must keep you very busy."

"Yes, it does. I appreciate your being so considerate."

"Ahhhh," he said, his voice as warm as melting butter, "to what greater service can we use our gifts than to be of help to others?"

"That's beautifully put," I said. "Where is your office?"

"I work out of my home." He gave me the address. It was in Brentwood, a few blocks from the Redding house.

I told him that I'd see him at four, and we said good-bye.

Galen Light's home was a small Spanish hacienda with a well-kept front yard on Bundy Drive, just south of Sunset Boulevard, and not far from the house in which Marilyn Monroe died. That sad place was still on the list of "sights" pointed out to vans full of tourists.

The life coach opened his door, barefoot, wearing a royal purple velour running suit that I doubt had ever felt a drop of sweat. It was zipped up to just below his collarbone, exposing a few tendrils of dark chest hair.

"Della, you're right on time. Welcome to Casa Light."

"Thank you for making an appointment on such short notice."

"On television, I've seen a certain touch of melancholy in your eyes. I sensed you need some guidance. In fact, if you believe in such spiritual matters, I sent vibrations inviting you to come to me."

It took monumental self-control, but I managed not to laugh.

He stepped aside to allow me to enter the house, but it was a narrow doorway, and when I brushed past him I caught a hit of alcohol on his breath.

Light was a good-looking man, if one made the assessment by wide-set dark eyes, a broad forehead, an abundance of black hair, full lips, and prominent cheekbones. But his complexion was florid, with a few tiny red veins dotting his well-shaped nose. His name, Galen Light, didn't match his face, which suggested a mixed heritage of Mediterranean and Slavic. It was an attractive melding of ethnicities, but if he had been a salesman, there is no way I would have bought whatever he was selling.

His living room was dim and cool, with a high beamed ceiling, handsomely furnished with deep couches and carved Spanish chairs and small tables. Spanish tiles framed the fireplace, and brightly colored woven rugs covered portions of the deep red tiles on the floor.

"This is a lovely house," I said politely.

"I'm glad you like it. Come, let's go into my office to talk."

I followed him down a short hallway to a room on the left. He opened the door and ushered me inside.

His office was small, but beautifully furnished. Another deep couch, upholstered in burgundy velvet, and a pair of wing chairs in gold suede. A carved wooden coffee table rested in the center of the seating. There was no desk, but two of the four walls were covered with floor to ceiling bookcases of polished oak, filled with books in colorful jackets.

He turned on the brass lamp on the end table beside the couch and told me to have a seat.

I took one of the wing chairs.

"May I offer you something to drink?"

"No, thank you. Unless you have coffee?"

"My housekeeper just made a fresh pot. I'll be right back."

While he was gone, I went to the bookshelves to see what he liked to read. Novels, mostly. Nothing that seemed recent. Three volumes of poetry in one corner. Most surprising was a copy of *Love Letters,* edited by Lady Antonia Fraser. I was holding it when he returned, carrying a tray with a coffee cup and a cream and sugar set. Next to it was a crystal glass with a generous portion of some dark liquid. I suspected that it wasn't Coca-Cola.

He saw the book in my hand and grinned. "The letters of Abelard and Héloïse are in that collection. Now *there* was a couple who could have used a life coach. Then he wouldn't have been castrated and she wouldn't have ended up in a nunnery."

"But in spite of all that, they wrote beautiful letters," I said.

"You've read them?"

"A long time ago." I wasn't going to tell him that I owned this same book, and had read excerpts to Nicholas one night when we were in bed.

I put Light's copy back on the shelf.

He closed the door. "I don't want us distracted by the god-awful clatter my housekeeper makes in the kitchen. She's a treasure — anticipates everything I need, but she's not exactly easy on the ears." Handing me the coffee, he said, "Cream and sugar?"

"Yes, please."

Light doctored my coffee and I sat back down in the wing chair. He settled on the couch opposite me, took a swallow from his drink, and set the glass down on the table. "What inspired you to call me, my dear Della?"

"Roxanne Redding."

The smile vanished from his face. "Ah-hhh, Roxanne."

He picked up his drink and held it so that it was caught in a beam of sunlight coming through the window. After apparently studying how the illumination affected the color of the liquid, he took another swallow. When he put the glass down again, he said, "May I be frank with you, Della?"

"Of course."

"I feel sorry for the poor woman. She's not very stable," he said. "That was true even before her husband's shocking death."

"Really? What do you mean?"

"I shouldn't have said anything. You didn't come here to talk about Roxanne."

"Actually, I did. What I mean is, I heard that you were giving her advice, and I wondered what a life coach does."

He sat up straighter; his chest seemed to swell and his wide smile displayed a set of perfect teeth. "I help people make the most out of their lives, to identify the path that will lead them to happiness and encourage them to be brave enough to take the big risk that brings the big reward."

"Ah," I said, because he seemed to expect some response.

He drank more of whatever was in his glass. "Roxanne is a talented photographer. She should be at least as famous as her husband, but she lacks courage. I feel bad about that, because I liked her very much. I worked hard with her, but . . ." He shook his head in regret.

"What risk did you want her to take?"

"Let's talk about you." He leaned forward. "I know you have courage. I read about that situation you were in a few months ago. You defeated a killer."

"I was lucky," I said, dismissing the subject with a wave of my hand.

"It was more than luck, my dear. You are a remarkable woman. Tell me what you want to achieve and I will help you climb that mountain."

I suppressed a sardonic comment. Instead, I asked, "How much do you charge?"

"There is no set fee. It depends upon how excited I am about a project. What do you want? To continue cooking on television, or would you rather run the network? Or run for political office?"

"I hadn't thought about it. What kind of risk do you think Roxanne should take?" I asked.

"How well do you know her?"

"Casually," I said. "But we talked quite a bit while she was taking new professional pictures for me."

"Did she speak about me?"

"Just girl talk." I gave him a smile I hoped would imply that we had discussed him.

He drank the last drops in his glass. "Roxanne is a lovely woman, underneath that brittle exterior. But she remains a mere acolyte of her husband. I wish she had come to me earlier — I could have made something magnificent out of her." He got up and went around to the bookcase behind the couch. "Come," he said. "I want to show you something."

I put down the coffee cup — I'd barely taken a sip — and stood to follow him.

He was running his fingers along the spines of the volumes on the middle shelf, but when I was beside him, he turned toward me. "God, you're beautiful," he said. His voice was husky, the smell of liquor on his breath so strong I stepped back, but he grabbed me by the shoulders, pulled me against him, and planted his mouth on mine.

This can't be happening!

I clamped my lips shut, and struggled to get away from him, but his fingers were so strong they dug painfully into my upper arms as he crushed my breasts against his chest.

Coming up for air, he whispered, "You want this."

"No! Let me go!" I screamed.

He slapped my face so hard my cheek burned and I heard ringing in my ears.

"Shut up. Or scream as loud as you want — there's nobody here."

He yanked me off my feet, rolled me over the back of the couch and down onto the cushions. Before I could get up or twist away, he threw his body on top of mine, grinding himself against my thighs as he ripped at my blouse.

One of my arms was pinned against the back of the sofa, but with my free hand I lunged for his eyes. He jerked his head back. My fingers missed their target, but my nails raked a path across the side of his face, leaving a little trail of blood on his cheek, and bits of his skin under my nails.

Enraged, he slapped me again, harder. His eyes blazed. Even more frightening than the power of his superior strength and the weight of his body was what I saw in his eyes: *excitement.* My stomach lurched with revulsion. I knew he wasn't going to stop until he'd raped me or killed me. Or both.

While he held my wrist in an agonizing grip, he groped for the hem of my skirt and pulled it up.

Fighting for my life, with more strength than I ever guessed I had, I freed the arm he had pinned against the back of the couch. Balling my hand into a fist, I delivered a hammer-blow to his nose that smashed it flat. I heard the crack of bone. Blood gushed from his nostrils. He bellowed in pain and reared up enough for me to raise my knee and slam it into his groin. He shrieked and clutched at himself, giving me the chance to heave him off me. He tumbled sideways and crashed into the coffee table.

His head caught the wooden edge with such force it up-ended the table and sent all that was on it clattering to the floor.

I looked down.

Galen Light lay on his side on the carpet. Eyes closed.

Not moving.

30

My heart pounding, breathing heavily, terrified of what had almost happened to me, and terrified to think I might have killed him, I scrambled to my feet. In spite of my fear, I was about to lean down to feel for a pulse when I heard him groan. One of his hands moved slightly.

Thank God, he's alive.

I grabbed my purse and ran from the house, but pulled the door only partway closed and didn't let it lock. Safely inside my Jeep, watching Light's front door, I used my cell to dial nine-one-one.

When the dispatcher answered, I said, "We need an ambulance. A man has been injured in a fall." I gave the woman Light's address. "He may not be able to come to open the door, but it's unlocked. Go in." I disconnected, and sped away from the house.

At Sunset Boulevard, I headed east, but swerved into the next street. I stopped just inside the corner and killed the motor. Behind me, I heard the wail of a siren. Through my rear window, I saw a red paramedic's van race along Sunset Boulevard and make a sharp turn onto Bundy Drive.

I knew that I should drive to the West Los Angeles police station and report Light's assault on me, but I was embarrassed that I had been so stupid as to go alone to the home of a strange man. In my defense, he was a well-known media personality with much to lose if he were accused of rape. He had mentioned his housekeeper, so I assumed we were not alone. And I certainly had not given Light any indication that I had any sexual interest in him at all. Even if he'd taken something I'd said or done as an invitation, the moment he heard my emphatic "no" he should have backed off.

It took a few minutes for my heartbeat to return to near normal. Even though I felt sick to my stomach at the thought of going to Butler Avenue to file a complaint against Galen Light, I steeled myself to do it. I imagine he counted on shame or embarrassment to make any woman he forced himself on reluctant to report the assault. For my own self-respect I couldn't remain silent, but also I felt a kinship with other women who had faced what I just went through, or worse.

It was close to five o'clock on Sunday afternoon. Butler Avenue was quiet. I saw only two pedestrians, a couple pushing a stroller. I took the rare open parking space near the police station's red-tiled entrance. When I reached up to hold my torn blouse together, I saw that the knuckles of that hand were swollen and smeared with blood. Light's blood, from when I'd smashed him in the nose with my fist. I'd been vaguely aware while I was driving that my hand hurt, but it was only now, when I'd calmed down, that I could assess the damage. A bruise was developing, and it was painful to flex those fingers.

I knew how lucky I was, that my wounds were only superficial. Those would heal quickly, but it would take longer before I forgot being thrown onto that couch like some raging giant's rag doll, those terrifying moments of helplessness before I was able to fight him off and escape.

Inside the station house, I was relieved to see that the desk sergeant on duty wasn't anyone I'd met before. This officer was bald, with a thick neck and bushy black eyebrows. He was on the phone when I came through the door and barely glanced at me until he finished his call. I must have looked even worse than I thought because those dense eyebrows twitched when he focused on me.

"Are you all right, miss?"

"Yes, but I need to report a crime. An assault."

"Do you need medical attention?"

"No. Just someone to take my report."

"Sure." He picked up the receiver, punched a couple of digits, and requested a detective to "see a woman" at the front desk. Replacing the receiver, he gestured toward the empty bench beside the door. "Take a seat. A detective will be out soon."

It must have been a slow day for crime in Los Angeles, because I'd been sitting for only a few seconds when a man emerged from the direction of the detectives' squad room.

Oh, no.

It was John's partner, Hugh Weaver.

The desk sergeant pointed to me, but he needn't have bothered because I was the only person waiting.

When Weaver saw me and registered my disheveled condition, his usual scowl morphed into a frown of concern. "Hey, what happened?"

"A man tried to rape me —"

"We need to get you to the hospital."

"No, Hugh. I said he tried. He didn't suc-
ceed, but he hit me and ripped my clothes.
I want to swear out a complaint."

"Jeez. Thank God it wasn't worse. Come
on in."

He steered me into the squad room and
over to the pair of desks he shared with
John. I was profoundly grateful that John's
side of their unit was empty. In fact, the
squad room itself was practically deserted.
Only one other detective was there, typing
at a computer keyboard on the other side of
the room.

Weaver hauled the nearest straight-back
wooden chair over to his desk so I could sit
next to him. "Can I get you something? The
coffee here smells like rotten eggs today; I
don't know what the eff happened to the
machine, but we got some cold sodas."

I realized how dry my throat felt. "Yes.
Anything cold."

A minute later he was back with a small
bottle of orange juice. He twisted off the
top and handed it to me. "This'll be better
for you."

"Thanks." I took a sip and winced when
the juice touched a cut on my lip. Ignoring
the burning sensation, I drank half the
bottle. "That helped." I couldn't see any
place to put it down on his cluttered desk,

so I set it on the floor beside the chair.

Weaver pulled an official form from a pile behind his telephone, picked up a pen, and wrote my name on one of the lines. He was all business. "Okay. Who attacked you?"

"Galen Light." I gave him the address.

"Galen Light? I bet he wasn't born with that stupid name. What's the story?"

I kept to the basics: that I'd made an appointment to see Light, who was a well-known television personality. "He's a life coach," I said.

"What the eff is that?"

"Someone who gives people advice about how to live their lives. It's the in thing, apparently. A lot people seem to be going to them."

Weaver snorted with contempt. "I could do that easy. Somebody comes an' tells me they're thinkin' about doing something. I just say don't do it, an' tell 'em, 'Pay the secretary on your way out, sucker.' Except I don't say 'sucker' out loud." Again serious, Weaver said, "Tell me what happened. Details."

"We were talking in his office when he grabbed me." The last thing I wanted to do was relive the experience, but I told Weaver what Light did, and what I did.

"When I pushed him off of me he fell over

and hit his head on the edge of the coffee table. I thought he was unconscious, but he started to move. I ran outside, called paramedics for him, and came here. I want him arrested and charged with . . . assault, certainly. Attempted rape?"

Weaver looked up from his scribbling. "Let's see if he's got a record." He shoved the report to one side, pulled his computer keyboard toward him, and typed. After a minute or two, he said, "He got a DUI two years ago."

"Nothing else?"

"Not under the name Galen Light," he said. "I'll see what I can dig up about him. Right now, you need to get photographed, then I want a doc to treat those cuts an' bruises."

I extended my hand. "Some of his skin is under my nails. Can you get one of the SID techs to take scrapings?"

Movement at the entrance to the squad room caught my eye. Simultaneously, the last person I wanted to see at this moment saw me.

31

John O'Hara stared at me. "My God . . .
What happened?"

Weaver said, "She got attacked."

"But I'm all right," I said.

"You're *not* all right!" His hand hovered
near my bruised cheek; he didn't touch me,
but his hand was so close I was sure I could
feel heat from it on my face. "Who did this?
D'Martino?"

"Of course not! How could you even think
such a thing?" I pushed his hand away.

"Kiddies, don't fight." Weaver held up the
form he'd filled out. "Della made a report.
A guy smacked her around and tried to . . .
but she got away before he could. It sounds
like she gave as good as she got."

"What guy?" John stretched for the paper,
but Weaver jerked it back, out of his reach.

"Cool your jets. I'm gonna take a uniform
an' arrest him."

"I'm coming with you," John said.

"Oh, no. I'm not letting you anywhere near the bastard."

Weaver's tone was so hard it shocked me. All the other times I'd seen them together, he had deferred to John as the senior partner, but now Weaver declared himself in charge. "Stay with her," he said. "Get pictures taken, have somebody from SID scrape under her nails, then get a doc to treat the cut on her lip." He said to me, "When the tech finishes, go home and put an ice pack on your face."

Through most of the routine of documenting my injuries and taking physical evidence, John was silent. When the SID tech told me he had to take my torn blouse, John got an LAPD sweatshirt from the locker room for me to wear in its place.

I refused to go to an emergency room just to have the tiny cut on my lower lip looked at. John started to protest, but the SID tech agreed that I didn't need a doctor. He dabbed the nick with disinfectant from a first aid kit, repeated Weaver's suggestion about the ice pack, and told me I was good to go. He left with my blouse and nail scrapings.

Back at Weaver's desk, I picked up my handbag.

"I'll drive you home," John said.

"Thanks for the offer, but my car's outside, and you can see that I'm fine."

"Okay. You win. But sit down for a few minutes and talk to me."

He dragged the chair Weaver had commandeered for me over to his side of the desk. As I settled into it again, John took his own seat.

"I'm calm now," he said.

"Yes, I can see that. I'm sorry about —"

He held up a hand in a "stop" gesture. "While you were with SID, I read Weaver's report. Who is this Galen Light? You were at his house, but it doesn't say why you went there. Your reason may not be relevant to this complaint, but it is to me."

"Roxanne Redding paid him three thousand dollars in two checks made out to cash instead of to his name. He lives only a few blocks from the Redding house. I hoped to learn what kind of relationship he and Roxanne have, and if he could have had a reason to kill her husband."

John put his hands on the top of his desk — it was much neater than his partner's — and laced his fingers together. "What did you find out?"

"Not much," I admitted. "He said he worked hard with her, but that she lacked courage to take risks. I got a definite vibe that there was, or maybe there had been, something going on between them. More than just his giving her advice."

"What were you doing when he assaulted you?"

"We'd been talking about Roxanne, then he went over to one of his bookshelves and said he wanted to show me something. I thought whatever it was had something to do with Roxanne, but it was just a trick to get me out of the chair where I'd been sitting."

John was about to say something when Weaver strode into the squad room. He was seething. And he was alone.

John and I got to our feet.

"Did you pick him up?" John asked.

"No. The bastard's in the hospital. He's got some scumbag shyster holding his hand and threatening to sue our friend here."

I couldn't believe what I heard. "Sue *me?*"

John said, "Sue her for what?"

"Assault."

I felt like Alice after she'd tumbled down that rabbit hole. For a moment, nothing seemed real. Then my head cleared and I heard Weaver's voice.

"Light's story is that Della came to his house, pretending to want his professional services. She flirted with him, sat with her skirt hiked up, an' crossed her legs — coming on to him. He said he'd had a little too much to drink an' made a pass at her because he thought she was inviting it. But instead of her just saying 'down boy,' and letting him apologize for misunderstanding, he says she attacked him. She broke his nose, shoved him into a table, and knocked him out. In addition to the nose, he's got a gash on his forehead, a possible concussion, and swollen nuts where she kneed him."

John frowned at Weaver. "Why didn't you put that he'd been drinking in the report?"

"She didn't mention it."

"I forgot. I was pretty shaken up when I got here."

"But you knew he'd been drinking when you were with him?" Weaver's tone sounded accusatory.

"I smelled liquor on his breath, but he was speaking clearly, not slurring his words, and he wasn't clumsy. There was no reason to think he was drunk."

John said, "Even if he was, being drunk is no excuse for sexual assault."

"What she *says* was sexual assault."

That made me so angry I practically sputtered. "Hugh! Look at me. Do you think I did this to myself?"

"Calm down," Weaver said. "I believe you.

But you better get yourself a lawyer."

"Why do I need a lawyer? I'm the *victim!*"

"Not according to Light's shyster, Wylie York. He swears he's gonna make you — an' these are his exact words: 'rue the day you did bodily harm' to his 'f***in' client. The 'f***in' part's my word. Between you an' me, I'd like to shove a big handful of 'rue' up his day."

I turned to John. "This is outrageous. What can I do?"

John sighed heavily. "It's not fair, Del, but you're going to have to get yourself a lawyer."

I didn't wait until I got home. As soon as I drove around the corner, out of sight of the station house, I phoned Olivia Wayne.

"What is it?" she sounded sleepy. "I'm getting a massage."

"A man tried to rape me this afternoon and now he's threatening to sue me for assaulting *him.*"

"You may be a one-dollar client, but at least you're not dull." The sleepy voice was gone. "Hold on a moment." I heard her mumble something to the person giving her the massage, then I heard a door close. Back on the line, she said, "Give me the basic facts. I'll ask whatever I need you to fill in."

I gave her the abridged version, and

answered her questions.

"Who's this creep's lawyer?" she asked.

"Wylie York."

Olivia hooted. " 'Wile E. Coyote' we call him. He gives 'sleazy' a bad name, but he's not stupid."

"Galen Light hit me, tore my clothes, and tried to rape me. How can he possibly sue *me?*"

"Being indignant is just a waste of energy, Della. Anybody can sue anybody for anything in this country. The problem with democracy is that it gives people the freedom to abuse the system. Where are you? At home?"

"In my car, parked around the corner from the Butler Avenue station."

"Go home. I'll see what I can find out." She disconnected.

My cheek was throbbing. I felt dirty, and from the smell of the sweatshirt, I realized someone had worn it before me.

I turned the key in the ignition.

At least for the moment, my problem was in Olivia's hands. Right now I needed the cleansing of a hot shower, the comfort of my pets, and the ice pack in my freezer.

32

It was eight o'clock and dark by the time I got home. The carriage light glowing over the front door was a cheerful sight, and I could see through the front window that the floor lamp in the living room was on. Tuffy was lying on the couch. He probably had been sleeping, but now he was sitting up, alert. By the time I let myself into the house, he was just inside the door, wagging an excited greeting.

I stooped down to pet him, and he licked my bruised cheek. That was a surprise because licking my face was something he never did.

"You trying to heal my wound, Tuff?" I really think that was it.

I found a note from Eileen on the hall table — our traditional message center — saying that she had given Tuffy and Emma fresh water and food at six o'clock, had taken Tuffy for a walk, and that she would be out for the evening, having dinner and catching a movie with friends.

I wondered if one of those friends was the man with whom she'd had the coffee date.

"Eileen deserves some good luck with men," I told Tuffy. I've been talking to him since he was a puppy and he seems to understand most of what I say.

In my bathroom, I stripped off the LAPD sweatshirt and my underwear and tossed them into the laundry hamper. I folded the skirt I'd worn to Galen Light's and put it into the bag I used for items to be dry-cleaned, although I didn't think I'd ever want to wear it again. No, I was sure I'd never even want to look at it again.

But it's a good skirt. I'll donate it to a group that helps women make a new start.

I took a shower, put on a clean pair of sweatpants and a soft, pale blue Better Living Channel sweatshirt — one of Phil Logan's new promotional items — and lay down on the bed with the ice pack pressed against my cheek.

It felt good, but I remembered the rule about ice packs: twenty minutes on and twenty minutes off. I glanced at the numerals on the clock radio; it was eight thirty-five.

When I took the ice pack off at five minutes to nine, I returned it to the freezer. Before the next twenty-minute application, there was a phone call I dreaded, but one I knew I had to make.

Phil Logan, the Better Living Channel's head of publicity, picked up his cell on the second ring.

"Hello, Della," he said. "Your timing is perfect. I just got in from Vegas."

"How did you do?"

"Better than most, not as good as some," he said. "On the plus side, I came back with two hundred dollars in winnings — and I met a magician's assistant. She's pretty, smart, fun to be with."

"That's wonderful, Phil. I hope you get to see a lot of her."

"Their show is going on tour, but I'll meet her next weekend in San Francisco. Enough about me. What's going on with you?"

"It's not as happy a story as yours." Briefly, I told Phil what happened at Galen Light's house.

He interrupted to ask if I was all right, and if I needed anything.

"I'm fine, really. But you haven't heard the rest." I told Phil that Galen Light's lawyer was threatening to sue me for assaulting Light.

He listened quietly. When I finished he

muttered, "That bastard. First, you need a lawyer."

"I have one: Olivia Wayne."

"You couldn't do better. She's a tiger. But you need me, too — to keep this out of the media."

My mind had been roiling with so many emotions: fear, anger, outrage, the realization of what *could* have happened to me, that I hadn't thought about publicity. Having the world know about my experience with Light was the last thing I wanted. A wave of hope washed over me. "Do you think you can do that?"

"Are basketball players tall? Seriously, I want to jump on this right away before the story gets out."

"I'll be grateful for whatever you can do."

"Keeping stories out of the media is sometimes as important as getting stories in. I want to protect you from embarrassment, but if our mutual boss, Mickey Jordan — Mr. Hot Head — hears about this he might go after Light with a lethal weapon. *That* would be harder to cover up. Okay, I gotta get busy and do damage control."

"Thank you, Phil."

I took the ice pack out of the freezer and went back to the bedroom to lie down.

■ ■ ■ ■

The next thing I knew the phone was ringing and the ice pack had melted on the pillow beside my head. Fighting my way up to consciousness, I squinted at the beside clock: five minutes past eleven. Who could be calling at this hour? I reached for the phone.

It was Nicholas.

"Honey, did I wake you?"

"No. I mean, yes, but I hadn't gone to bed." I shook my head to clear it. "Where have you been?"

"Vienna," he said. "I took an overnight Friday and just got back about an hour ago."

"You weren't supposed to leave the state! If the police found out you'd left the country —"

"I didn't fly commercial. There's a CEO who owed me a favor — with a private jet big enough for overseas flights. The cops didn't confiscate my passport."

"But if you're arrested they probably will confiscate it, and then they'll see the entry and exit stamps."

"The trip was worth the risk. Look, Del, I'm parked outside your house. May I come in? Not to stay, just to talk for a little while?"

I wanted to see him — of course I did; my heart did an automatic flutter when I heard his voice — but I didn't want him to see my face and have to explain what happened. But I couldn't think of any way to avoid seeing him tonight. And, I wanted to know what he was doing in Vienna.

"All right," I said.

"Are you mad at me, hon? I didn't call from Vienna because I couldn't afford to have any record that I was out of the country. If you didn't know where I was, you wouldn't have to lie."

"I understand," I said, but my tone was cool. "Come to the door so I can let you in."

Emma stayed curled up in the wing chair next to my bed, but Tuffy escorted me to the front door.

33

Before I reached for the doorknob, I turned the hall light off, but I left the living room light on because Eileen hadn't come home yet.

I greeted Nicholas in three-quarter profile, managing to keep the bruised part of my face averted.

"Hi, honey. Hi, Tuff." He brushed my forehead with his lips and gave Tuffy a quick ear scratch.

I said, "You look exhausted. Coffee?"

"Thanks. I feel like I'm running on empty."

It wasn't going to be possible to keep my injury from him. As soon as we reached the bright lights in the kitchen, I turned to face him.

His eyes narrowed with concern. "Della — what happened?"

"I'm all right. It's just a bruise. Tell me about Vienna."

Using the knuckle on his index finger to gently lift my chin, Nicholas studied the damage. "You first. Were you in a car accident? Or are you going to joke about it and tell me I should see the *other* guy."

"That's not funny. Sit down and I'll tell you everything. The coffee's ready to go. All I have to do is push the button."

He straddled a chair, watching me as I moved around the kitchen.

I asked, "Are you hungry?"

"No. Talk to me."

As soon as I sat down across from him, he reached for my hands and covered them with his.

"I'll get to what happened, but I have to explain something first. I've been trying to turn up other people who might have had a motive to kill Alec Redding." I told him about my session with Roxanne, and the financial records Liddy found, which led me to Galen Light. He listened quietly up to that point, but when I told him what Light tried to do, his face hardened and his fingers tightened on mine.

"I got away from him," I said.

"How?"

Showing my bruised knuckles, I said, "A punch in the nose and a knee in the groin. I went to the police station to swear out a complaint. Now here's the punch line, or as you writers might say, the twist to the story. Light is claiming that I attacked *him.* He's threatening to sue me for assault."

"That's ridiculous," Nicholas said.

"So I thought, but Olivia's taking it seriously. She's going to handle it. Somehow."

I saw fury in Nicholas's eyes. "I'll go have a talk with Light."

"Absolutely not!" I snatched my hands away from his. "Don't go all caveman on me and make the situation worse."

"I should have been here to protect you."

"Stop that right now. Don't you know me *at all?* I'm not some delicate medieval maiden who needs protection from the Big Bad Wolf."

"You're mixing your metaphors," he said.

"I'll mix anything I damn well please!"

I glared at him.

He sat back in the chair and raised both hands, palms out, in a gesture of surrender. "I'm beginning to feel sorry for Galen Light."

In spite of the stress of what I'd gone through that day, I began to laugh. It was only a soft chuckle, but it released my tension and I felt better.

Mr. Coffee finished brewing, and the warm scent filled the kitchen. That aroma had the effect of a tranquilizer on me. I got up to fill our mugs; I would deal with tomorrow's problems tomorrow.

As part of the comfortable-with-each-other pair we had become, or at least were before Celeste's arrival, Nicholas went to the refrigerator and took out the container of half-and-half for me. He always drank his coffee black.

I put two steaming mugs on the table and added the cream and Sweet'N Low to mine. Careful to use the uninjured side of my mouth, I took a welcome swallow.

"Did Olivia know you went to Vienna?" I asked.

"Of course not. As an officer of the court she would have had to report the trip because I'd been ordered to stay in California. If she knew about it and didn't report it, and if I'd been caught, we both could have gone to jail." He drank some coffee. "I went to find out everything I could about Prince Freddie. It's not the kind of research you can do on the phone." Nicholas grinned. "And I learned a lot."

"Can we make the case that he's a viable suspect?"

"Possibly. He's broke and desperate for money," Nicholas said, "which seems to be the reason he's marrying Tanis."

"But why is she eager to marry him?"

"My guess is she wants to be a princess. When Tanis and I were together, she was obsessed with Princess Diana. Dressed like her. Copied the same hairstyles. But most fairy tales have a witch in them, and Freddie's mother fills that role. From what I learned from my journalist contacts, Freddie's momma seems to have a reasonable claim to the title of grand duchess, and she's a maniac on the subject of scandal. She and Freddie are professional house-guests. That ski chateau in Switzerland isn't his; he's the respectable front for the real owner. Mother and son live on loans extended because of their 'expectations' — that's how it's phrased — from commoners who want to be in their social circle. Freddie has to marry money, but he can't without his momma's approval. They were apparently about to make the big announcement when they came back from Rio and found that Celeste had gone to Los Angeles."

"So Tanis and Freddie came to make sure she stayed out of trouble?"

"At least until after the 'royal wedding.' " Nicholas's lips curled with distaste. "By Hollywood standards, that photo of Celeste with the pie isn't all that shocking. It upset the hell out of me for a while — I'm her father — but according to my sources in Vienna, salacious photographs of Freddie's potential stepdaughter would make the grand duchess snatch her little boy out of Tanis's reach. I think Freddie could have gone to Redding, tried to get the photos. Redding said no, and Freddie picked up the stool and killed him in a rage."

"I hate to say this because she's your daughter's mother, but doesn't that scenario fit Tanis, too? She could have tried to buy the photos, been refused, and killed him. Since the weapon was the stool that was already in the studio, that doesn't sound like premeditated murder."

Nicholas shook his head. "Celeste swore that she and her mother were driving around Los Angeles Thursday night."

"So Celeste didn't back up Freddie's claim that they were all together, playing cards in the suite?"

"She doesn't like Prince Charmless. With Celeste telling a different story, Freddie's just left with the butler as an alibi. I know Celeste is telling the truth about being with Tanis because the hotel's garage attendant confirms that the two of them left at seven o'clock and returned at ten thirty."

"What if Celeste is lying about what she and her mother did during the three and a half hours they were away from the hotel?"

"My daughter didn't kill Redding!"

"Oh, Nicholas — I'm not suggesting any such thing. But I am saying that perhaps she's lying to protect her mother. Maybe they separated for a while that night. Or maybe they went to a club together and while Celeste was dancing, Tanis slipped out."

"And took a taxi to Redding's? No, Tanis is much too smart to do something that could so easily be exposed."

"She could have taken Celeste's new car. Celeste wouldn't have known about it."

He shook his head in vehement denial. "No. Tanis wouldn't take such a risk. She'd think of all the ways she could be found out."

I wasn't thrilled that he was so adamant about his ex-wife's innocence, or how highly he seemed to regard her intelligence, but I wasn't going to argue about it. At least not at the moment. I began to consider how Prince Freddie could have killed Alec Redding.

"Because you were out of touch, you may not know this, but there is a private back elevator from the Presidential Suite that goes to the underground garage. And there's a pedestrian exit to the alley behind the hotel. Suppose, while Celeste and Tanis were out, Freddie left the hotel that way. No one would have seen him."

"How did he get to Redding's?"

"His butler, Mordue, lied about the four of them being together all evening in Freddie's suite. Mordue could have met Freddie out in the alley with a car, driven him to Redding's, waited while Freddie was talking to Redding, and then driven back to the hotel. He probably didn't know what happened in the house, but he would have figured it out when he learned about the murder. Keeping quiet about his part — being an accessory, albeit unknowingly — could assure Mordue of a luxurious retirement after Freddie married Tanis."

"Interesting idea," Nicholas said.

"If that turns out to be the case, I can just see one of your *Chronicle* headlines: 'The Butler *Almost* Did It.' "

"I'll have to tell that to Herb Zaslow. He's the one who writes our headlines."

I said, "I still remember my favorite headline from years ago. It was over a story about the city of Malibu getting a sewer system: 'Malibu Now an *Effluent* Community.' "

Nicholas laughed.

"I was teaching English in a public school

311

then and brought that headline in. But nobody got the joke. For homework I had each of them use the word they didn't understand in five different sentences. Half the class stayed home sick next day."

"Teachers don't get paid enough," Nicholas said.

"Getting back to our problem, after my experience with Galen Light, he's the one I'd most like to nail for the murder."

"When I go to the paper tomorrow, I'll see what I can find out about him. And I'll tell Olivia that whatever she's going to charge to fight the lawsuit, I'll pay. Since you won't let me beat him up, it's the least I can do. You went there to help me."

Nicholas finished his coffee, declined a refill, and told me he was going home to sleep.

"I haven't been to bed for forty-eight hours," he said.

Tuffy and I walked him to the door.

"Thanks for being down here in the foxhole with me," Nicholas whispered. He gave me the lightest little kiss on the good corner of my mouth and said good night.

Monday morning the swelling on my cheek was down, but the bruise was more vivid than the day before.

I called Liddy and told her what happened with Galen Light.

"My God, Della! Are you all right?"

I assured her that I was, but that Light was now planning to sue me over *his* injuries.

"Oh, that's horrible! He's a pig. But he couldn't possibly get away with that, could he? I mean, he couldn't *win,* could he?"

"Stranger things have happened in courtrooms," I said. "Somewhere in California a year or so ago a man attempting to burglarize a jewelry store got hurt breaking in. He won a settlement from the store's owners. I'm trying not to think about it and leave that problem to Olivia Wayne."

Liddy sighed. "You never expect a celebrity to try to rape a woman. I mean, Galen Light isn't a rock star, but he's been on television a lot."

"Speaking of TV — I've got to tape two shows today," I said. "With your makeup expertise, do you think you could hide the bruise well enough so it won't show on camera?"

"I'll be right over," she said.

Liddy did such a good job that even when I leaned in close to the mirror, I couldn't see a trace of skin discoloration.

"I'm going to the studio with you," Liddy said. "Those lights are so strong you'll need a fresh makeup job between shows."

The two half hours went as smoothly as any I'd ever done. I got through the talking and the demonstrations without making any mistakes, or having to shoot anything over because of technical glitches. Even Tuffy, who always appeared on the taped shows, knew without anyone prompting him when he was supposed to get up from his dog bed and come over to the preparation counter to watch what I was doing. By the time we'd completed the second show, I was more exhilarated than fatigued. It was one of the easiest days I'd ever had.

"You've got two more shows to tape tomorrow," Liddy said. "I'm coming with you to take care of the makeup."

"But Car Guy's using the studio to film a special on sports cars, so I can't begin taping until five. You'd be away from Bill all evening."

"Tuesday's his poker night," Liddy said. "If I don't come to help you, I'd just be alone."

The Tuesday half-hour shows should have gone as smoothly as did the Monday episodes, but that night every technical thing that could go wrong, did go wrong, from a power outage at the studio to camera operator Ernie Ramirez being hit with an attack of food poisoning. Our director had to call in a substitute cameraman who didn't know our setups. It was close to eleven o'clock when Liddy, Tuffy, and I were finally able to leave.

On the way home in my Jeep, Liddy and I were talking about Galen Light, when the eleven o'clock news came on the radio. I was barely paying attention to a story about problems in the Los Angeles County Jail when the correspondent announced breaking news.

"A reporter for the *Los Angeles Chronicle* has been found dead in Westwood."

34

Those words struck me like a blow to my chest. "Nicholas . . ."

Liddy cried, "Oh, no!"

Gripping the wheel hard to keep my hands from shaking, I pulled over to the side of Ventura Boulevard and cut the engine. In those few seconds my heart pounded so loudly it drowned out the news reader's next few words. I began to hear the report again as she said, ". . . was found at approximately nine o'clock this evening by two restaurant busboys who went outdoors to smoke."

What restaurant?

"The name of the deceased has not been released pending notification of next of kin, but according to an anonymous source close to the investigation, an identity card in the victim's wallet indicates employment by the *Los Angeles Chronicle.* Also, according to our source, it appears that the victim died from head injuries. Anyone in the vicinity of the alley behind the Olympia Grand Hotel between seven and nine PM this evening is asked to call the West Los Angeles Police Department at 555-1600. Stay tuned to KABC-AM 790 for news on the hour, the half hour, or when it breaks."

The reporter went to a story about the discovery of a meth lab in Van Nuys.

As I reached to turn off the radio I realized that Liddy was gripping my arm.

"Oh, dear Lord," she whispered.

A lump in my throat felt so huge I wasn't sure I could speak, but I gently pried Liddy's fingers away, pulled the cell phone out of my bag, and pressed the speed dial number for John O'Hara.

He answered on the second ring. "Del?"

"On the radio . . . I just heard . . . John, that murdered *Chronicle* reporter — it's Nicholas, isn't it?"

"D'Martino? No. It's a woman."

"A woman . . . ?" The news hit me like another physical blow. Praying I was wrong, I asked, "The reporter — is her name Gretchen Tully?"

"How did you know that?"

"I met her. . . . Oh, John, I'm afraid this could be my fault — I encouraged her to investigate the Redding murder."

"That's just great." I heard anger and exasperation in his voice. "This wasn't our case, but it's linked to ours now. Where are you?"

"In the valley, coming from the studio."

"Get to the station as quick as you can. I was on my way home but I'll meet you there."

On the way to my house, where Liddy had parked her car, I filled her in about my visit from Gretchen Tully the previous week.

"Gosh," she said. "This is terrible."

When we got to Eleventh Street, Liddy said, "Since we walked Tuffy at the studio, I'll use my key and put him in the house so you can get right to John."

I thanked her and told her I'd call her in the morning.

John was waiting for me by the front desk when I entered the West Los Angeles police station on Butler Avenue.

"I called Detective Keller, who got the Tully case. He's waiting for you inside."

The detectives' squad room was livelier than it had been late Sunday afternoon when I'd gone to report Galen Light's attack on me. At close to midnight, three detectives were at their desks. Separately, one man and one woman were taking reports from aggrieved Los Angelinos. Another detective, a male, was working at his computer.

A man was perched on the edge of John's desk, but stood when he saw us come in. He was thin, with sharp features, frizzy blond hair, pale eyes, pale skin. A head shorter than John, he looked to be in his thirties and had probably been hired when the LAPD lowered its height requirement in an attempt to inject diversity into the force. He wore the standard attire of detectives on duty: jacket and slacks, shirt and tie, although his clothes appeared to be more expensive than most.

"Della, this is Detective Keller. Val — Della Carmichael."

Detective Val Keller extended his hand and I took it. His grip was appropriately firm; what surprised me were the calluses I felt on his palm. He dressed like an upper-income business executive, but his hands were those of someone who did manual labor.

John got a chair for me from a neighboring empty desk.

He took his accustomed place and Keller moved over to Weaver's, shoved some of the clutter aside, and parked his rear on the edge of that desk. I was an inch or two taller than Keller, but in our new positions, he towered over me. Up close, I noticed that while his teeth were unnaturally white, his fingers bore the discoloration typical of a heavy smoker. His jacket reeked of cigarettes.

"O'Hara tells me you knew Gretchen Tully," Keller said. "How well?"

"I met her for the only time last Friday, when she came to my house to interview me."

"Interview you? What for?"

"A feature article in the paper. It was arranged by the publicist for my TV show, *In the Kitchen with Della.* I thought she wanted to talk about the bake sales for charity contest our network is promoting, but she came to see me six days early and all she only wanted to talk about was Alec Redding's murder."

"Why would she want to talk to *you* about that?"

I glanced at John, but he had his poker face on. I had no clue what he'd told Keller, so I said, "She brought it up because Nicholas D'Martino and I discovered Redding's body."

"Correction," John said. "D'Martino discovered the body. Della got there later."

"Only a few minutes later," I said firmly.

"Anyway, Gretchen Tully said she wanted to move on to hard news stories — not stay stuck in women's features — so she asked me what I thought about the murder."

That wasn't strictly true — she had wanted to know why I thought *Nicholas* killed Redding, but I wasn't going to reveal that. Before Keller could ask, I said, "We discussed the fact that a murder investigation was a great opportunity for a reporter. She was excited about the possibility of discovering information that could lead to her getting an exclusive."

"You talked her into trying to find the killer?" he said.

"Yes, I did," I said softly. I felt tears beginning to well in my eyes and fought them back. "I'm so sorry."

"You're *sorry?*" Keller's tone rang with contempt. "Fat lot of good your being sorry is going to do Tully's family."

"That's enough, Val." John stood up. "The young woman was an ambitious reporter after a story. She couldn't have been talked into something she didn't want to do."

Keller's pale face flushed an angry red. He faced John like a furious terrier challenging a mastiff. "Yeah, well, what we don't need is private citizens thinking they can work a case better than the cops!"

"We're on the same team, Keller," John said calmly.

"Maybe."

The other people in the squad room were looking at us as though expecting someone to start swinging. After a moment of highly charged silence, Keller focused on me again. "Who was Tully planning to talk to?"

"I have no idea."

"Why was she outside the back of the Olympia Grand?"

"I don't know," I said. The only positive thing about his hostility was that it had squelched my impulse to cry.

"When was the last time you saw her?"

"I told you — on Friday. After she left my house I never heard from her, talked to her, or saw her again."

"And you've told us everything you know?"

"Yes," I said. *Everything I know about Gretchen Tully.*

Keller turned to John. "I talked to the captain. Since our two cases have turned into one case, we're stuck with each other."

"I'll let Weaver know," John said. "Where's your partner?"

"Still questioning the hotel's kitchen help. I'd be there if you hadn't called to tell me about this . . . person. What a wasted trip.

I'm going back to my crime scene."

We watched Detective Keller stalk out of the squad room. There was a moment of awkward silence.

"John, I feel terrible about this."

"Don't blame yourself too much — you couldn't know she'd get close enough to the perp to get herself killed."

"When did Gretchen die?"

"We don't have a TOD yet. It appears she was killed somewhere else and her body hidden behind the hotel's Dumpster some-time after seven tonight, when a load of kitchen trash was emptied, and before nine o'clock when two of the busboys went outside to take a smoke and discovered her."

"John, if Gretchen Tully was found in the back of the Olympia Grand, isn't it likely she'd been investigating the group in the Presidential Suite?"

"Or someone put her there to make us think that," he said. "In any case, first thing tomorrow, we'll be talking to Prince Charm-ing and his future princess again. And to D'Martino and his daughter."

"And Roxanne Redding," I said.

"Speaking of the widow, there's something I meant to tell you. Those photos of the unknown man? Mrs. Redding said she and her husband took the shots of each other.

Because of the style, there's no doubt that he took the pictures of her, but according to the medical examiner, the limb and hand measurements of the man don't match her husband's."

35

Even though it was a few minutes after one Wednesday morning, as soon as I got into my Jeep I dialed Olivia Wayne.

"I'm sorry to call so late," I said.

"I just got home. What's the problem?"

"John O'Hara plans to question Nicholas and Celeste again. I thought you should have a heads-up." I told her about the murder of *Chronicle* reporter Gretchen Tully sometime Tuesday evening. "Or maybe yesterday afternoon. There's no official time of death yet. John told me they don't think she was killed in back of the Olympia Grand, but elsewhere, and then her body was dumped there between seven and nine last night."

"Other than working on the same paper, does Nick have some kind of relationship with Tully?"

"Not that I know of. He's never mentioned her." I told Olivia how I met Gretchen, and the horrible feeling that I had sent her on the trail that led to her death.

Olivia's reply was instantaneous and sharp. "Don't be ridiculous. Reporters go after stories. Often there's risk involved. But don't go around telling people you feel responsible or we might have another lawsuit on our hands. She could have litigious relatives."

Litigation . . . I'd almost forgotten about Galen Light's accusation against me.

"Is Light still in the hospital?" I asked.

"They released him Sunday evening, right after that detective, Weaver, left. I've been negotiating with Wylie York."

"How's that going?"

"One of my most useful qualities is the ability to frighten the other side. Old Wile E. Coyote can't carry my briefcase as a lawyer, but he doesn't scare easily."

"What do you think is going to happen?"

"I don't speculate, I act," she said. "I want to talk to Nicholas. Is he there with you?"

"No. Try him at home."

There was a second's pause on her end before she asked, "Trouble in paradise?"

"No, but it's a complicated time."

"A surprise teenage daughter and an ex-wife on the scene, and now two murders? I'd say 'complicated' is an understatement.

I'll call you." As usual, she hung up without saying good-bye.

I put the car in gear and drove a few blocks away from the police station before I stopped to use my phone again. Guessing that Olivia would be talking to Nicholas on his landline, I called his cell.

Four rings and the call went to voice mail. "I'm in my car and I have to talk to you," I said to the recording.

In less than a minute, Nicholas called back. "What are you doing driving around so late?"

"Do you know about what happened to Gretchen Tully?"

"Of course I do. Just about everyone who's still working at the paper has been called in. The front page is being torn apart for the murder story, with a feature piece inside about Gretchen. I can't work on the story because I've been exiled to the rewrite desk until I'm no longer under suspicion."

I told him about Gretchen's unexpected visit, and how I'd persuaded her to look into the Redding murder. "I wanted to tell you about it last week, but you were out of touch. By the time you came to the house Sunday night, so much else had happened that I forgot about her. Are you at the office now?"

"I'm in my car, on my way to Gretchen's apartment. If the police haven't got there yet, I'm going to see if I can find out what she was doing that could have gotten her killed."

"Are you crazy? What if the police think she might have been murdered at her place? They'll be all over it."

"I just checked. The lead detective is Val Keller. He's still canvassing at the Olympia Grand."

"I met him. He has the personality of a shark with a toothache. Tell me where Gretchen lived and I'll meet you there."

"No, Della —"

"Don't fight me on this. Give me the address."

"You're crazy," he said.

"Probably. What's her address?"

I heard him sigh with resignation. "Four Twenty-three Hollywood Boulevard, just east of Laurel Canyon. I went through her desk at the office and found her spare key," he said.

When I got to Gretchen Tully's address, the first thing I looked for was — mercifully, absent — police or SID vehicles.

So far, so good.

Gretchen lived in a three-story pink stucco

apartment building on the north side of Hollywood Boulevard, in a line of small but well-kept multitenant structures. The apartment house had a name displayed in large letters above the main entrance: "The Holly Woods." That was either an intentional pun, or an odd name for a building flanked by palm trees surrounded by low-lying flower beds, a landscaping choice that didn't remotely resemble a "woods."

There was an empty space a few doors east of the entrance. I pulled into it just as I saw Nicholas park his silver Maserati on the opposite side of Hollywood Boulevard. His wasn't the perfect vehicle for going house-breaking, but at least he managed to wedge it in between two SUVs. He wasn't near the streetlight, so his car wouldn't be easy to spot unless one was looking for it.

After grabbing my flashlight from the glove compartment, I hurried to meet him in front of number 423.

Nicholas had a flashlight, too; he carried it down along the side of his thigh, pointing toward the ground, the way detectives carry their weapons when they don't want it to be obvious that they're armed.

We saw a pair of headlights coming toward us fast and stepped into the darkness close to the outside wall, behind a palm tree. To my relief, the car zoomed past us and swung right into Laurel Canyon.

Nicholas took something from his jacket pocket. When he opened his hand I saw he had two pairs of thin latex gloves, the kind worn by surgeons, detectives, medical examiners — and your smarter burglars.

"I stopped at an all-night drugstore on the way here," he whispered.

I gave him a thumbs-up sign and he smiled.

We slipped on the gloves and he pointed to a narrow flagstone path running along the side of Gretchen's building, concealed from the neighboring apartment house by a tall hedge.

"Her place is the ground floor rear, garden apartment on this side," Nicholas whispered. "Let's hope there's no alarm system." He gestured for me to follow him.

We didn't need our flashlights on the path because the moon provided enough illumination until we reached Gretchen Tully's door. Back there, the building next door blocked the moon and plunged us into inky blackness.

I shielded part of my flashlight's beam and aimed it at the door. "No burglar alarm keypad," I whispered.

"Turn off the light."

I did, and in the darkness I heard the faint scrape of metal against metal, followed by a barely perceptible click.

Nicholas pushed the door open wide enough to enter. I followed him inside and quietly closed the door behind us.

We stood still, side by side, barely breathing. Listening. After a full minute during which we heard no sound inside the apartment, Nicholas snapped on his flashlight. He had it pointed down, toward the floor. I did the same, although I aimed my beam just a little higher.

As my eyes became accustomed to the minimal light, I saw that we were in a small living room. To the left, there was a kitchenette along the wall. It could be concealed by a screen, but the screen was folded back, exposing the stove, sink, counter space, and refrigerator. At the end of the room there was a sliding-glass door that opened onto a private patio. A shaft of moonlight showed the outline of two reclining chairs with a tiny table between them. Against the back wall of the patio were several large pots with some kind of plants in them.

There were two doors off to the right. The far one opened onto the bathroom and the nearer led to the bedroom. The space between the doors had been made into a little office area: a desk with a computer on it, a chair, and a two-drawer filing cabinet on the floor next to the desk.

By unspoken signals, we agreed that Nicholas should take the desk and I would go into the bedroom.

There was a window in the bedroom, but it was covered by slatted shutters. They were closed, but if I turned on a lamp bars of light would be visible from the outside. Partly shielding my flashlight's beam with one hand, I surveyed the room: a double bed, made up with a floral-patterned comforter. Above the comforter were two pillows; both of them looked slept-on. So Gretchen either didn't live alone, or had had a recent visitor.

There was a small table on either side of the bed, each with a lamp. Several thick books were on one surface. A copy of *Sports Illustrated* was on the other. Definitely, two people shared this bed. I didn't know anything about her personal life, but she wasn't wearing a wedding ring when she visited me.

An old-fashioned bureau with a mirror on top faced the bed. The bureau's surface held two sets of combs and hairbrushes. One set was similar to what I had at home. Next to that was a pair of "military style" brushes that I guessed must belong to the man in Gretchen's life.

He's not here; I wonder if he knows what happened to her. If he loved her . . .

Firmly shutting off that line of thought, I concentrated on looking for anything that might tell me who she was investigating.

I pulled the top drawer of the bureau open just enough to see that it contained female underwear and stockings, and only those things. The second drawer held sweaters, T-shirts, socks, and workout clothes. Kneeling down, I found that the bottom drawer was full of men's sweaters, shirts, and underwear. Nothing hidden beneath the folded stacks.

As I straightened, the beam of my light caught something shiny on top of the bureau, beside an open box of facial tissues. Back against the bottom of the mirror was an object I hadn't noticed during my first quick survey of the surface. It was a small silver picture frame. I picked it up to look closely and saw a picture of a man and a woman, smiling in sunlight, arms around each other. The young woman in the photo was Gretchen.

When I realized who the man was, I had to suppress a gasp.

Clutching the photo, I hissed, "Nicholas,

come see what I found."

He appeared in the doorway and held up an eight-inch-by-eleven-inch manila envelope.

"This was taped under her desk," he whispered. "Look what's in it."

Our heads together, we bent over the top of the dresser to prevent the light from our torches from leaking out through the window. Nicholas pulled several pages out of the envelope; they were lists of phone numbers. I recognized immediately what these lists were, but before I could say anything, a hard voice behind us commanded:

"Hold it right there!"

The person flicked on the wall switch and the room was flooded with light.

"Put your hands up and turn around."

I pivoted to see the barrel of a 9mm pistol pointed at us.

And above that weapon, I saw a familiar face.

36

The man holding the 9mm was as surprised to see us as we were to see him.

He mumbled, "Oh, crap."

I said, "Officer Downey." Downey was the big blond farm boy who was one of the first two uniforms on the scene of the Redding murder.

Nicholas recognized him, too. "Downey? What are you doing here?"

"Look." I showed Nicholas the photograph of Gretchen and Downey, arms around each other, and said, "Now I know who Gretchen's 'source' in the LAPD is." *Was.* Past tense. That word caused a fresh pang of guilt in my heart.

Nicholas brandished the pages from the manila envelope. "So that's how she got a copy of the Reddings' phone call lists. Put your weapon away, son."

Downey lowered the pistol and replaced it in his holster; he was still in uniform, but perhaps for not much longer.

"Leaking information on a police investigation can cost you your badge," Nicholas said.

Or worse. He might go to jail.

Downey's eyes started to water. He wiped them with the back of his hand. "I wasn't betraying the department. I mean, it's not like I was selling stuff to bad guys. All I did was try to help Gretch." He sank down onto the edge of the bed and put his face in his hands, a picture of dejection.

"What else did you give her?" Nicholas asked.

"Nothing. Just a copy of the phone dumps."

I asked, "When was the last time you saw Gretchen?"

"This morning — I mean yesterday morning. Tuesday. She was studying the phone numbers when I left to go to the gym."

"Can you prove you were at the gym?"

"Sure. Everybody saw me. Wait a minute — you don't think I killed her. Do you?" He stared at me, horrified, his face gray.

I said gently, "We're just trying to sort things out."

"When did you get back to the apartment?" Nicholas asked.

His eyes were watering again. "About

eleven. Gretch was gone. She said she'd try to be here so we could have lunch together. I lay down to wait for her. When I woke up it was almost three and she wasn't back. I had to hustle because I'm on the four to midnight."

Nicholas said, "Do the cops know you two were living together?"

Downey shook his head. "No. I was just coming off duty when I heard about — heard her name. I didn't believe it. I came right here. . . ."

"They're going to find out about the two of you, and you'll be under suspicion unless you can account for your time yesterday before you went on duty," I said. "Can you?"

He frowned in thought, and pinched the bridge of his nose with his thumb and forefinger. "I was at the gym from eight o'clock. Lots of people saw me. I worked out with some guys. I told you I came home about eleven and fell asleep. When I woke up, I was hungry. I called Barry — that's my partner, Officer Willis. We met at the Burger King near the station right about three fifteen. While we were eating, Gretch called, all excited. Said she was on her way to see somebody and would tell me about it when I got home. She wanted me to be sure to wake her up if she was sleeping."

Nicholas was skeptical. "I don't know if the cops will buy that story."

"They have to. I'd gone to the crapper, left my phone on the table. When she called, Barry answered. He talked to her first."

"He knows her voice?" I asked.

"Sure. Gretch and me go out a lot with Barry and his girl. Anyway, right after she called, Barry and me went to the station to check in. We were together all the time until midnight."

Downey looked from me to Nicholas and back to me, a plea in his eyes. "I know my making a copy of the phone dumps looks bad — okay, it was really wrong — but I swear to God, on my mother's life, Gretch promised whatever she found out that could help clear the Redding case, she'd turn it right over to Lieutenant O'Hara or Detective Weaver. All she wanted was to make a name for herself as a reporter."

Something seemed to occur to Downey and he sat up straighter. "You two . . . you're doing an illegal search. I live here. I got home and found you with —" Apparently he realized where that sentence was heading. He slumped again.

"You found us with material that *you* stole from an LAPD investigation," I said.

The room was silent for a moment. Nicholas's expression was thoughtful. I guessed we were thinking pretty much the same thing: that we should turn Officer Downey in for what he did, but then we'd have to confess how we found out. For my part, I felt queasy about the hypocrisy of destroying Downey's career. Nicholas and I had been investigating on our own, in spite of John's telling us to drop it.

But Nicholas and I couldn't stay out of it; the stakes were too high. He had risked going to jail by leaving the country to learn what he could about Prince Freddie, and I'd been physically assaulted for trying to get information out of Galen Light.

And for her ambition, Gretchen Tully had paid with her life.

With the surprise of discovering her relationship with Downey, and almost simultaneously being confronted by him at gunpoint, I'd lost sight of the most important human element in this scene.

"Have Gretchen's next of kin been told what happened to her?" I asked Downey.

"Her folks died in a car accident couple years ago. She only has a sister, Jolene, up in Wisconsin. Married, with a little kid. I guess somebody should call her. . . ."

"Let one of the detectives do it," Nicholas said. "They'll want to question her to find out when she last talked to Gretchen, and if she knows what Gretchen was doing the past few days."

"Officer Downey, I have a suggestion," I said. "Right now, before they find out on their own, go to Detective Keller, and to John O'Hara. Tell them that you and Gretchen were living together, but don't tell them you gave her a copy of the phone dumps."

"Thanks. I really appreciate —"

"This isn't a charitable contribution," I said. "It's a deal."

"What do you want?"

"To keep the phone list," Nicholas said.

Downey considered his options, then shook Nicholas's hand. Next, he shook mine. "Okay," he said.

I put the silver frame with their photo on the top of the dresser.

Nicholas slipped the pages of numbers back into the manila envelope.

We told Downey that we were very sorry about Gretchen, and left the apartment.

Outside, Nicholas walked me to my Jeep and took me in his arms. "Those poor kids — Downey and Gretchen."

Our arms tightened around each other as we stood in the darkness.

"I don't know what I'd do if I lost you,"

Nicholas whispered.

"We have some things to talk about," I said, stepping back. "But first we need to get you out of this mess. Maybe those phone numbers will help."

"I'll take them home and fax copies to you."

"No. John and Weaver are going to bring you in for questioning again. If they get a warrant to search your house, they mustn't find these. Let me have them."

"Good thinking." He handed the envelope to me. "Today's Wednesday. You're not working, are you?"

"No."

"Get some sleep. I'll call you as soon as I know when I can go over those numbers with you." He leaned forward; we kissed, and said good night.

I locked myself in and watched Nicholas hurry across the street to his car. It was only when I inserted the key in the ignition that I saw I was still wearing my burglar gloves. Stripping them off, I was about to throw them into the little receptacle I kept beneath the dashboard for trash when I changed my mind. I folded them neatly and put them in the glove compartment under the flashlight.

Were they going to be a memento? Or a memory? I didn't know.

37

After a few hours' sleep, I woke at seven and was just coming out of the shower when Liddy called.

"Sorry to phone so early," she said, "but I'm working on a set today and have to leave soon. What happened at the police station last night?"

I told her about my conversation with Detective Keller.

"Yikes. He sounds like a real charmer," Liddy said. "Do they have any idea who killed her — Gretchen Tully?"

"Not yet. No exact time of death, either, but it looks like she was killed somewhere else and dumped behind the hotel after dark."

"Oh, that poor girl."

I told Liddy about meeting Nicholas at Gretchen's apartment, and discovering that she was living with one of the two uniform officers who were at Alec Redding's house the night of his murder. I didn't tell her about Officer Downey stealing a copy of the phone lists for Gretchen, and that they were now in my possession. I couldn't tell Shannon or Eileen, either, because it wouldn't be fair to ask them to keep such a secret from John.

"You thought there was a leak at the department," Liddy said. "Now we know it was Gretchen Tully's cop boyfriend who tipped her off about Nick being under suspicion."

If I hadn't encouraged her to investigate Redding's murder . . .

I gave myself a mental shake. It was useless to speculate on what might have happened. "That's the quickest way to drive yourself crazy," I said.

"What is?"

I didn't realize I'd spoken aloud. "What I meant was that we can't go back and change the past."

"Good thing, too — we'd probably screw up the future," Liddy said. "I've got to leave in a minute, but did Gretchen have family here?"

"All I know is that there's a sister in Wisconsin, but Nicholas said the paper is doing a feature article on her life and career. There should be a lot of information in it."

343

"I'd like to send a donation in her name to a charity. Maybe her obituary will mention some cause she was interested in."

"When we find out, I'll send a contribution, too." *Guilt money,* I thought ruefully.

"Well, I'm off to be the 'Woman Who Gets out of Cab' just before Leonardo DiCaprio gets into it. They told me to wear a flared skirt because they've got a wind machine and want to show some leg. Thank God panty hose hides cellulite!"

"Panty hose — one of the Western world's great inventions," I joked.

"You're not kidding, Del. Remember how people were stuffing them with human hair to help clean up the oil spill in the Gulf? And last weekend, I saw a woman wearing them with her tennis outfit."

"I can beat that. Once when I was out of cheesecloth, I cut the leg off a pair to squeeze the liquid out of some ricotta when I was making a cheesecake."

We laughed, I wished Liddy good luck on her shoot, and we said good-bye.

Tuffy and I were coming back from our long morning walk just as Nicholas drove up. He got out of his car carrying a bulging plastic grocery bag.

Indicating the bag, I said, "Those are just

about outlawed. I'll give you a cloth reusable."

" 'It's not easy being green,' " he said.

"That's cute, Kermit. Thank you for not singing it."

"I've got to meet Olivia at Butler Avenue at ten, but first I brought something to make our investigating a little easier."

"What is it?"

"Not out here. Come on inside and I'll show you."

I unlocked the front door and unhooked Tuffy's leash. Nicholas followed us down the hallway and into the kitchen. I offered coffee, but he declined.

"Where's that list of phone numbers?" he asked.

"Hidden." I opened the door of the freezer and from the bottom shelf removed a roll of what looked like premade biscuit dough wrapped in aluminum foil. Stripping off the foil covering, I unrolled the manila envelope and smoothed it out flat on the table.

Nicholas gave me an admiring smile and said, "Pretty clever." Opening his plastic grocery bag, he took out a thick book. "Here's what I'm bringing to the party."

I felt my eyes widening in surprise. "A reverse phone directory? I thought only the police and the phone company had those.

Where did you get it?"

"Can't reveal my source," he said. "Even to my partner in crime, who's also the woman I love." He tipped my chin up to examine my face. "You're looking better. How does your mouth feel?"

"The cut's healed."

"Good." He drew me into an embrace and gave me a gentle kiss. I put my arms around him and responded with enthusiasm.

When we came up for air, Nicholas said, "I want you so much it's a physical ache." He stepped back, but took my hand and held it. "Before we get to finding out who the Reddings have been calling, there's something I need to say."

"You have another child I don't know about?" I kept my voice light.

"No. Seriously. A couple of minutes ago I called you my partner in crime, but I admit lately I haven't been the real partner you deserve. It's created a wedge between us; I saw that when I came back from Vienna. I couldn't let you know where I was because I didn't want to put you in a more difficult position than I have already. But being away from you — not being able to talk to you — made me realize how you must have felt on the other end of my silence. What I want to say is that I'm sorry I cut you out for a while. I hope you haven't given up on me because I promise not to do it again."

"You're right about the wedge," I said. "I won't settle for a fair weather relationship. Whatever problems are thrown at us, if we can't be truly together in dealing with them — and that's not a matter of geography — then we're not my idea of a couple."

"I won't let Celeste come between us," he said.

"Oh, Nicholas, *please.* I'm not in competition with your daughter. I told you I'm very happy she contacted you so you can build a relationship with her, and I meant it. But right now we have to concentrate on getting you both out from under suspicion of murder."

"This is the first time in my life, and I'm including my marriage to Tanis, when I've felt like half of something complete. I've been a bit of a slow learner."

"Don't sell yourself short. I think you've learned pretty fast." I stretched up and gave him a quick kiss. "Now let's get to work."

He sat at the table and removed the pages of numbers from the envelope while I got one of my white legal pads from the desk next to the computer. I tore off a few sheets for him to use, and took the chair opposite.

Nicholas was skimming through the pages.

"The cops got the phone records from the day Redding was killed going back for three months," he said.

"They had two landlines and three cell phones," I said. "Let's separate the pages into the calls from each number."

The landlines and two of the cells had several pages of numbers each. One cell had only two pages. Suspecting that was the mystery phone, I picked them up.

"I'll start with this phone," I said. Nicholas nodded and began studying one of the other piles.

There was a list of twenty-two calls on my pages. Twelve of them were to the same number. Six were to another number. Those eighteen were all to numbers in the 310 area code, which meant the Los Angeles area encompassing Beverly Hills, Westwood, Brentwood, Bel Air, Santa Monica, and Malibu. The final four were all to one number in the 949 area code, a location considerably south of Los Angeles, in the vicinity of San Clemente or Del Mar, in Orange County. I knew that because one of my cooking students lived in Del Mar and had a 949 number.

On my pad, I made note of the three numbers and reached for the reverse directory to find out to whom the majority of those calls had been made.

I felt a lurch inside my chest when I saw that the greatest number of calls had been placed to Galen Light.

"This must be Roxanne's cell," I said. "She called Galen Light twelve times. The last call was the day before her husband was murdered."

"Who else did she call?"

"I'm looking . . ." I turned pages in the reverse directory until I found a name to go with the 310 number that was called six times. "It's a doctor," I said. "Sanford Udall, MD."

Nicholas's eyebrows rose. "Sanford *Udall?*"

"Yes."

He chuckled. "I don't think that phone belongs to Roxanne," he said.

"Why? And what's so funny?"

"You don't recognize the name? Sanford Udall. He's fat, bald, in his sixties, glasses with big black frames. He wears a white jacket when he does commercials on cable TV about his specialty."

"I've never seen one," I said. "What's his specialty?"

"Erectile dysfunction." Nicholas handed his cell phone to me. "Look at the keypad and see what his phone number spells out in letters."

I looked. It took a minute of mental juggling, but then I saw . . . "Oh, no. I don't believe it." When translated from numerals into letters Doctor Udall's phone number spelled out "Har-dnow."

Nicholas grinned. "I can tell from your face that you got it: 'Hard Now.' He announces that in his commercials. It's the mnemonic he uses so prospective patients can't forget his number."

"I'm surprised the phone company, or is it the FCC, allows him to say that."

"It was a fight, several years ago," Nicholas said. "I remember the case. The ruling was that those two words are not obscene — only suggestive. Anyway, I doubt that Roxanne Redding was a patient of his."

"But if this is Alec's phone, why did he call Galen Light so often?"

"It's something we need to find out about." Nicholas indicated the pages in my hand. "Who was the third person called on that line — the 949 number?"

I flipped through pages until I came to the right one. Running my finger down the list of numbers I found what I was looking for. "This is interesting. The number belongs to a house in San Clemente, owned by April Zane. The actress."

"She could be just a photographic client. What's his business number?"

I told Nicholas, and he scanned the four other piles until he found the calls for that number. "Here it is. He called her on the business line twice three months ago, then once the month after that. . . . Then nothing."

"That's when he started calling her on the cell."

"When I get back to the office I'll go through the paper's archives and see what I can find out about her. Maybe something will indicate if they were having an affair."

"If so, she could be another suspect," I said. "He cut off the affair and she killed him. Or Roxanne found out about the affair and *she* killed him. Or Galen Light had some kind of a twelve-call relationship with Redding, and *he* killed him. Or Prince Freddie killed him in an attempt to prevent the picture of Celeste from going public and ruining his chances to marry money. Or Tanis and Freddie killed him together."

Nicholas shook his head. "No. Tanis didn't kill him. Absolutely not. I might consider that if the photo of Celeste was missing, but it's still in the Redding house. Tanis wouldn't do anything so extreme unless she got what she wanted. Freddie might be a

351

bungler, but she most definitely is not."

We spend the next hour checking phone numbers against the reverse directory and writing down the names of people called on all five of the lines. At nine o'clock, Nicholas put down his pen, folded the sheets of paper on which he'd been making notes, and tucked them into his jacket pocket.

"I've got to put this book back before it's missed," he said. "Then I'm meeting Olivia at the police station. Call you later?"

I nodded.

We kissed good-bye at the front door. I was on my way back to the kitchen when the phone rang. When I picked up the extension in the living room and said, "Hello," I heard Olivia Wayne's voice.

"I've been going head-to-head with Galen Light's lawyer, Wylie York. He's been demanding fifty thousand dollars to drop the charges against you," she said.

I felt my face flush with anger.

38

"Fifty thousand dollars! Light assaulted *me*. All I did was defend myself. That's outrageous."

"You were an English teacher," she said. "You should listen to the tense of my verbs. I said he 'has been' demanding that. Pending your agreement, I've reached a settlement with the slimy little toad."

"What *settlement* are we talking about?" My voice had a distinct edge to it.

"Retract your claws, Della. Okay, I shouldn't have told you what he wanted before I told you what he's getting, which is nothing. Nada. He drops the charges against you and you drop the charges against Light."

"That's better than my having to pay him anything, but it means that Light gets away without being punished for assaulting me."

"Not really. You gave him a broken nose that's going to require plastic surgery to make him look good again. I'd like to have had a big red 'R' branded on his chest, but we're too civilized to do that."

Now that I'd had a moment to process the information about the resolution of the case, I asked, "How did you make York back off?"

I heard a self-satisfied little chuckle on her end of the line. "Wile E. Coyote had a vulnerable underside that I exploited," she said. "I heard a rumor that he's a rooster with a taste for underage chicks, so I maneuvered him into a situation with one of my PI agency's operatives who's twenty-four but looks fourteen. All we let him do was touch her, but we got pictures. Even if he finds out her real age someday, flashing those shots was enough to scare the fight out of him. From the guilty way he reacted, I know that if I wanted to spend the time and money, I could come up with the real thing in his past."

"What a disgusting creep."

"And it's a lucky thing for us that he is. Della, I've defended a lot of people I wouldn't have dinner with, but I've always drawn the line at rapists and child molesters. It helps me sleep at night to think that the ones to whom the law doesn't dole out what they deserve to get, pay for it some other way. If a doctor ever tells me I have a terminal illness, I might decide to become a vigilante, like Charles Bronson in *Death Wish*."

"I'm in favor of evil being punished, but I don't want it to be because a doctor told you to put your affairs in order."

"Much to my surprise, I like you, too," she said.

"You're surprised?"

"Months ago, when Nick brought me over to meet you, my first impression was that you were a kind of Stepford Wife — or Stepford Widow. Too damn nice to be real. But I've learned you can be almost as much of a badass as I am. You just conceal it better."

"Sisters under the skin?"

"Just don't expect me to be all girly and go shopping with you."

"I hate to shop," I said.

"Before we get sloppy, I've got to meet Nick at the cop house. Try to stay out of legal trouble for a while." She disconnected.

I went back to the kitchen and the pages of telephone numbers and names that matched the numbers.

So much information, but what did it mean?

I told Tuffy, "I've got to see if there's some kind of a pattern to the calls."

He looked at me as though he understood, and sauntered to his dog bed to settle in and leave me to it.

Going through the lists of names that matched the phone numbers, I started crossing out the calls that seemed of doubtful relevance to the murder investigation, such as those to photo supply houses, framers, a plumber, the Reddings' pool service, the Home Shopping Network and QVC, Neiman Marcus, a watch repair company, weekly calls to Jenson's Market in Century City, and a call to Publishers Clearing House.

One call two months ago was made to a gynecologist, presumably Roxanne's. Two separate calls, from two different phones, went to a dentist in Beverly Hills. I guessed that the Reddings used the same dental professional.

In all of those names and numbers I couldn't find one call made to Gretchen Tully. If they had communicated it must have been either by Gretchen calling Roxanne, or showing up at Roxanne's door, as Gretchen had done to me.

It was tedious work. By the time I finished eliminating the calls that it seemed reasonable to ignore, my neck ached from bending over the pages and my right hand was cramped from lining through numbers.

But I had much shorter call lists for each of the Reddings' numbers.

Getting up, I stretched and rotated my neck. I let Tuffy out into the fenced back-yard, filled a bowl with fresh, cool water, and put it outside for him in a shady area beside the door.

It was noon and I was hungry, but I didn't want to bother making anything compli-cated. After surveying the contents of my pantry, I decided to have sardines on toast. One can of skinless, boneless on a piece of twelve grain bread. It would be delicious — and it was brain food.

Emma must have smelled the sardines when I opened the can, because I heard her trotting down the hallway. In seconds she was beside me in the kitchen, rubbing against my leg. "Okay," I told her, "I'll share. But too much won't be good for you." I put one sardine on a clean dish and placed it between her dry food and her water dish. She attacked the tiny fish, finished it in what might have been record time, and licked up every drop of oil. Then, purring, she stepped into Tuffy's bed, curled up, and went to sleep.

I went outside to run around the yard with Tuffy for a few minutes to get my blood circulating. When I'd had enough of the game we played where I chased him and then turned around and he chased me, I began to throw tennis balls for him. After about a dozen tosses, he took the ball in his mouth, but instead of bringing it back to me he sat down under the big shade tree with it between his front paws. That was my signal; he wanted to relax and I should get back to work.

Whether it was the sardines or the exercise, I returned to my task with fresh energy. I wished that I had Alec and Roxanne's actual cell phones, because then the logs would also tell me about incoming calls. Unfortunately, all I had were the lists of outgoing.

It was a beginning. Turning my white legal pad sideways, I began making charts of the people the Reddings called, and the dates and times of the calls.

And, at last, a pattern began to emerge. . . .

39

The cell phone number that I'd decided must belong to Roxanne, the one used to call the gynecologist, also showed multiple calls to Galen Light. I began to match the dates of Roxanne's calls to Light against those of Alec Redding's. Then I matched the times and durations of each of their calls.

Before I jumped to any conclusions, I moved over to my desk, attached the cable from Liddy's spy camera to the computer, and zipped through her dozens of shots until I came to the pages she'd photographed from Alec Redding's monthly appointment book. Fortunately, it had been on his bedside table. Had it been in the studio, Liddy would not have been able to touch it.

According to his book, Alec Redding had photographed Galen Light five months ago. While I was studying his appointments, I saw that April Zane had also been photographed by Redding. So, too, had some of the other names that had come up on the phone lists. But only Light and Zane had been contacted subsequently from the cell phones. Alec and/or Roxanne had communicated with every other Redding client via the landlines.

I wished I had records of e-mails and text messages, but the police surely had those. All I had was the information in the appointment book and on the pages of phone calls. Maybe it would be enough to, at least, allow me to come up with a theory of the crime. *Crimes.* The murders of Alec and Gretchen had to be connected. John thought so, and it seemed Detective Keller agreed.

When I finished making a chart of the dates and times of the cell phone calls, I saw that the first two calls to Galen Light had been made by Roxanne. On the day of Roxanne's second personal call, but an hour earlier, Alec had called Light.

Roxanne's calls to Light occurred either during the middle of the day — typically, the lunch hour — or late at night.

As for Alec's calls to Light, beginning with the second one, each of those calls were placed Mondays, Wednesdays, and Fridays at four o'clock in the afternoon, and lasted between twenty-eight and thirty minutes. Alec's final call to Light happened the afternoon of the day before Alec was murdered.

Was he getting life coaching on the telephone?

Alec's calls to the office of Sanford Udall, the erectile dysfunction doctor, were made between eight thirty and nine in the morning, and lasted three or four minutes. His calls to the San Clemente number for April Zane were placed late at night; each lasted from fifteen to twenty minutes.

That conjured up an image in my mind of Roxanne and Alec, in separate parts of the house, each thinking the other was asleep, doing their private phoning. They wouldn't have used a landline because they had two old-style lines where a light would appear on the instruments when one of those receivers was picked up. Anyone in the house who was near an extension would know someone was on the phone.

Redding's late night calls to a beautiful actress from one of his cell phones suggested that they might be having an affair. But his morning calls to an erectile dysfunction specialist suggested that he might be having some trouble in that area. Perhaps Redding was planning an affair and getting himself ready to consummate it. The actress lived more than one hundred miles south of here, and Redding had had appointments to photograph subjects almost every day. They could be in that stage of exciting each other with anticipation until they could manage to get together.

If I'm right about this, did Roxanne know what her husband was planning?

And his erectile dysfunction. How long had that been going on? How had it affected his marriage? The regular communications with Doctor Udall seemed to imply that he was being treated for it. But how? With injections? Not with pills, unless Alec had hidden them somewhere. The medical examiner who went through their bathroom cabinets found that the only prescription medications were Roxanne's birth control pills.

Did Roxanne's many calls to Light, at times when her husband was likely either to be occupied or asleep, mean that they were having an affair? My guess is that they were. But had something happened to that relationship shortly before Alec Redding's death? Was that why Light had spoken of Roxanne in the past tense, and in a negative tone? Was that why he had been drinking? Or was he simply covering up what was going on between them?

Roxanne had claimed to be at a movie theater in Little Tokyo watching *Seven Samurai* while her husband was being murdered. It's a long movie, and an old one, shown many times in theaters and on television. She could have seen it before that night, and been able to answer any questions about it. She produced a ticket stub, but it's easy to slip out of a theater without being seen. She could have come back to Brentwood, parked in the alley, come in through the back gate, killed Redding, and left the same way. Officer Willis had said that the gate at the back of the property wasn't locked.

Where had Galen Light been that night?

And where — *really* — had Tanis, Prince Freddie, Celeste, and Freddie's butler, Mordue, been that night?

Mentally, I crossed Celeste off my list of murder suspects. Also Mordue. I could imagine the butler, who had no connection to Redding, as an accessory after the fact, but not as a killer. It didn't seem likely that Freddie could have made it to Redding's house unless someone, Mordue or Tanis, drove him there.

I could imagine Freddie and Tanis going together to Redding in an attempt to buy the pictures of Celeste. If they were refused, and they would have been because the salacious pie photo was still stored at Redding's after his death, one of them might have been angry enough to pick up that white stool and hit Redding with it.

But who killed Gretchen Tully, and why? It seemed likely she had discovered something about Redding's murder that threatened the killer with exposure. But what?

John or Weaver or Detective Keller must have her cell phone. If it wasn't with her body, then they must have obtained her records from the phone company.

This exercise in trying to formulate a theory was frustrating because of the things I didn't know. I wanted to go to John and tell him what I'd pieced together, and ask him to share what he had learned. But if I told him that I had the Reddings' phone records it wouldn't be more than a minute before he would deduce that someone had stolen copies for Gretchen, and who would have done that except her live-in boyfriend? Then Officer Downey would, at the very least, be fired from the police force. He might even be prosecuted.

I was in the middle of a collision of wrongs. Downey had been wrong to steal the phone records for Gretchen so she could try to solve a murder and win a promotion to hard news reporting. To be honest about it, Nicholas and I had been wrong to make an illegal search of Gretchen's apartment. We'd been wrong to blackmail the grieving Officer Downey — there was no other word for it — into giving us the envelope of numbers.

Downey, Nicholas, myself: we'd all had good intentions . . .

Now I'd hit a wall.

I needed to know what John, with his much greater resources, had learned. And what I had figured out, and charted, could be helpful to him in constructing the picture that would lead to the solution.

How could I confide in John, and protect Officer Downey? Not to mention Nicholas and myself.

The phone was ringing. So deep in thought was I that for a moment I didn't realize what that sound was.

I answered and heard Roxanne Redding's voice.

"Hi, Della. I've been looking at your pictures, and I think they're good. Before I make any prints, I'd like you to pick the ones you like best. Can you come over to the studio this evening?"

A glance at my wall clock showed it was a

few minutes after two. "I can come over now," I said.

"No, I'm busy until seven. How about after that?"

I didn't want to go to the Redding house at night. Call me paranoid, but I wasn't going to be one of those too-stupid-to-live females in horror movies. I didn't know there was a murderer lurking at 190 Bella Vista Drive, but on the other hand, I didn't know there wasn't.

"That's not going to work for me," I said. "Tomorrow night I do a live TV show and have to prepare for it during the day. Why don't you e-mail the proofs to me?"

"I'd rather we be able to go over them together so I can answer any questions you may have, and I can show you how I'd like to crop them, and what retouching I suggest."

"I'd rather not have my picture retouched."

"Aren't you the one who said you wanted to look like yourself but a little bit better?"

I had to admit that I was. "But I can't come over tonight or tomorrow. What about Friday morning?"

"Let me check my book," she said.

We settled on ten o'clock Friday morning. Returning to the kitchen, I picked up my chart of names, numbers, and times of the phone calls that seemed most relevant.

John had more information than I did. What I knew made a picture with large holes in it. Whatever John had learned probably would fill in at least some of those holes. But maybe he wasn't yet able to see a picture — he may not have had time to organize the phone calls the way I did.

It was a daunting task, but I had to think of some way for us to merge what we knew without destroying Officer Downey's career, or involving Nicholas. Or, for that matter, me.

How could I make a bargain with John without landing all of us in hot water?

40

Then the idea came to me.

I dialed a number I no longer had to look up. Olivia wasn't in her office — she was most likely at Butler Avenue with Nicholas and Celeste — so I asked her assistant to have her call me as soon as possible.

Turning to a fresh page in my pad, I began to make a need-to-know list.

First: What had Gretchen Tully been doing between leaving my house on Friday afternoon and when her body was discovered on Tuesday night?

Next: Where was her car? If she wasn't killed in her apartment, and there wasn't any indication that she had been, then she must have driven to the place where she either met her killer or the killer surprised her.

If Gretchen's vehicle was anything like mine — full of reminders to myself, receipts for gas and other items I'd bought — there could be useful information in it.

I didn't have her and Officer Downey's home phone number. Why hadn't I thought to make a note of it when I was in their apartment?

Maybe she's listed.

Los Angeles telephone books are divided into various areas of this sprawling metropolis, which is more like a collection of smaller communities rather than one big city. Most households are provided with several targeted phone books. On the shelf above my desk I found the one for the area that included Hollywood, and flipped to the "Ts."

There she was: G. Tully, at her address on Hollywood Boulevard.

It was only two thirty. Officer Downey was on the four to midnight shift. Unless he was still answering questions about his relationship with Gretchen, he should be at home.

When he answered his voice was thick with sleep.

"This is Della Carmichael, Officer Downey. I'm sorry if I woke you."

I heard him yawn. "It's okay."

"Are you going on duty this afternoon?"

"No. After I told the bosses about me and Gretch, they gave me a couple days off. What do you want?"

"I was wondering where Gretchen's car is."

"Her car . . . ? Gee, I don't know. It's not here."

"Do the police have it?"

"Maybe . . . They didn't say . . . I wasn't thinking about . . ."

"What's the make and model? And do you know the license number?"

"It's a Toyota Camry, white, three years old." His police training kicked in and his voice was stronger now. "The taillights don't match: one's red and one's amber. The dealer didn't have the right one in stock, but it's on order. Plate number's Three-Bravo-Yellow-Ernest-One-Six-Zero. If it wasn't recovered, I'll put it on the Hot Car list."

"Before you do anything, tell Lieutenant O'Hara and Detective Keller that you don't know where her car is. Let them take it from there," I said.

"Yeah, right. Okay."

After hanging up, I thought about where Gretchen's car might be. If someone from Parking Enforcement spotted it and thought the vehicle had been abandoned, it could have been towed to the police impound yard.

Or, whoever killed Gretchen might have

driven to a high-crime area and left the car there. If so, it would have been stripped to the bare frame and sold for parts quicker than a school of piranha could reduce an unlucky swimmer to a skeleton.

But there was another possibility. . . .

I brought Tuffy into the house, told him I'd be back soon, and grabbed the keys to my Jeep.

What had Gretchen stumbled upon that would make Alec Redding's killer believe she was a threat?

The fact that her body had been dumped behind the Olympia Grand Hotel suggested that either she was concentrating on the trio in the Presidential Suite, or the killer had wanted detectives to think she was. Or Tanis and Prince Freddie put her there so that the police would think they *wouldn't* have done that and thereby implicated them-selves. Oh, no — that was too convoluted. I could make myself crazy going in circles like that. Better to find some facts.

Whatever the reason Gretchen's body was found in back of the hotel, the five people she would most likely have been checking on were all either in Westwood, where the hotel was situated, or in the adjacent enclave of Brentwood, where Roxanne Redding and

Galen Light lived less than a mile apart.

The police theory was that she had been murdered in a different location. It meant that whoever killed her had to move her car away from where she had been parked. It seemed logical to me that it hadn't been moved too far away, or how could the killer have returned to his or her own vehicle, or residence, without using public transportation? He or she could have had an accomplice, but my guess was that Gretchen's murder was a spontaneous reaction to a perceived threat, not something planned in advance.

Of course all of this was conjecture. I had no evidence, but trying to find Gretchen's car was at least something proactive I could do. It beat staying home and worrying.

Driving east from my home in Santa Monica, I reached Brentwood first and began a slow cruise up and down streets, looking for that white Toyota Camry.

There were quite a few of them; I hadn't realized what a popular vehicle it was.

Each time I spotted one, I stopped to read the license number. Just in case the plate had been switched with one from another car, I also looked for mismatched taillights.

This went on, block after block, for nearly an hour when my cell phone rang. A glance at the faceplate indicated it was Olivia, returning my call.

My phone was hands-free, but fearing I might miss Gretchen's car if I tried talking and searching at the same time, I pulled over next to a fire hydrant and cut the motor.

When I answered, Olivia asked briskly, "What's up?"

I told her that Nicholas and I had searched Gretchen Tully's apartment in Hollywood and what we'd found.

"Nick filled me in about your little midnight B and E stunt. It was a stupid risk."

"We didn't *break* and enter because Nicholas had a key. We just entered."

I went on to explain that I'd made a chart of the Reddings' phone calls from the lists that Nicholas had found taped to the underside of her desk.

"Here's why I called you," I said. "Part One: I'd like to share with John what I've put together because I think it would help him, but I don't know how to do that without destroying the police officer who stole the phone lists for Gretchen. Part Two: I want to know if John and Keller have found out anything that would eliminate Nicholas, Celeste, Tanis, Prince Freddie, Roxanne Redding, or Galen Light from suspicion of the Redding murder."

"Part Two is easy to answer. No, they haven't come up with anyone outside their viable suspect list. No jealous husbands, nobody to whom it would be dangerous to owe money, no women scorned."

That was a surprise. "I don't believe he was Mr. Clean."

"Oh, no — he'd been a naughty boy. Redding sowed his 'wild oats' pretty liberally until about six months ago, but there's no indication his wife knew about it. I have to give O'Hara and Weaver credit — they did a thorough job of questioning people who worked for the Reddings, their neighbors, and their business associates. Nobody saw or heard signs of marital discord. Everybody thought the Reddings were a happy couple. Several volunteered that they envied them, and thought the harmony was because Roxanne and Alec worked together. Of course, nobody knows what goes on behind closed doors."

I told Olivia about Redding's calls to the erectile dysfunction doctor.

"That could be why Redding-the-player quit playing; he was benched, so to speak." Her tone was wry.

"Do they suspect Nicholas of killing Gretchen Tully?"

"Good news there. Nick was at the paper during the hours when Gretchen could have been killed. A dozen people saw him, worked with him. No way he could have slipped out, even if he had a motive to murder her, and nobody at the *Chronicle* thinks he did. But the not-good news is that Detective Keller is trying to get the two murders un-linked and treated as separate cases."

"That's ridiculous. How could he imagine they're not connected?"

"I don't know how his mind works, but he's a glory hound who wants to clear the Tully case and knows he can't pin it on Nick. He's been grilling her boyfriend's partner, Officer Willis, all day, trying to get him to say that Willis and Downey weren't together for their whole shift."

"Do you know if he succeeded?"

"I was still at Butler when he finally let Willis go. From the expression on their two faces, I could tell Keller struck out." Olivia chuckled. "That Willis is one tough cookie. I wouldn't be surprised if he ends up chief someday, and if I were Keller, I'd damn well pray he doesn't. Keller could find himself back in uniform, in one of those areas where white cops aren't popular. Look, we're wasting time. Re your Part One: Let me think

375

about how to approach O'Hara regarding an informal deal for an information exchange. I'll let you know."

"Thanks, Olivia."

She disconnected, and I continued cruising for one particular white Camry.

Another hour later, on a residential street called Midvale, south of Wilshire Boulevard, I found the car I'd been searching for. The right plate number and mismatched taillights. I'd almost missed it because it was parked under a tree that had shed leaves and purple berries all over it.

I steered the Jeep into the space between the back of the Toyota and the beginning of someone's driveway and was about to get out when I remembered that I still had the latex burglar gloves. I glanced around to be sure no one was watching me. All clear. Slipping the gloves on, I approached the Camry and peered in through the driver's side window.

Gretchen didn't keep a "neat house" in her car. The front seat had several slips of paper, an empty McDonald's box, a bottle of water, a *Thomas Guide* for Los Angeles, and an accordion-style map of Southern California that had been folded into a square.

I expected that the car would be locked,

but I tried the door handle anyway.

The door opened.

A set of car keys lay on the floor below the driver's seat, beside the gas pedal. I left them there; I had no intention of driving it, nor of getting in because I didn't want to disturb any evidence — fibers, possibly, or traces of blood — that SID techs were equipped to find.

By bending over the front seat I saw that the road map had been folded, with a red highlighter tracing the route to San Clemente. April Zane lived in San Clemente. It looked as though Gretchen had thought it worthwhile to visit the actress whom Alec Redding had been phoning late at night. But had she actually made the long trip south — or was that something she had planned to do?

The *Thomas Guide* was closed, with no little pieces of paper sticking out of it to indicate what streets she might have looked up.

From the McDonald's bag, it was obvious that she'd had at least one meal in her car. Of the pieces of paper, one was crumpled from a pad, another looked like a gas station receipt. Those might be useful to the police, but not to me.

I saw something metallic on the floor

below the passenger seat. Only a bit of it was visible from the side I was on because the leafy tree under which the car was sitting had darkened the well on the passenger side. I couldn't get any closer without getting into the car, so I closed the driver's door and went around to the opposite side.

The floor on the passenger side was littered with empty packages of trail mix and flattened Starbucks cups, but just under the lip of the seat was the object I'd spotted: a camera.

Leaning in, I could see the camera was a Canon with a 55–250 mm zoom lens. It looked like Gretchen had been doing surveillance, which explained the empty food and coffee containers. I had to see if that was a film camera or digital, and if there was film in it, or pictures. Glad I was wearing the latex gloves, I picked it up. It was a single lens reflex. Digital, with a slot for the SD card.

But no card.

Gretchen must have been caught photographing, and whoever killed her must have stolen the record of what she shot.

"Is this your car, ma'am?"

Startled, I turned to see a uniformed patrolman. So intent had I been on examining Gretchen's camera that I hadn't heard his car pull up and double-park beside my Jeep. He had one hand on his holstered weapon.

"My car? No. It belongs to a friend," I said.

He stared at me, his expression grim. "Put that camera back in the car where you got it, ma'am, and let me see some ID."

"I've been looking for this car, and I was about to call —"

"Hey! What's that you're wearing on your hands?"

Now he drew his weapon and pointed it at me.

He sees the latex gloves and thinks I'm a thief. "Officer, I'm wearing these because I didn't want to disturb any evidence." I started to strip them off.

"Don't do that," he commanded. "Leave the gloves on. Just like that, put your hands on top of your head and lace your fingers together."

41

"Please, Officer, I'm trying to tell you that I was about to call Lieutenant John O'Hara at West Bureau. This car belongs to a murder victim. He'll want to have SID go over it."

The patrol officer looked dubious. As well he might, I thought.

"Lieutenant O'Hara's on my speed dial," I said. "Just look at my phone."

"Where is it?"

With my hands clasped on the top of my head I had to point my elbow in the direction of my Jeep. "In the cup holder. My driver's license is in my wallet — in my handbag, on the passenger seat. Use my phone and call West Bureau and ask for Lieutenant O'Hara, or Detective Weaver. They need to know where this car is."

He gave a quick glance back at my Jeep, but instead of going to it for my handbag, he kept his attention focused on me while he activated his mobile to call the station house and asked to speak to Lieutenant O'Hara or Detective Weaver.

Keeping my tone pleasant and trying to sound helpful, I said, "My name is Della Carmichael. They know me."

I saw recognition flicker in his eyes and hoped that was a good sign. I said, "I'm not very comfortable like this. May I put my hands down?"

"Okay," he said, "but place them flat on the trunk of the car where I can see them."

Someone came on the other end of his line and I heard the officer tell whoever it was my name, and that he had "apprehended" me going through a car that wasn't mine.

A moment of silence while the officer listened. He gave them Gretchen's license plate number, then said, "Yes, sir," and thrust the phone toward me. "Detective Weaver wants you."

I took the phone. "Hello, Hugh? I found Gretchen Tully's car and was about to call its location in when your officer came along."

"Jeez, Della!" He gave an exasperated snort. "If our mayor finds out about all the stuff you do, he may think he can fix the city's budget by laying off more of our guys."

I ignored his sarcasm and told him where I was. "Gretchen Tully was watching someone, Hugh. I'm sure she saw something that got her killed."

Weaver told me to stay put, and to give the phone back to the uniformed officer.

The patrolman listened for a minute, nodded, and said, "Yes, sir." He hooked the phone on his belt and holstered his weapon.

"You've got to stay here until the detectives arrive, ma'am. Please go sit in your vehicle."

A familiar unmarked Crown Victoria pulled up in front of Gretchen's car and parked. I saw Hugh Weaver at the wheel, but it wasn't John in the seat beside him; it was Detective Val Keller.

The uniformed officer, Judson — I'd seen his nameplate when I passed him to get into my Jeep — stepped away from Gretchen's car to meet the detectives.

I got out and stood on the pavement just behind Gretchen's mismatched taillights while the three of them conferred briefly, looking over at me.

Weaver and Keller pulled on their latex investigator's gloves and Weaver gestured for me to join them. Officer Judson went to his patrol car.

Acknowledging Keller with a nod, I spoke mostly to Weaver. "Gretchen must have been doing surveillance."

"So that's what it looks like to *you.*" Keller's voice had a nasty edge. "What did you do to mess up whatever evidence might be in that car?"

"Nothing." It would have been more politic to act meek and apologetic to a bully like Keller, but I couldn't do it. I responded to his unpleasant tone with ice in my own. "The car doors were unlocked. I put on latex gloves —"

"Yeah?" Keller smirked. "What were you doing with them? You just carry a pair around?"

"My profession is cooking," I said. "Anyone who handles food —"

Weaver interrupted. "Forget that. What did you touch?"

"Only the camera. And I put it back on the floor in front of the passenger seat, exactly where I found it. It's digital, and the SD card is missing."

Keller said, "What if we get a female officer out here for a full body search? We might find that card."

"By all means, have me searched." I stared at him defiantly. "But why wait? You have my permission to do it yourself."

Keller knew I was daring him. He blinked first, shrugged, and turned away. Without a further word to me, he opened the driver's side door and peered into Gretchen's car.

Weaver said, "What made you figure the girl's car was here?"

"I had no idea where it was. I spent the last two hours going up and down streets in a kind of grid pattern because I theorized that whoever killed Gretchen moved her car from wherever it had been. Whether it was someone at the Olympia Grand Hotel, or Roxanne or Light in Brentwood, they wouldn't have driven it too far away from their home base because they could get back without leaving a trail by using public transportation."

"The killer coulda had an accomplice with wheels," Weaver pointed out.

"That's possible, but then wouldn't the car have been driven a long way away? Whoever drove here left the doors unlocked and the keys on the floor next to the accelerator. The killer probably hoped that the car would be stolen and you'd never find it. Or if you did, it wouldn't be in any condition to be useful to the investigation."

"Go home," Weaver said, making a shooing gesture. "We'll take it from here."

"You're welcome," I said curtly.

Weaver glanced at Keller, who by now was on the passenger side of the car, examining Gretchen's camera. Leaning toward me and keeping his voice low, Weaver said, "We had an APB out on this car, but you found it first. Thanks."

I was three blocks from home when my cell rang. It was Liddy, and she sounded upset.

"Del, where are you?"

"In the car, just turning onto my street. What's the matter?"

"Have you seen today's *Los Angeles Observer*?"

"No." The *Observer,* a racy tabloid similar to the *New York Post,* had begun publication in Southern California as an afternoon paper about a year ago. I subscribed to the city's morning daily, the *Chronicle,* and bought the *Observer* once in a while when it caught my eye on a newsstand. "Why? What's in it?"

"Go find a copy," she insisted. "Call me as soon as you get home."

"Liddy, I'm tired. What are you talking about?"

"You've got to *see* it." I heard the urgency in her voice. "It's on the front page."

I knew that Liddy seldom got upset over minor things. With a growing sense of apprehension, I told her that I would, and turned the Jeep around.

The corner of Montana and Eleventh had a line of vending machines in front of a popular coffeehouse that had several small tables outside where people were allowed to have their dogs sitting with them. I nosed the Jeep into the only empty spot I saw — a passenger loading zone — and kept the motor running.

The coin-operated box containing the *Los Angeles Observer* sat between similar machines selling the *Chronicle* and *USA Today*. I inserted three quarters, pulled the glass door open, and took out a copy of the *Observer*.

I felt my mouth drop open in shock.

Below the paper's logo, and covering most of the front page, was Alec Redding's photograph of Celeste holding the pie. Her nude derriere was concealed by the *Observer*'s judicious use of a black bar, but it was clear that she wasn't wearing anything beneath the chef's apron.

The headline above the picture read: "Motive for Murder?"

42

"Hey, lady, you're going to get a ticket."

A young man in a Dallas Cowboys sweat-shirt, sitting with an English sheepdog by his side at one of the curbside tables, had called out the warning.

I looked up to see a Parking Enforcement person in one of those white golf cart–type vehicles approaching. My Jeep couldn't stay in the passenger loading zone.

"Thank you," I said, quickly folding the paper in half and shoving it under my arm. I jumped back into the Jeep. With seconds to spare, I managed to zoom into a momentary gap in the line of traffic on Montana Avenue and get away before the woman could cite me.

I drove straight home without stopping to read what went with Celeste's picture. In red type just below her image, it said, "Sensational story on pages four and five."

My cell phone rang as I put my key in the

front door lock. Inside, I heard my landline ringing, too. I ignored both phones — voice mail would pick up the messages — rewarded Tuffy's enthusiastic greeting with a quick pat, and headed for the kitchen to read the newspaper article. It was a good bet that the calls were about that. I didn't want to talk to anyone, even to Liddy, until I'd read it.

In the kitchen, I opened the door to the backyard for Tuffy and told him we'd go for a walk a little later. Seeming to understand, he trotted outside.

It was close to five thirty. Not dark yet, but the sun was going down. I turned on the strong kitchen light and opened the paper.

Pages four and five had a large photo of Celeste in one of the fully dressed modeling poses that Redding had taken. Also accompanying the article were pictures of Alec Redding, from some Hollywood event, a shot of his home on Bella Vista Drive — they captioned it "the murder house" — and also a photo of Nicholas, taken two years ago, when he won a Pulitzer Prize for his series of articles in the *Chronicle* called "The Making of a Monster," about the history of a serial killer.

Because of the tabloid size of the *Observer,*

and the emphasis on photographs, there wasn't a lot of room left for text. Unfortunately, there was enough to be damaging to Nicholas. Three reporters shared the byline. They had managed to find out that "prize-winning *Los Angeles Chronicle* journalist Nicholas D'Martino's long-estranged teen-age daughter" had come to Los Angeles from Europe to live with him, that Nicholas was "reputed to be enraged" when he saw the "scandalous" photos of his "child" taken by "celebrity portrait artist" Alec Redding.

That term — "celebrity portrait artist" — told me that the photo and the information had surely come from Roxanne Redding. One of the tricks good photographers use to relax a subject is to get them to talk during a session. While Celeste was sitting for Redding, I imagined that she had talked about not having known her father.

The *Observer* article then recounted gory details of the "rage-fueled slaying" of Redding: "his handsome head in a pool of blood, with the bloodstained bludgeon" discarded nearby. It went on to say that the "young girl's angry father, Nicholas D'Martino, was discovered at the murder scene when police arrived, but claimed to have found Redding already dead." The reporters added, "Arriving following the discovery of the body was glamorous TV chef Della Carmichael, with whom D'Martino has been keeping company. Because Redding's time of death eliminates Ms. Carmichael as a suspect, her presence at the murder house is not considered significant by authorities."

I didn't think the article could get any worse for Nicholas, until I read the next paragraph, about the murder of "fellow *Chronicle* reporter, Gretchen Tully." The *Observer* referred to her as "a rising young journalist rumored to be moving in on D'Martino's crime beat territory." The story concluded with this: "An unnamed LAPD source who was not authorized to speak on behalf of the department stated that D'Martino had not been taken into custody because the investigation was ongoing."

My cell phone rang again. Just as I answered and heard Liddy's voice, the landline started to ring again, too. I ignored it.

"Did you see that awful story?" Liddy asked.

"Yes, but you've got to remember that paper's in competition with the *Chronicle,* so they're trying to make Nicholas look bad."

"They succeeded. Where did they get all that information?"

I told Liddy my belief that Roxanne Redding had sold the photos, probably for a lot of money, and that Celeste had talked about personal matters while she was being photographed. "Either Roxanne put a negative spin on whatever Celeste said, or the *Observer* reporters did."

"At least they called you 'glamorous,' " Liddy said.

"I should be flattered?" I said dryly. "I doubt whoever wrote it has ever seen me. Somebody throws in a bit like that to make their sleazy story a little more titillating."

"I'm going to send an e-mail to the editor telling him that this story is so disgusting I'm never going to read their rotten paper again."

"You're wonderful, Liddy. Go get 'em."

"I will. I can be very stern when I see an injustice being done."

"Oh, I just realized — I should call Olivia Wayne about this. She may not have seen it."

Olivia had seen it, and had already been on the phone with the *Observer*'s owner.

"Why go to the editor, when I can try to scare the hell out of the person who has much more to lose in a lawsuit?" she said.

391

"Are they going to retract this libelous story?"

"The problem is that they've stayed just this side of libel, quoting unnamed sources and only *implying* that Nick is a murderer. The piece was vetted by a lawyer before it went to press. I couldn't win a case against them in court, but I persuaded the paper's owner that I could make enough trouble for him — and cost him enough to make me go away — that he agreed to have the paper do a *positive* story about Nick."

"What good will that do? This is so frustrating! People who read this will think Nicholas killed Redding, and maybe even poor Gretchen."

"The public tends to remember only the last thing they read," Olivia said briskly. "The moment the real murderer is caught, or there's a new celebrity scandal, Nick will be forgotten. Until then, just keep your head down. Don't talk to anyone from the *Observer.* You've got a live show to do tomorrow night, don't you?"

"Yes."

"Look on the bright side: You'll probably get a bump up in ratings from this," Olivia said. I could imagine her wry smile.

There were three messages on my landline;

two were from *Observer* reporters wanting to interview me. I erased those. The third was from Eileen. She left the number of our little bakery in Hollywood, Della's Sweet Dreams. When she answered she sounded breathless.

"Hi, partner," she said. "We're selling out here today, and it's not even a holiday week."

"Do you need me to come down and help?"

"No, we're handling things. I called to tell you about the e-mail you got from Harmon Dubois." One of Eileen's duties was to read my business e-mails and deal with whatever she could.

Harmon Dubois. My mind blanked on the name for a moment, but then I remembered: Harmon Dubois was the spry, eighty-year-old, poetry-writing student from my Saturday afternoon adults' cooking class. Eileen had nicknamed him "the suck-up" for his habit of bringing me flowers from his garden and following me around in class, offering to help.

I asked Eileen what he wanted.

"He said it was going to be a surprise, but then he thought he'd better warn you."

Oh, Lord, what now? I said, "To borrow a line from Dorothy Parker: 'What fresh hell is this?' "

"Actually, it's kind of sweet," Eileen said. "Your whole cooking class got tickets for the live show tomorrow night, but Harmon decided to break their 'code of silence,' as he put it, so that the sight of them there wouldn't throw you off. But he wants you to 'act surprised.' "

"That is sweet," I said. "I appreciate them wanting to come to the show. Please e-mail him for me, thank him, and tell him I promise to act absolutely stunned." I debated whether or not to tell Eileen about the *Observer* piece, and decided that I should.

"There's an article in today's *Los Angeles Observer* —"

"I saw it," she said. "It's sold in one of the machines on the street outside the shop. A customer brought it in."

"What did you think?"

"Two things. First, them calling you a 'glamorous TV chef' can only help our business. Second, that Daddy's going to be furious when he reads it and learns somebody in the department is talking to the press."

For a moment, I was taken aback, but then I thought, *It's true, what I've always believed, but was too upset to remember earlier: People view things through the prism of their own self-interest.* Eileen saw the article as helpful to our shop. John would want the LAPD leaker exposed. Maybe Phil Logan's mantra — "there's no such thing as bad publicity" — was right, and that ultimately Nicholas wouldn't be damaged.

"Tanis has gone berserk," Nicholas said.

I'd taken Tuffy on a long walk and was on my way up Eleventh Street, heading home, when Nicholas drove down from the opposite direction and flashed his lights at me.

"Get in," he'd said. "A guy from the *Observer* is parked in front of your house. When I spotted him I drove on past and turned around. I figured this time of night, you might be out with the big Tuff."

"You're a good detective."

"Not as good as you," he said. "You're the one who found Gretchen's car."

"How do you know about that?"

"Weaver told me; I was at the cop shop when you talked to him. Detective Keller had pulled me in again for questioning. That didn't last long, because he hasn't been able to shoot holes in my alibi for Gretchen's murder."

Nicholas turned into the alley behind my house, parked outside my back gate, and cut the motor. We sat there in the darkness with Tuffy in the rear seat.

"What do you mean about Tanis going crazy?" I asked.

"That picture of Celeste on the *Observer*'s front page. Reporters have been calling Tanis at the hotel. They want to do a 'mother's perspective' on both the Redding murder and on 'the corrupting effects of Hollywood on young girls.' Those vultures."

In the moonlight, I saw him gripping the steering wheel so hard his knuckles were white.

"I'm so sorry." I reached out in a gesture of comfort and found his forearm muscles as tight as steel cables. At my touch, he relaxed a little, letting go of the steering wheel and taking me in his arms.

"Thank God for you, Della." He sighed, released me, and leaned against his driver's side door. "The only good thing about today is that Celeste has come back to me. She said Tanis is hysterical, Freddie is having anxiety attacks, and the phone was ringing so often Tanis told the hotel to hold all their calls." Nicholas's lips curled in a hint of a smile. "The grand duchess in Vienna got through on Freddie's cell. Celeste said she could hear the old woman screaming in German because Freddie had to hold the phone away from his ear."

"How did she find out about the picture?"

"She *saw* it — it's on the Internet. The *Observer* publishes an online international edition. They referred to Celeste as the 'wild-child future stepdaughter of a prince.' With the subhead 'Another Pretty Commoner Disgracing the Royals?' " He grunted. "It's — I can't call it *journalism* — it's filth. But their kind of repulsive sensationalism has resulted in the *Observer* having a larger circulation than the *Chronicle*."

"But if it's just for this issue —"

"No, hon. I haven't told you because I didn't want you to worry, but since that rag started publishing here, it's consistently outselling my paper by thirty percent. We've lost advertising dollars and had to cut staff. Next month we'll be putting out fewer pages, and the size of the paper's going to be slightly reduced. The bosses are hoping our readers won't notice, but they will."

"Oh, Nicholas . . . you don't think the *Chronicle*'s going to go out of business, do you?"

"I'm afraid I do. For a decade, we haven't had any local competition. I used to think that because of our record of integrity and political fair-mindedness, we could survive despite the availability of online news options. But ever since the *National Enquirer* gained credibility and the *New York Post* expanded its reach, readers are voting with their dollars. They're signaling that they want a *livelier* read than we're giving them by our choice to stay on the so-called high ground. What's left of it."

" 'The post of honor is a lonely station. . . .' "

"That sounds familiar."

"I think it's from Cato," I said. "What are you going to do?"

"Long term, if the *Chronicle* folds, or lets me go — I don't know. All over the country, papers are tanking, jobs for reporters are drying up. I don't like the news-lite bits on TV. Are people making money writing blogs?"

"I think they can if they get advertising," I said.

He gave a short bark of a laugh. "Can you imagine me trying to sell myself to an advertiser?"

I had to admit that I couldn't, and said with a smile, "Your charm is an acquired taste."

"Like eating haggis — thanks a lot. But I can't think about the future right now. I should get home to Celeste. She wanted to go to a club, 'to be seen,' she said, but I told her absolutely not. We're going to stay home tonight and start getting to know each other. High time. I've already missed her first eighteen years."

We kissed good night, deeply, and with passion that left us both wanting more, but when we came up for air, Nicholas said, "That's going to have to last us for a few days."

"It's a good thing we're mature enough not to need instant gratification."

"Speak for yourself," he said. "I want you so much I'd make love to you even if it meant I would be hanged for it in the morning. But right now . . ."

"I know," I said. "Go home to your daughter."

Tuffy and I got out of the car. Nicholas watched us until I unlocked the back gate and we were safely inside.

Listening to his car start up and the silver Batmobile drive away, I felt a wrench in my heart. What would Nicholas do if the *Chronicle* went out of business or if he were let go?

43

Thursday morning, after we had breakfast and I walked Tuffy, Eileen and I drove to the market with our reusable grocery bags to buy the large number of items I needed to prepare food in advance of the TV show. The two main dishes and the dessert would be made on-camera during the one-hour broadcast, but I had to do a lot of work at home today in order to have enough for members of the audience to sample at the end of the show.

After we'd managed to separate two shopping carts from the line of them that had been jammed tight together, Eileen looked at her half of the shopping list. "I can't figure out what your theme for tonight is."

"I'm calling it 'Budgeting Your Calories.' The idea is that you can eat a high-calorie dish — in this case it's going to be the sweet potato pie dessert — if the rest of the meal is low-calorie. Same principle as budgeting money. If you want to spend more on one thing, you should spend less on others."

"Sweet potato pie . . . yum. I wish you could make your friend Mira Waters's recipe. The sweet potato pie she sent us last Christmas was the best I've ever had, but when we called to tell her, she said it had a secret ingredient she wouldn't reveal."

"She was just joking," I said. "Several months ago she sent the recipe and permission to make it for the show, but this is the first time I've been able to do that."

"What's her secret ingredient?"

"Rum," I said. "Not enough for anyone to be aware of it specifically, but it enhances all the other flavors."

I gave Eileen half of the reusable bags and we pushed our carts through the automatic doors.

Inside the store, I said, "I'll start picking out the produce. You find whole wheat tortillas."

After we got back to the house and lugged in the heavy bags of groceries, Eileen went off to oversee our retail shop, and I set to work in the kitchen.

The chopping, cooking, baking, and wrapping would consume most of the day, leaving me just enough time to take a bath and put on some makeup. My bruised face had healed so well I didn't need Liddy's expertise tonight.

I had to bake the pies first. They needed time to cool thoroughly before they could be packed. The low-calorie tortilla wrap main dish sandwiches would be made later, and kept fresh in tight envelopes of foil.

The first step in Mira's recipe was boiling the sweet potatoes in their skins. I filled four big pasta pots with water and put them on the stove. Then I set sticks of butter and the eggs I'd need out on the counter so they would get to room temperature by the time the sweet potatoes were cooked and cooled enough to peel.

As I worked, I thought about Mira Waters; I'd missed her since she'd moved from Los Angeles to Florida a few years ago. An actress, and a good one, she had appeared in a lot of television shows, and had played Muhammad Ali's wife in *The Greatest*. I made sure to catch the movie whenever it played on TV.

I do my best thinking when I'm cooking, and I should be thinking about who might have killed Alec Redding. And Gretchen Tully. So why am I thinking about Mira?

Because I'm boiling a ton of sweet potatoes? No. It's something else. . . .

I let my mind bounce around — free associate images of Mira in the parts she played . . . images of other actresses . . . movies I'd seen. . . .

Then one image came to the center of the pack, like a movie special effect that sent an object zooming to the forefront of a scene. I remembered a shot of Mira in one of her roles. A close-up on her eyes. In that moment I noticed something going on behind the mask of her lovely face. Unspoken. A communication without words.

In my head I did a freeze-frame on the expression in those eyes. Then, without my conscious direction, another picture was superimposed onto it. Another actress, another unforgettable emotion — a *message* — in the depths of her eyes. I squeezed my own eyes shut and focused on that new photograph. Gradually, the camera in my head moved back to reveal the whole face, and I saw it was a picture of the British actress Judi Dench from one of her early roles . . . Lady Macbeth. What was I seeing in those eyes? Intelligence? Strength? Yes . . . and a need so intense that behind the intelligence was a flicker of madness.

It jolted me to realize that I'd noticed that same look in another pair of eyes. Not in a still picture, or from an actress's performance. I'd seen it in someone I knew. It had been there for just a moment, but my brain had registered it, and filed the impression away. . . .

Suddenly, on the "screen" in my mind all three of those images merged and became *one particular pair of eyes.*

Roxanne Redding's.

I'd glimpsed that Lady Macbeth flicker the day I met her, at the Film Society luncheon, when she came to our table to take Alec away because a studio executive wanted to talk to him.

Here in my kitchen, standing over pots of boiling sweet potatoes, steam frizzing my hair, I knew with certainty that Roxanne Redding had murdered her husband. I didn't have any idea whether or not she'd killed Gretchen. Maybe I wasn't going to get more than one blinding revelation in this lifetime.

Any sane person was going to tell me that my belief in her guilt wasn't evidence. Of course it wasn't, but the picture in my mind of Roxanne hitting Alec on the back of his skull with the white stool was so real that I could see it, as if in a hologram. It was as vivid to me as if I'd been in the room when it happened.

But that's a vision; it's not evidence.

I had nothing concrete to present to the police. Despite our years of friendship, John was likely to laugh if I told him I knew Roxanne Redding had killed her husband because I'd seen a deadly spark in her eyes weeks ago and now I'd had a vision. This wasn't some kind of psychic gift. It wasn't a paranormal experience. Ordinary people could *feel* an event sometimes. I felt this one.

If I tried to explain it to John, I'd be lucky if he didn't lock me up in the psychiatric wing at UCLA on a seventy-two-hour hold.

I felt helpless, and frustrated, *knowing* something but not being able to prove it. One thing was sure, though: When I kept my appointment with Roxanne tomorrow morning to review the pictures, I was not going alone. I would try to persuade John to go with me. Or Hugh Weaver. Or maybe John would arrange to let me take Officer Willis — Downey's partner — whom Olivia described as a tough cookie. In desperation, I might even ask Detective Keller to come. Whoever I had to drag along in order to feel safe, I was *not* going into the Redding house by myself.

44

When John returned my phone call, I told him about my appointment to go over photos with Roxanne Redding, but that I didn't feel comfortable going alone.

"Why not?"

"I believe she killed her husband."

On the other end of the line I heard an exasperated sigh. "Feminine intuition? The spouse-as-most-likely-suspect theory?"

"I can't explain it so it will make sense."

"Is there something you're holding back?" I heard his voice start to rise in anger. "If you've found evidence —"

"No, I haven't got any evidence. What can I say that will get me an escort? Feminine intuition? Or that I'm clinging to the spouse theory?"

A moment of silence.

"Hugh and I are too busy. So is Keller."

"What about Officer Willis?"

"Let me see what I can work out. Call you later."

He did call later, and told me that it had been difficult because of budget cuts and new deployments at the department, but he'd talked privately to Officer Willis, and Willis had "volunteered" to accompany me.

"He doesn't go on duty until four," John said, "so he'll be in street clothes. He'll pick you up at your house at nine forty-five, drive you there and back."

"Thank you, John. Name the night and I'll cook dinner for you and Shannon. I'll invite Liddy and Bill, too. Like old times."

John didn't ask if Nicholas would be there. He just said he'd talk to Shan and let me know.

At a few minutes past six that evening, when I reached the security gate at the Better Living Channel's taping facility in North Hollywood, I asked, Angie, the desk guard who'd answered my buzz, to have one or more of the stagehands meet me in the back because I had a lot of food to carry inside.

"You got it. What's the best thing tonight?"

"Sweet potato pie. I'll have some saved for you in the on-set fridge."

"You're a doll, Miss Della. Hey — your Mr. D'Martino? I saw his daughter's picture in the paper. She could use a good whuppin' right where they put that black bar across the page."

"I'm afraid it's much too late for that, Angie."

"Well, that picture really wasn't so bad. You kin tell him for me we've all seen worse."

"He'll appreciate that," I said, although I didn't intend to relay the message.

Driving onto the channel's property I saw people in line, waiting to get into the audience part of the studio for the seven PM broadcast. Although I drove facing forward, in my peripheral vision I recognized several of my cooking school students, but I pretended not to see them.

At the back of the airplane hangar-shaped building, I stopped next to the big double doors that opened onto Car Guy's garage set. Two men, wearing the navy blue uniforms of the BLC's stagehands, came outside. Theirs were familiar faces; they knew how to unload the custom racks I'd had installed in the Jeep behind the rear passenger seats.

"You got a lot of stuff today," the one whose name was Roy said. "It'll take us a couple trips. Why don't you go inside and when we finish I'll put the Jeep in your parking place."

I thanked him, and gave him the keys.

When I made my way between Car Guy's stacks of tires and past his hydraulic lift, I saw the gaffers were just finishing the lighting of my kitchen set. A quick check of my preparation counter showed that a production assistant had laid out the ingredients and seasonings I would use on the show, plus the necessary bowls and spoons, and the hand mixer.

I greeted my regular camera operators, Ernie Ramirez and Jada Powell, waved at our TV director up in the glass booth above us, and showed the stagehands where to place the premade pies and stacks of tortilla sandwiches.

Not because I don't trust our excellent crew, but because I try not to leave anything to chance if I can help it, I checked that the oven was preheating, the refrigerator was working, and the electrical outlet for the hand mixer was functioning. I was relieved to find that everything was operating perfectly.

A few minutes in the tiny dressing room behind the set to refresh the makeup I'd applied at home, then out onto the set where I stashed my handbag below the preparation counter. I put in the earpiece that connected me to the control booth, and told both the director and the camera operators that I was ready to run through the movements I'd be making as I cooked.

Six fifty-nine PM. I stood behind the back wall of the kitchen set, peeking through the crack that allowed me to see the audience. My cooking school students were in the first row. Harmon Dubois was sitting right in the middle, clutching a bouquet of peach-colored roses.

Six fifty-nine and fifty seconds. My theme music began. So did the countdown from the control booth that I heard through the earpiece concealed under my hair.

"Nine . . . eight . . . seven . . ."

I walked out onto the set, smiling.

". . . four . . . three . . . two . . . Go!"

"Hi there, everybody. I'm Della Carmichael. Welcome to *In the Kitchen with Della.* I have to share this with you — I've just had a delightful surprise. Walking out here, I see that people from my Santa Monica cooking classes are with us here in the studio tonight. Ernie, can you turn your camera around and let my guys wave hello to the folks at home?"

Of course, that had been prearranged with

the director. As Ernie made a show of reversing the position of his camera, simultaneously the lights on the audience came up from low to transmission bright.

"Aren't they a nice looking group there in the front row?" I lifted an eyebrow at them and joked, "Because you didn't let me know you were coming, I'm going to make you all wash the dishes after our next class."

The audience — both students and strangers — laughed and applauded.

"Okay, now." I looked into Jada Powell's lens while Ernie pivoted back into his usual position facing the set. "We've got a lot to do tonight, so . . . let's get cooking."

More applause.

I quieted them and explained that tonight's show was about "Budgeting Your Calories" and explained what I meant.

"Dessert tonight is a fabulous sweet potato pie. That's not exactly on anyone's standard weight-loss diet, but you can spend some of your calorie budget on a piece *if* you 'pinch' your calories, like you pinch your pennies, on the rest of the meal. Naturally, I don't mean to suggest this to anyone in the audience who might have a particular medical challenge or prohibition — you should follow your doctor's instructions — but for the rest of us who really like

411

to eat but want to stay in reasonable shape, this is how I do it."

As I talked, I filled a pot with water, put it on the stove with the burner turned to high, and demonstrated what I was explaining. So that the studio audience had no difficulty seeing exactly what I was doing, two large TV monitors had been set up.

"The sweet potato pie takes the longest," I said, "so we're going to make it first and get it into the oven. While the potatoes are cooking, I'm letting the stick of butter and the two eggs we'll need get to room temperature. As that is going on, we'll make the crust for our pie. Don't worry if you can't write the directions down. Tonight's recipes will be up on the Web site tomorrow."

I said it was perfectly okay to use a prepared piecrust, but that I liked to make my own, and explained how simple it was. As I worked with the flour and the shortening, I gave Mira credit for the sweet potato pie recipe, and told them a little about my actress friend who was also a great Southern cook. . . .

During the commercial breaks, I stayed on the set and answered questions from the audience. Happily, all of the questions were either about cooking or planning meals. No one mentioned the story in the *Observer.*

After the pie went into the oven, I told them about the low-calorie main dish I suggested pairing with the dessert.

"I call what we're going to make now a Greek Chicken Tortilla Wrap. Simple ingredients, and they won't bust either your household budget or your calorie budget: Greek yogurt, chopped cucumbers, some fresh dill, cut-up grape tomatoes, salt and fresh ground black pepper, a couple of cups of leftover chopped-up chicken — or you can get a little rotisserie chicken already cooked at the market. Actually, think of this as a Greek salad with chicken, all wrapped up in a whole wheat tortilla. If you try to explain it to your friends, say it's a kind of Greek salad soft chicken taco. . . ."

The pie I'd made on the set came out of the oven a couple of minutes before the show ended. Just in time for what's called the "beauty shot," where the cameras focus on the dishes that have been prepared during the show.

As the end credits rolled on the TV screen, but while we were still on the air, I said to the people in the studio, "Now comes your reward for being such a great audience. We get to eat!"

The red lights on the cameras went out. We were off the air.

Studio staff came onto the set and began unwrapping the sandwiches and cutting pieces of the pies I'd made at home.

While paper plates and napkins were being passed out in the audience, and the food served, I put the pie I'd just made and eight of the sandwiches into the refrigerator where the crew knew to go to help themselves. They also knew to take food out to Angie at the front desk.

I was still on the set when Harmon Dubois put his piece of pie down on his front-row seat and came toward me with the bouquet of roses.

"These are for you," he said. "From my garden."

"They're beautiful, Harmon."

"They're a special type, called brandy roses because their color looks like a snifter of brandy if you hold it up to the light."

"That's fascinating. Thank you." I made sure I wasn't near a live microphone, but I lowered my voice anyway to tell him that I appreciated his thoughtfulness in tipping me off about the class visit.

Harmon beamed. "You really did look surprised. Nobody would know you expected us."

It was almost an hour before the last of the studio guests had gone and finally I was able to leave. No longer having to smile and perform, I realized how tired I was. All I wanted was to go home, take Tuffy out for a quick march around the block, and fall into bed.

Only a few cars were left in the BLC lot when I climbed into my Jeep, and the traffic on Ventura Boulevard and through Beverly Glen Canyon was moderate. The drive was so unexciting that I put on the car radio, to an all-news station, to stay alert. Fortunately, none of the "Breaking News" segments involved anything relevant to my life.

I was on Liberty Avenue, a dark street with mostly closed shops, south of Wilshire Boulevard when I braked for a red light.

Suddenly, I was thrown forward against the chest strap on my seat belt.

A car behind had rear-ended me.

After the first moment of surprise, I realized that it wasn't a bad collision. Probably minimal damage.

I pulled over to the side of the street. Through the rearview mirror I saw the car behind me pull over, too. It looked as though there was only the driver in it, a blonde woman.

After taking my insurance information from the glove compartment and the wallet with my driver's license out of my purse, I climbed out of the Jeep. I imagined the conversation to come: She would apologize, tell me her husband was going to be upset with her, and ask plaintively if we really had to get insurance companies involved.

The blonde woman who emerged from the car looked vaguely familiar. I couldn't see her very well because some bureaucrat I considered an idiot had replaced the streetlights all over Los Angeles with much weaker bulbs.

Tanis? Hair the same shade of blonde, and cut shoulder-length. She was turned partially away, searching through her handbag that she'd placed on the hood of her car.

"Damn it, I can't see anything in this stupid light," she wailed.

It wasn't Tanis. No pretentious mid-Atlantic accent.

I was within three feet of her when she looked up, and I saw that the "blonde" was Roxanne Redding.

At that same moment, I felt a sharp poke in the small of my back — and heard Galen Light say, "Payback time."

45

Roxanne Redding and Galen Light. Together — and surely planning to kill me.

It was the two of them against me, and Light had a gun.

Tiny hairs on the back of my neck prickled. Drops of icy perspiration formed on my scalp and begin to trickle down my back. My heart thumped so hard in my chest I thought they would hear it. I willed myself to slow my breathing.

Act calm. Fake it until it's real.

The area we were in offered no realistic help. Liberty Avenue was crowded and busy during the day. It took too long to drive its length then, but at night, with the businesses closed and traffic sparse, it was a quick route from Wilshire Boulevard down to Montana Avenue.

The perfect place to stage a minor nighttime auto accident.

The few drivers that passed us took no

interest in three people standing between two parked cars. Why would they? There was no visible accident, no shower of glass in the street, no body to be gawked at.

At least, not yet.

Galen Light dug the barrel of the pistol deeper into my back.

"Ow! That hurts. Just tell me what you want."

"Walk around to the passenger side. Get in the backseat," he said.

Roxanne joined us on the sidewalk and opened the rear door. "Wait a minute." She snatched my wallet out of my hand, dropped it into her purse and took out a man's necktie.

"Hands behind your back. Wrists together," she said.

While Light held the gun on me, Roxanne tied my hands tightly.

I asked sarcastically, "Did the hardware store run out of duct tape?" I was pleased I'd been able to keep a tremor out of my voice.

"Silk ties don't leave a trace," she said.

"People who watch *CSI* make it tough on us hostages."

"You won't be a hostage for long." Light gave a raspy chuckle.

There was no one to hear me scream. No

possibility of overpowering this man whose tone communicated his hatred of me. Sandwiched between two probable killers, I did as I was told. The way our bodies were positioned on the far side of the car, even if drivers going by glanced at us, they couldn't have seen what was happening.

With Light facing me now, I saw the weapon in his hand was a Glock. An easy pistol to recognize. Mack had had one. I'd given it to John after Mack died.

Light had a heavy plaster bandage over his broken nose. The hatred I'd heard in his voice was visible in his eyes. His pupils were constricted; I wondered if he was high on pain pills. Those eyes frightened me more than the gun he pointed at me.

Stay alive as long as you can. Look for any chance to escape.

Roxanne pushed me into the backseat. Light climbed in close beside me. Roxanne got behind the wheel, turned the key in the ignition, and accelerated out into the empty street.

Using his free hand, Light buckled the seat belt around me.

I made my inflection humorous. "So you don't want me to get hurt before you murder me?"

"Shut your smart mouth before I shut it

for you."

Observe. Memorize as many details as you can.

The car was a heavy sedan, a late model something. Dark blue outside. Pale blue interior. Full size. Luxurious. This wasn't either of the vehicles I'd seen at the Redding house: not Alec's black SUV, nor Roxanne's tan Lexus. I don't know what Light drove, but they surely wouldn't stage a kidnapping and murder in a car that they owned. This vehicle must either have been stolen, or rented. I hoped it was a rental because I was pretty sure that they wouldn't kill me in a car that could be traced back to one of them.

However long this ride takes, is how long I have to live.

Could I have avoided getting into this mess? I didn't think so. If I had seen a man driving the car that rear-ended mine, I wouldn't have gotten out of the Jeep to exchange information. Not at night, on a street with few other vehicles. I would have made sure my doors were locked and called nine-one-one — or, if I had sensed danger — I would have driven away fast to the nearest police station to report the accident and explain why I was afraid to stay at the scene. If possible, I would have memorized the offending car's front plate number. If I couldn't do that — if there was no front plate, or if my vision had been obscured — then I would have paid for the necessary repair myself. That was a better choice than having my insurance rates go up, and a *much* better choice than getting out of my car at night on a quiet street to talk to a strange man.

But I had seen only a woman by herself in the other car. We weren't in a gang area. Exchanging information hadn't seemed dangerous. For a moment, I'd thought the woman was Tanis Fontaine, the former Mrs. Nicholas D'Martino. We weren't that far from the Olympia Grand Hotel.

Surprise! It was Roxanne Redding in a blonde wig.

Light must have been crouched in the back of this car, and slipped out while I was climbing down from the Jeep. With my attention focused on the woman, he'd been able to get around behind me.

Roxanne was driving south, keeping to the speed limit, obeying traffic laws. With my hands tied behind me, my torso secured by the seat belt, the doors locked, and Light beside me with the pistol pointed at my chest, I doubted that even Houdini could have escaped.

I'd have to wait until we stopped some-where.

Make conversation. "Where are we going?"

"A place where we can talk," Roxanne said.

"We can talk here. Why do you have me trussed up like a Thanksgiving turkey?"

"Because you nearly ruined everything," Light said. "You kept Rox busy while your friends searched her house."

"I realized that when I found some of my things out of place after you left. There was no one else in the house," she said.

"You sent that girl to spy —"

Roxanne glanced back at us. "That's enough, Galen. We're talking too much, like some stupid TV show where everything is explained to the victim." She turned back to concentrate on her driving. "God, I hate those shows. Idiot scriptwriters who don't know how hard it is to —"

"To what?"

"Never mind!"

Keep them talking. Say anything.

I let a few seconds pass before I said, "Roxanne, those photos you took of Galen — the ones in the box under your bed — they're beautiful art studies."

"How did you know they were me?" Light demanded.

Lucky guess. "Because you have beautiful hands," I said, suppressing a shudder at the memory of him pawing me. "I saw the photos before we met, but later I remembered them."

"So that's why you set the girl reporter on Roxanne. That's why she was watching us!"

"Shut up, Galen!"

"Don't talk to me like that, Rox. Who's she going to tell — Saint Peter at the pearly gates?"

"I might as well," I said. "You won't be meeting him."

He raised his arm to strike me. I flinched, pulling away from him as far as I could — but Roxanne's voice stopped him before the blow fell.

"Not in the car!" she yelled. "For Christ's sake, Galen, have some self-control. In another twenty minutes it'll all be over."

Twenty minutes. Wherever they're taking me is another twenty minutes away.

Up ahead, I saw the Pacific Coast Highway, and the ocean beyond. Little diamonds of moonlight sparkled on its surface. I felt a fresh stab of fear in my chest. Would this be the last night I'd ever see the ocean?

Get a grip! The trip's not over yet.

Roxanne turned north onto Pacific Coast Highway and increased her speed.

We're in Malibu. What's twenty minutes from here?

I was on the opposite side of the car from the ocean, on the land side of PCH. There wasn't much to see: two- and three-story small apartment complexes; a few single family homes, lights on inside but no one visible; cars in driveways.

Ticking off the time in my head, I figured twenty minutes had passed when Roxanne began to ease up on the gas pedal. She slowed down, and made a sharp turn onto a side road.

Now we were going up. From the way the car bounced I knew the surface wasn't paved, but I could see that it was wide enough to accommodate one vehicle traveling in each direction. Unluckily for me, ours was the only car on this road.

We passed a signpost. I just caught a glimpse of one word — "Wild" — but that was enough to tell me we were on Wild View Drive.

Now I knew exactly where we were, and what the destination was — and that we would reach it in less than a minute.

All this time in the car, I had been trying to work my hands free, but even though I'd stiffened my wrists to make them a little bigger, Roxanne had tied the knot too tightly. Still, I might have managed it if Light hadn't strapped me so hard against the back of the seat.

Several narrow roads branched off Wild View Drive. I kept hoping that someone would come out of one of them, see us, and wonder why anyone was going to the top of this popular hiking area *at night.* Maybe they'd wonder enough to stop us and ask.

Dots of soft, steady lights off in the distance signified houses. People inside, but no place was close enough for anyone to hear me scream.

We were traveling up a canyon that was about half a mile north of Malibu Bluffs Cliff, heading to a higher elevation that would dead-end at Malibu Falls. I hadn't been here in five or six years, but I knew the location because Mack and I had hiked it a few times.

" *'I wandered today to the hill, Maggie, To watch the scene below. The creek and the rusty old mill, Maggie, Where we sat in the long, long ago . . .' "*

Mack had sung those first few lines of the old song "When You and I Were Young, Maggie" to me on our tenth anniversary, when we were reminiscing about the crazy day we'd made love beside Malibu Falls —

and paid for our recklessness with a bad case of poison oak.

I told myself not to retreat into memories. Stay in *now*.

Two small, man-made parking areas had been bulldozed into the side of the canyon; each was about the size of a lot in a lower-income housing development. Roxanne passed the first one, but turned into the second and cut the motor.

We were about a hundred yards below Malibu Falls. In the distance I heard the faint sound of rushing water. During Southern California's many periods of drought, the water would diminish to little more than what would come out of a bathtub faucet, but the heavy rains of a few weeks ago had replenished the falls.

"Last stop," Light said. He unbuckled my seat belt. "Everybody out. Especially you, Della. This is your last stop, ever."

The moon was partially obscured by clouds, but there was enough illumination for me to see the grim smile on Galen Light's face, and the lines of strain on Roxanne's.

"Your TV fans are going to be sad to lose you," Light said cheerfully. "When your body is recovered it won't be in good enough shape for an open casket. Maybe there will be rumors — like with Elvis — that you really aren't dead."

Roxanne said, "Please don't joke about this, Galen." She untied my hands.

"Thanks," I said, massaging my wrists.

"I didn't do that for you."

"Now don't get cute," Light warned me, waving the Glock for emphasis.

Roxanne stuffed the necktie into her handbag. She took out a letter-size envelope, held it up in front of me, and said, "As unhappy as you were, you were thoughtful enough to write a suicide note — typed on a computer that no one will be able to trace. Not to yours, not to any of ours. No one will be able to prove you *didn't* write this. At some point, the letter will be found underneath your wallet, weighed down with rocks." Her voice was tense, without inflection, as though reciting something she'd memorized.

"Let's go." Light dug the Glock into the small of my back, forcing me forward, up the trail toward the top. Roxanne was beside me, with Light close behind us.

I asked Roxanne, "What was I thoughtful enough to say in the note?"

"You are overwhelmed with guilt because you know Nick D'Martino killed Alec and you can't go on covering for him anymore."

"Did I say 'Nick'?"

"Why?"

"Everyone who knows me knows I never call him Nick. They'll know I didn't write the note. To me, he's *Nico,*" I said, using Tanis's name for him.

"Doesn't matter," Light said. "You were upset enough to kill yourself."

"That's a big mistake," I said, chiding her. "If you want to go back and retype the note, I'll wait."

Light gave me another painful jab. "Shut up."

We were almost at the top of the falls. The sound of rushing water was strong. The moon had come out from behind the clouds, making the scene bright enough for me to see that the three of us were trudging along a path bordered by shiny plants sporting a familiar three-leaf pattern.

Poison oak.

Galen Light and Roxanne Redding didn't seem to know it.

If I don't manage to live through this night, at least when my body is found, their miserable rashes will tie them to the murder scene.

Light was breathing hard through his mouth by the time we reached the top. Roxanne was puffing, too. It gave me a certain feeling of triumph to discover that I was in better cardio shape than the two of them.

After taking in a few deep breaths, Roxanne bent down and put my "suicide note" under my wallet. She found a couple of brick-size rocks nearby and stacked them on top of the wallet.

Light prodded me closer to the edge of the falls. The water flowed out from a cave a few feet below where we were standing, splashed onto several outcroppings of rocks, and finally into a pool near sea level.

It was a long way down.

But if my memory was correct, it wasn't a *sheer* drop onto the rocks. Not if I could get over to my left . . .

I heard Light's harsh chuckle before he asked me, "Any last words?"

"Oh, Galen, for God's sake. Just get on with it."

He snapped his head around to face her. "Damn it, Rox! I said don't talk to me like —"

This was my moment! Instead of standing still until Light pushed me over the falls, I gave him a mighty shove into Roxanne. She stumbled backward and he fell on top of her.

Taking my one chance to stay alive, I sprinted to my left —

And JUMPED!

46

Jumped out into the darkness — praying that what had been there years ago still was there.

Terror at having nothing under my feet but air!

Until I plunged into a thick outcropping of bushes! I grabbed at them, gripping their rough branches. Nettles and thorns pierced the palms of my hands.

I dangled for precious seconds.

My thundering heartbeat was beginning to slow . . . when the bush I was hanging on to moved — and started to pull away from the face of the cliff. Little pellets of dirt from around its base hit me in the face. I bent my head, taking most of the particles of loose earth on the top of my skull.

Then I was going down again, my knuckles scraping the face of the cliff, my feet flailing.

Suddenly, the branches of another shrub

slapped me. I grabbed it, clung to it, and regretted every dish of pasta or piece of pie that might have added a few ounces to my hanging weight.

This bush, too, began to move, pulling slowly from where it had taken root.

I looked down and could make out a dark shape a little ways below me: a rock shelf!

Bracing my feet against the cliff, I eased my palms — scraped almost raw from my slide — down the branches. A few agonizing inches more . . .

I released my grip, and dropped.

Oh, please God . . . I landed on the ledge, fell to my knees, and grasped the edge so I wouldn't go hurtling over.

The edge was surprisingly smooth. The ledge itself was narrow, but solid. The impact of my body hitting it hadn't caused a tremble.

Water from the falls sprayed me, soaking my face and hair and clothing. I was about to brush water from my eyes, but remembered the poison oak and put my hands back down.

I strained to listen for voices above me, but all I could hear was the rush of water.

I waited, counting seconds into minutes.

Five minutes. Six. Seven.

Did Roxanne and Light think I was dead?

Had they left? Or were they still up at the top, waiting for me to emerge so that Light could shoot me?

My hiding place was a pretty good one — on a narrow shelf of rock beside the falls, below a thick outcropping of bushes that had grown straight out from the side of the cliff.

Unlikely survivors, those shrubs. I was an unlikely survivor, too.

Tension and terror had given me a powerful thirst. My mouth and throat felt dry as sand, but I didn't dare drink the water that sprayed me; I knew it wasn't pure. There had been newspaper articles about people who'd acquired serious internal parasites because they thought that what was gushing from a natural waterfall was safe to drink.

I took inventory of my situation. Against big odds, I was still alive, but I couldn't stay on this narrow ledge. If exhaustion overwhelmed me and I fell asleep, I might well tumble over it to my death.

From what I could see of the face of the cliff below me, I couldn't go down. No more life-saving branches to cling to.

There was no hope of rescue because no one knew where I was. My car was parked on Liberty Avenue, but it wouldn't get attention from Parking Enforcement until tomorrow, when one of those people saw that the meter had expired and slipped a ticket under my windshield wiper. My handbag was on the front seat — as were my cell phone and Harmon Dubois's bouquet of brandy roses. Would the parking person glance inside and become suspicious that something had happened and report the contents of the car to police? I doubted it. Generally, those warriors against parking scofflaws were single-minded in their search for expired meters and other forms of vehicle sins.

Eileen would call John to tell him that I hadn't come home, and that I hadn't answered my cell phone, but it probably wouldn't occur to her to worry until midnight.

My best chance to get out of this situation alive would be to climb back up the cliff — but not at the place where I came down. If Roxanne and Light were still up on top, they would be trying to spot my body, and were probably looking down from where I'd taken flight. I couldn't predict how long they would wait before concluding that I was dead.

The narrow ledge I was on stretched to my left perhaps another dozen feet, but there was no covering brush above that part of it.

If I couldn't go left, I would have to go right and explore the cliff behind the waterfall.

Feeling my way along, I saw there was a depression behind the cascade. But first I'd have to plunge through that chute of water.

Yikes — was it *cold!* But behind the sheet of water was a dry hollow that went about four feet deep into the cliff.

Out on the ledge, I'd been dampened by the spray from the side of the rushing water; having gone through the deluge, I was soaked. Not a bad thing, actually. A thorough dousing would probably wash away most of the poison oak, but I still had to be careful not to touch my face.

The red wool jacket I wore over my pale blue sweater and navy slacks was my favorite, but it was too heavy to wear now that it was soaked. I shrugged out of it and let it drop to the rock floor of this little cave. Immediately, I felt lighter, and my arms were no longer constricted by the jacket's sleeves.

As I explored behind the falling of water, I saw it was a shaft that went way up the face of the cliff. It looked as though it reached to the mouth of the opening through which the water gushed from the underground spring that was its source.

Running my hands along the face of the shaft, I felt a few rocks jutting out. I grasped the closest one, tested it for strength, and found that it held my weight. Bracing my feet against the wall, easing myself up another foot, I found other chunks of stone — big enough to hold on to.

Could I climb up the cliff behind the waterfall until I reached the roof of the cave from where the surge was coming? If I could manage that, I'd be only a few feet below the top of Malibu Falls. If I got that far, I would hide there, invisible, until daylight. Then I'd have a good chance to attract the attention of someone below or of hikers above.

No one was coming for me. What choice did I have?

Pulling myself up by the first jutting rock, forcing the toes of my shoes into any crevice, I mentally gave thanks for all those sessions at the climbing wall on the Santa Monica Pier. My times there had begun as a friendly competition with Nicholas. Later, I used it in an attempt to keep my arms from acquiring the dreaded "middle-age flap."

Ironic that Roxanne's caustic warning about loose underarm flesh might be what saved my life — after she and her lover tried to kill me.

I put fierce concentration into inching myself up without sliding back down. When I finally reached the crude ledge just below the gush of water from the underground spring, I had no idea how long it had taken. All I knew was that my arms and my thighs burned as though my bones were on fire.

But it was a pain I could stand — no, almost welcomed — because it meant I was still alive. I lay on the floor of the last shallow cave beneath the opening in the cliff from which the Malibu Falls poured, taking long breaths, exhaling slowly. In a few minutes my pulse had retreated from its pounding high back to a near normal steady beat.

Thirsty, hungry, and shuddering with cold, I felt wonderful. *It's amazing,* I thought, *that one can be thankful for epic discomfort.* Given the alternative . . .

Looking through the sheet of water, I was startled to see what looked like bright light.

I sat up and leaned forward. It was bright light — a search light.

My ears had become so accustomed to the sound of the falls that suddenly I could hear another sound: *voices.* Yelling. Calling my name! And yet another sound: the *whup, whup, whup* of a helicopter!

Crawling to the side of the rush of water, I fought my way through to the other side where there was just enough room to stand.

"Here!" I shouted. "Here I am! Down here!"

A man peered over the top of the cliff.

I waved at him wildly.

He turned his head and called, "Here she is!" Back down to me: "Stay where you are!"

I laughed. Then I felt hot tears filling my eyes and making rivulets down my cold, wet cheeks.

The helicopter hovered over my head, the lights from it pinning me. A rope ladder, with a man on it, was lowered down. Closer. Closer . . . Close enough for me to grab the man's extended hand. He held on to me as the helicopter began to rise and I was able to grasp the bottom rung of the ladder with my other hand.

Once again, I felt nothing but air beneath my feet — but this time, instead of going down, I was being pulled up to safety.

The man who had come down the ladder helped me up into the body of the helicopter.

I yelled "Thank you!" There was too much noise for him to hear my words, but he grinned and gave a thumbs-up in acknowledgment.

In what seemed only like moments, the helicopter settled onto the ground. Another man — now I could tell he was dressed in some kind of uniform like the first — helped me down.

My feet touched solid ground, and suddenly my knees buckled under me. He kept me from falling, and steadied me for the seconds it took for me to be able to stand on my own.

Looking around, I saw at least a dozen more men wearing those same uniforms. Sheriff's department, I thought. They were smiling and high-fiving each other. And then I saw yet another man. I knew him, but his was the last face I would have expected to see: Harmon Dubois.

Harmon Dubois? What was my elderly cooking school student doing *here?*

47

Harmon rode with me in the Fire Department Rescue Squad's all-terrain vehicle.

He said, "I was following you from the TV studio —"

"Following me?" I sat up on the gurney.

"Please don't be angry," Harmon said quickly. "I wasn't following you for any bad reason. You see, I had a present for you, but I didn't want to give it in person, so I was going to leave it on your doorstep. Or put it through your mail slot, if you have one of those. But I didn't know where you lived."

"So you followed me?"

"I was a few cars behind, but there wasn't much traffic. When I saw you stop and talk to those people, I thought they were your friends. Then you got into their car, but you didn't take my roses. That seemed strange because I didn't think you'd leave them in your car to wilt. But you might have forgotten. So I followed your friends' car . . . not thinking anything was wrong. But when they went so far, and up that canyon, I began to worry."

"You followed us all the way up? I didn't see your car."

"I turned off my headlights when we left PCH. I parked below them, and walked the rest of the way, avoiding the poison oak. I recognized the plants because I taught botany before I retired. At the top, I saw the man had a gun pointed at you. I didn't know what I could do to help you — I'm not brave around guns, but I had to do something. I went back down to where their car was parked and unscrewed the valve stems on their two back tires, to let all the air out. Then I hurried back to my car and dialed nine-one-one. I told the operator that there were two people up on top of Malibu Falls and I was afraid they were going to kill a television star. I gave them your name and begged them to hurry."

I took his hand and gave it an affectionate squeeze. Touching him was safe because the paramedic, aware of the poison oak, had cleansed my exposed skin with disinfectant and slathered me with some kind of lotion. "Harmon," I said, "you caught two killers and rescued me."

He beamed, but then, suddenly shy, he

withdrew his hand from mine.

To cover the awkward moment, I asked, "What were you going to give me?"

He looked puzzled for a moment. Then he beamed again, reached into the pocket of his jacket, and withdrew a booklet. "This is an epic poem I wrote for you. Only forty stanzas. I could have gone on longer, but brevity is important in poetry. I had the pages printed into a booklet for you."

I took the booklet. It had a laminated cover, with a color photograph of a bouquet of brandy roses. Superimposed on the flowers was the title of the poem: *Della Bella.*

"This is the nicest thing anyone has ever done for me, Harmon."

"Please don't think I have expectations," he said. "I recognize that we were born at incompatible times, but I wanted you to know how very much I admire you."

John O'Hara and Nicholas were waiting for me in the emergency room at St. Clare's Hospital in Santa Monica. I introduced them to Harmon and told them everything he had done for me. Then I asked, "What happened to Roxanne Redding and Galen Light?"

"In custody," John said. "Being interrogated separately by Weaver and Keller.

When I left they'd started rolling over on each other, proclaiming their own innocence and claiming the other one did it."

Nicholas said, "Roxanne found out about her husband's affairs, and that he was planning to leave her to marry a movie star."

"April Zane," I said.

"That's the one. Marriage to April would have catapulted Redding onto Hollywood's top social tier, leaving Roxanne as just another photographer in a town crammed to the rooftops with them."

"The young woman reporter got a photo of April and Light kissing in the alley behind the Redding house. She recognized Light because she'd interviewed him a few months before," John said. "According to Roxanne, Light invited Ms. Tully into the house, pretending he wanted to explain what she saw. While they were talking, Ms. Tully mentioned having visited you for an interview, and that you encouraged her to investigate Alec Redding's murder. Roxanne said that's when Light went ballistic, killed her, and hid her body until it was dark enough to dump her behind the Olympia Grand. Roxanne — I call her the Black Widow — said that she was terrified of Light. When he said they had to kill you because you must have found out too much, she only went along because she thought she could figure out how to stop him before he actually did harm you."

I shook my head. "That's ridiculous. She was as eager to get rid of me as he was. I know because I was in that car with them, and on that path with them."

"I love it when the bad guys turn on each other," Nicholas said. "*His* story is that Roxanne killed Gretchen and that all he did was transport the body, and he only did that because he'd seen Roxanne kill her husband in a rage and he was afraid of her."

"That man is no gentleman," Harmon Dubois said.

All three of us turned to look at him. We'd forgotten he was there.

Nicholas stood and took out his reporter's notebook. "Mr. Dubois, why don't we find a quieter corner. I'd like to interview you for the *Chronicle*."

The *Chronicle*'s banner headline Friday morning read: "Hero Poet Saves TV Star." The story was accompanied by pictures of Harmon and me taken at the hospital. Fortunately, they were snapped after I'd washed the lotion off my face and borrowed a comb from one of the nurses. I didn't look too terrible.

443

The phone started ringing early. First, not surprisingly, was Liddy, and she had Shannon on the line, too. Liddy had arranged a conference call.

I gave them all the details that weren't in the paper and then said, "You two were wonderful. Your search of the Redding house was vital to uncovering evidence that led to the arrests of Light and Roxanne."

"We have to celebrate," Liddy said. "I'll organize a party for Saturday next. How's that?"

"Sounds wonderful." In my ear I heard the Call Waiting sounds. I hated Call Waiting, but hadn't been able to disable it, and the phone company told me it was "bundled." Whatever that meant.

Simultaneously with the Call Waiting bleeps, my cell phone rang. I was sure it wasn't a coincidence, and only one person I knew called on both phones simultaneously.

I said good-bye to Liddy and Shannon, pressed "Answer" on my cell phone, and said, "Hello, Phil."

"Great news, Della!" Phil's voice conveyed such excitement that I pictured him jumping up and down with glee. "Your story's on the wire services, and all over the Internet. This'll be fantastic for our ratings! And I've got a fabulous second story that I'm issuing tomorrow."

"What other story?"

"The Better Living Channel is receiving an award from the Associated Charities of America. It seems our national bake sales have been producing so many donations from the teams of contestants that the ACA is amazed. And grateful. The money's going to help a lot of people now, when it's so badly needed."

"That's wonderful," I said.

"And because of that, *World Today* magazine is going to feature our beloved boss, Mickey Jordan, in a special holiday issue. The story's going to be titled 'One Person *Can* Make a Difference.' "

"I'll bet that was your idea, wasn't it, Phil?"

I heard him chuckle. "Well, yeah, I talked to the editor, but that's just between us. Okay? I want Mickey to think the magazine came to me."

"I won't say a word."

When Nicholas arrived at my house in the late morning, I waved the paper at him cheerily and said, "Take that, *Los Angeles Observer.*"

He grinned. "Yeah. We can be just as sensational as they can, once in a while."

We were in the kitchen, having coffee,

when Nicholas said, "Harmon Dubois."

"What about him?"

"Am I going to have to fight him for you?"

I laughed. "No. And after this story of yours, I have a feeling he's not going to be a lonely widower too much longer."

"That poem he wrote for you — are you going to let me read it?"

"No. It's private." To change the subject, I asked, "Do Celeste and her mother and her prince know about Galen Light and Roxanne Redding? Oh, I guess they must if they've read the paper."

"I told all three of them last night, after I filed the story."

"Are Celeste's mother and Prince Freddie going back to Vienna soon?"

"Tanis called this morning to say that Freddie's leaving this afternoon."

"*He* is?" I hoped Nicholas wasn't going to tell me that Tanis was staying in Los Angeles.

"Tanis said they need a few weeks for his mother to calm down. Freddie's going back to the grand duchess. Celeste is staying here with me. Tanis left for New York an hour ago."

"What's she going to do in New York?"

"Shop. Look around the social scene. She said that if Freddie really loves her he'll come to New York and persuade her to go back to Europe with him."

"And if he doesn't? Or if his mother won't let him?"

The corner of Nicholas's mouth turned up about a millimeter, but if he was trying to smile he failed. "She says she'll go to the south of France. She's heard that a woman she knows is about to be jilted by a Greek shipping tycoon who lives there."

I asked, "Do you want her back?"

"No," he said. "I want *you.*"

He leaned across the table and we kissed. A gentle kiss. When we separated he said, "I almost forgot. I have an invitation for you."

I smiled with pleasure. "To what are you inviting me?"

"Dinner. Tomorrow night. With Celeste and me. It was her idea. She wants to apologize for the way she's behaved toward you."

"That's nice. I'd like to get to know her."

He got up from the table, came around to my side, carefully stepped over Tuffy, and took me in his arms. We kissed again.

He said, "In a few days, when your scratches have healed and you're not aching all over, I'd like to show you how much I've missed you."

My answer was a kiss that left no doubt as

to how much I had missed *him.*

"How soon do you have to get back to the office?" I whispered.

■ ■ ■ ■

RECIPES

■ ■ ■ ■

CAROLE'S DEADLY CHOCOLATE NUT BUTTER PIE À LA MODE

Cookie Crust:

1 cup nut butter (smooth or crunchy, any kind: almond, cashew, macadamia, walnut and pecan, or peanut butter, which is a legume, not a nut)

1/2 cup dark or semisweet chocolate chips (to be melted)

1 large egg

3/4 cup Sucanat granulated cane juice powder (or packed light brown sugar)

1 teaspoon vanilla extract

1 teaspoon baking soda

1/2 cup dark or semisweet chocolate chips (to be left whole)

Position an oven rack in the center of the oven and preheat to 325 degrees F for glass or 350 degrees F for metal pie pan.

Pour off any oil accumulated on top of nut butter in jar and use a bit to oil pie pan.

Put chocolate chips into the top part of a double boiler over a pot of boiling water, and stir constantly until chips are melted. Turn off burner. Remove top part from stove and stir in nut butter.

While this mixture is cooling, in a small mixing bowl, beat the egg with a fork. Add the sugar, vanilla, and baking soda to the beaten egg and mix well. Add this mixture to the cooled chocolate and nut butter, then add the 1/2 cup whole chocolate chips and mix well. The mixture will become a stiff dough, Put about 2/3 of the dough on the bottom of a 9-inch glass or metal pie pan and flatten dough with back of spoon or rubber spatula. Bake crust until puffed and glossy sheen is gone, about 10 to 12 minutes, depending on your oven. Remove container from oven and cool on a rack.

Drop the remainder of the dough by spoonfuls onto a cookie sheet covered with parchment paper and flatten with back of spoon or rubber spatula. Bake cookies at 350 degrees F until puffed and glossy sheen is gone, about 10 to 12 minutes. Slide parchment from cookie sheet onto another rack to cool. When cool, enjoy cookies now or later.

Fudge Layer:

1/2 cup dark or semisweet chocolate chips

1/2 cup nut butter (same type as in crust)

1/4 cup honey (lightly coat inside of measuring cup with butter or oil off the top of the nut butter to make it slide out after measuring)

2 tablespoons sweet (unsalted) butter (about a 1/4 of a quarter-pound stick)

1 teaspoon vanilla extract

Put chips, butter, and honey into the top part of a double boiler over boiling water and stir constantly until ingredients are melted and thoroughly mixed together. Turn off burner. Remove top pot from stove and stir in butter and vanilla.

Pour fudge mixture onto the cookie crust and spread to cover. Chill in refrigerator until set, about 1 hour. No need to wash pot before next step.

Pudding Layer:

2 cups whole or 2% milk

1/2 cup dark or semisweet chocolate chips

1/2 cup nut butter (same type as in crust)

1/4 cup honey (coat inside of measuring cup lightly with butter or oil from top of nut butter jar to make it slide out after measuring)

2 tablespoons sweet (unsalted) butter (about 1/4 of a quarter-pound stick)

1 teaspoon vanilla extract

3 tablespoons cornstarch (or 1/3 cup kuzu starch, broken into small pieces)

Put all ingredients except starch and about 1/2 cup of the milk into the top pot of a double boiler. Add the starch to the saved milk, stir until dissolved, and then add that mixture to the pot. Place pot over, not in, boiling water and constantly stir the lumpy mixture until ingredients are melted, thoroughly combined, and thickened into a pudding with a glossy sheen. Turn off burner.

Remove top pot from stove. Cool for 10 minutes. Pour pudding over the (cooled and set) fudge layer and spread to cover.

Chill in refrigerator about 1 hour.

Serve each slice of pie with a scoop of dark chocolate ice cream. Optional: top with whipped cream. Enjoy!

MIRA WATERS'S
SWEET POTATO PIE

Mira Waters is an actress. Among her roles, she's played Muhammad Ali's wife in *The Greatest*. She's also a fabulous cook. Her sweet potato pie is my favorite version of this dish.

4 large sweet potatoes (boiled in their skins)
2 eggs
2 cups of sugar (or 1 1/2, depending on how sweet you want it)
1 1/2 teaspoons rum (Mira says this is the secret!)
1 stick of butter, room temperature
1 cup milk
1 teaspoon cinnamon
1/2 teaspoon nutmeg

Preheat oven to 350 degrees F.

When the sweet potatoes are cooked, and after they've cooled for a few minutes so you don't burn your hands, strip off the skins. Mash the sweet potatoes in a mixing bowl.

Add the eggs, sugar, rum, butter, milk, cinnamon, and nutmeg. Whip all the ingredients together and put into an unbaked pie shell. Mira says you can use a prepared pie shell, but she and I both prefer to make our own crust. My personal favorite crust is the Standard Pastry Crust recipe found in the *Betty Crocker Cookbook* — but be sure to use several tablespoons of ice water, not just "water."

Using whatever crust you prefer, bake the Sweet Potato Pie for 35 minutes. (Be sure the oven doesn't overheat.)

Mira says, "Enjoy!"

JOHN BOHNERT'S
BREAD PUDDING

John Bohnert is a retired elementary school teacher living in northern California. He loves to read crime fiction and also loves to cook. This recipe is his version of what he remembers his late mother's bread pudding tasting like when he was a boy growing up in Michigan.

3 cups whole milk
1 loaf cinnamon-raisin bread
1 cup brown sugar
2 eggs, slightly beaten
2 tablespoons unsalted butter at room temperature
1 tablespoon vanilla extract
1 teaspoons ground cinnamon
1/2 teaspoon ground nutmeg
1 cup raisins

Preheat oven to 375 degrees F.

Heat whole milk in saucepan.

Tear up cinnamon-raisin bread slices and add pieces to large mixing bowl.

Soak raisin bread in hot milk.

Add sugar, eggs, butter, vanilla, cinnamon, nutmeg, and raisins to mixing bowl. Mix with a large spoon.

Pour into 8-inch-by-8-inch baking dish that has been sprayed with cooking spray.

Bake for 45 to 50 minutes, depending on your oven.

DON'T BE A FOOL
EAT FRED'S PASTA FAZOOL

This recipe is from film producer Fred Caruso, who also gave us Pasta Caruso, which is printed in *The Proof Is in the Pudding.* That recipe drew so much praise from readers that I asked Fred for another of his pasta creations.

NOTE: Have all your ingredients ready — cans opened, veggies chopped. You will need a medium-deep pot or Dutch oven on the stove.

extra virgin olive oil
3 slices pancetta, chopped fine
1 medium onion, chopped fine
2 ribs celery, chopped fine
1 carrot (peeled or scrubbed) and chopped fine
4 garlic cloves, chopped fine
1/2 pound ground beef
1 tablespoon oregano

1 tablespoon Italian spices
pinch of red pepper flakes
salt and pepper
1/2 cup red wine
1 box (32 oz.) beef broth
1 can (28 oz.) diced tomatoes with juice
1 can (8 oz.) tomato sauce
1 can (14 oz.) cannellini beans with juice,
   pureed
2 cans (14 oz. each) cannellini beans whole,
   drained
handful of flat leaf Italian parsley, chopped
handful of fresh spinach leaves, chopped
1 lb. ditalini or tubettini (suggested pasta
   brands: Cecco or Brallia)
maybe, if needed later: 1 small can tomato
   paste (open at last minute)
grated Parmigiano or Romano cheese for
   the table
crusty Italian bread

Over medium heat, swirl the olive oil in the
bottom of the pot and let it begin to sizzle.

Add chopped pancetta. Brown slightly (stir
with a wooden spoon often to prevent
sticking).

Add the chopped vegetables (swirl in more
olive oil); stir often when added.

Add the ground beef in bits, mash with

spoon, and brown.

Add spices and red wine and stir.

Add beef broth, tomatoes, tomato sauce, and pureed beans. Let it all come to a slow, low simmer. Stir.

Add drained beans and continue to simmer. Stir.

Add Italian parsley and spinach leaves. Stir.

If fazool is too thick, add a ladle of boiling pasta water.

If fazool is too thin, add the tomato paste. Stir.

Cook pasta according to box's direction. Drain and place in a separate bowl. Sprinkle with olive oil so it won't stick.

Ladle the fazool into serving bowls; add a few scoops of the pasta to each. Top with grated cheese. Enjoy with Italian bread.

FREDA SMALL'S HAMENTASCHEN

This recipe for some of the most delicious cookies I've ever tasted comes courtesy of novelist and lawyer Abigail Shrier.

In A Large Mixing Bowl, Beat Together:
3 eggs
1 cup vegetable oil
1 cup sugar
1 teaspoon pure vanilla extract
1 teaspoon almond extract

Then Add:
1 teaspoon baking powder
3 cups all-purpose flour (or a little more, to create a workable dough)

Filling Ideas:

1. Mix in a saucepan over low heat until combined: cherry jam mixed with dried cherries.

2. Mix in a saucepan over low heat until combined: apricot jam mixed with diced dried apricots.

3. Freda's filling: mix in a saucepan over low heat until combined: 1 jar lekvar (prune butter), grated orange peel (Abigail says this is optional, but I like it), 1/2 cup sugar, 1/2 cup honey, 1/2 cup rinsed and soaked currants. Chocolate chips.

Divide the dough into quarters. Roll to 1/4 inch thickness on a lightly floured board. Using a 2 1/2- to 3-inch cookie cutter, cut rounds. Reroll scraps. Place filling of your choice in the center of each dough round. Fold three sides up for a triangle, leaving some filling exposed in the center. But don't let much filling show as you fold up the sides of the cookie.

Preheat the oven to 350 degrees F and place a rack in the center of the oven. On cookie sheets that have been sprayed with nonstick cooking spray, space cookies about an inch apart. Bake one sheet of cookies at a time until lightly browned and crisp, about 15 to 17 minutes. Transfer to a wire rack to cool.

Makes 40 small cookies.

NANAIMO BARS

"It's a better brownie." That's how *Los Angeles Times* columnist Chris Erskine described Nanaimo Bars (a Canadian Christmas treat) when he discovered them at the Vancouver Olympics. They were also touted on the *Today* show as one of the "must" items to bring back from Canada. This recipe comes from actress Jaclyn Carmichael, who was born in Nanaimo. Jaclyn got this recipe for the bars from the mother of one of her friends in Nanaimo.

(NOTE FROM DELLA: I use unsalted butter instead of margarine, but it's your choice. You'll need a total of 3/4 cup plus 1 tablespoon of either.)

1/2 cup margarine
1/4 cup granulated sugar
3 tablespoons cocoa
1 egg

1 teaspoon vanilla
2 cups graham cracker crumbs
1 cup shredded coconut
1/2 cup chopped nuts (usually walnuts)
1/4 cup margarine
2 cups sifted icing sugar (or confectioner's sugar)
2 tablespoons Bird's custard powder — not pudding (available from Amazon.com if nowhere else)
2 tablespoons hot water
4 ounces semisweet chocolate
1 tablespoon margarine

Cook the first five ingredients over hot water, then add graham cracker crumbs, shredded coconut, and chopped walnuts.

Press this into an 8-inch-by-8-inch square pan. Chill.

Mix 1/4 cup of margarine, icing sugar, custard powder, and hot water.

Spread over the cooled first mixture.

Melt semisweet chocolate with 1 teaspoon margarine and spread over the second mixture.

Place in a cool place to set. Enjoy! Makes

approximately 24 bars.

In 1986 the City of Nanaimo ran a contest to find the "ultimate" Nanaimo Bar. About one hundred recipes were submitted. I don't know who won, but I can't believe theirs tastes better than this.

BRINED POT ROAST

This recipe, for the most tender pot roast I've ever tasted, was contributed by actress/writer Julie-Anne Liechty. Julie-Anne lives in Los Angeles with her Chihuahua, Zelda, and her cross-eyed, half-Siamese cat, Gonghi.

2 to 3 lbs. beef roast
Kosher salt
cracked black pepper
dried basil flakes
olive oil
2 yellow onions, sliced into thick rounds
10 carrots, sliced on the diagonal into 2- or
  3-inch pieces

Brine the roast overnight for 12 or so hours in water with kosher salt, cracked black pepper, and dried basil flakes.

Next morning, remove roast from brine and

put into a cast-iron skillet with a bit of olive oil and some kosher salt. Sear roast until both sides are deeply browned.

Remove roast from skillet and put into Crock-Pot on the "Low" setting.

To the skillet: Add the onions and sear on both sides until browned, or even a little blackened. You'll probably need to add a little more oil to the skillet. Sprinkle with kosher salt. When onions are seared, put them on top of the roast, covering it.

In that skillet: Sear carrots until browned on two sides. (You may need a little more oil.)

When carrots are done, add them to the Crock-Pot on top of the onions.

Add to the combination of vegetables and roast some more kosher salt and basil flakes.

Cook on "Low" for 8 hours. Should be done just in time for dinner guests to arrive.

DELLA'S BROWN RICE & RAW VEGETABLES

2 1/2 cups water (divided into 1 1/2 cups and 1 cup)
1 cup uncooked brown rice
4 tablespoons butter or margarine
1/2 teaspoon salt

Chop Into Small Pieces:
1/2 bell pepper (green, red, yellow, or orange)
1/2 zucchini, unpeeled
1 small, firm tomato, seeded

Put 1 1/2 cups water, rice, butter (or margarine), and salt into 4-quart casserole. Cook uncovered in microwave for 10 minutes, stirring at 3 1/2 minutes, again at 3 1/2 minutes, and the third time after 3 more minutes. Now add 1 cup of water, stir briefly, cover with plastic wrap, put back in microwave, and cook for 5 more minutes.

Take out and carefully remove plastic wrap

covering. (Don't burn yourself with the steam.) With a fork, lightly fluff the chopped vegetables into the cooked brown rice. Cover again and let stand for 5 minutes outside the microwave. Serves 4.

Serve alone or with Zucchini Canoes.

DELLA'S ZUCCHINI CANOES

4 nice big zucchini (as straight as possible)
1/4 cup chopped pine nuts, walnuts, or almonds (whatever you prefer, or is cheaper)
1 firm tomato, seeded and chopped
1 tablespoon sweet onion, finely chopped
1 tablespoon Italian flat leaf parsley, chopped
1/2 teaspoon salt
2 tablespoons butter or margarine
1/4 cup seasoned bread crumbs

Wash zucchini, chop off the stem ends, place in a microwave-safe baking dish, and cook in microwave for 7 to 8 minutes. Let cool.

When you can handle them comfortably, cut off the top third lengthwise so that the zucchini look like little canoes. Rough chop the tops and set aside in mixing bowl. Hollow out the canoes and discard scooped-out matter. To the mixing bowl with chopped zucchini tops, add nuts, tomato, onion, parsley, and salt. Fluff together with a fork. Fill the zucchini canoes with this mixture.

Melt butter or margarine in microwave (about 25 to 30 seconds).

Take half of the melted butter and brush the filled zucchini canoes. Mix other half of the melted butter with seasoned bread crumbs and sprinkle this over the filled canoes.

Heat zucchini canoes, uncovered, in microwave for 2 1/2 to 3 minutes. Serves 4.

(NOTE: Each of the two previous dishes can be served as a side, or served together for a light, healthy meal.

These recipes are a tasty way to get children and "meat & potatoes" men to eat more vegetables.)

DELLA'S TOMATO-POTATO PANZANELLA

4 cooked red potatoes cut into chunks
4 ripe tomatoes, seeded and cut into chunks
1/2 red onion, thinly sliced
2 tablespoons Italian flat leaf parsley, chopped
1/2 cup black olives, sliced (optional)
8 to 10 fresh basil leaves, torn into pieces
1/2 loaf of crusty French bread, cubed

Dressing:
1/2 cup extra virgin olive oil
1/4 cup red wine vinegar
1 or 2 cloves garlic, minced
salt and freshly ground black pepper to taste

Wash, but don't peel, potatoes. Put into a pot of salted water to just cover. Bring to a gentle boil and cook until fork tender, about 15 minutes. Remove from heat, drain. When cooled enough to handle, cut potatoes into chunks — quarters or eighths, depending on size of the potatoes. (If you have some leftover cooked red potatoes from a meal the night before, take them out of the fridge, let them get to room temperature, and cut into chunks.)

In a large bowl, combine tomatoes, potatoes, red onion, parsley, black olives, basil, and cubes of French bread.

In a small bowl, whisk together olive oil, red wine vinegar, and minced garlic. When whisked into a dressing, add salt and freshly ground black pepper to taste. Whisk again briefly, to incorporate seasoning.

Add the dressing to the bowl of vegetables and bread cubes and toss. Let sit for a few minutes so the bread can absorb the dressing. Serves 4 as a side dish, or 2 for a hearty one-dish lunch.

NOTE: This is a versatile recipe. If you'd prefer to use your favorite vinaigrette dressing, then do. Or you can add some additional vegetables, such as green beans, kernels of fresh corn, chopped zucchini, or peeled and chopped cucumber. Personalize according to what you like.

DELLA'S STRAWBERRY CLOUD PIE

This is one of my favorite low-calorie desserts. Instead of sugar, I use granulated Splenda (the packets you might put in coffee). Splenda comes in a large bag and can be used in the same proportions as sugar: i.e., 1 cup granulated Splenda equals 1 cup sugar. On the back of the bag I have in my cabinet at the moment, there are delicious recipes for Blueberry Muffins and for a dinner party–worthy Banana Cream Tart. But below is my version of a refrigerated Strawberry Pie. (The only part of this dessert that's baked is the crust.)

Crust: (The World's Easiest)
36 to 40 vanilla wafers (or any plain cookies you prefer)

2 tablespoons and 1 teaspoon melted margarine (or butter)

white of 1 large egg

Preheat oven to 350 degrees F.

Lightly spray a 9-inch pie pan with nonstick cooking spray.

Crush the wafers or cookies (I put them in a Ziploc bag and crush with a rolling pin).

Combine crumbs with melted margarine. Stir.

Add egg white and stir.

Press the crumb mixture into the bottom and sides of the pie pan, using back of a wooden spoon, or what I do is press with my right hand inside a clean plastic baggie. (Or your left hand, if you're left-handed.) Bake 8 to 10 minutes, depending on your oven. Don't overbake.

Set aside to cool.

Filling:
3 cups fresh strawberries, sliced
1 cup granulated Splenda
1 1/2 tablespoons fresh squeezed lemon juice (not bottled)
1/2 cup light cranberry juice cocktail
2 envelopes strawberry gelatin
2 cups light whipped topping (plus more for garnish)

Mash the strawberries in a mixing bowl.

Add Splenda and lemon juice. Let Splenda dissolve for about 15 to 20 minutes.

Pour cranberry juice cocktail over strawberry gelatin. Heat to dissolve gelatin, then cool slightly. Combine gelatin with strawberry mixture. Cool completely. When cooled, fold in light whipped topping. Pour into pie shell and refrigerate for 2 hours, until firm. Garnish with light whipped cream and top generously with more sliced fresh strawberries. (Or blueberries, if available. The red, white, and blue colors make it perfect for national holiday parties.)

DELLA'S GREEK CHICKEN TORTILLA WRAPS

Here is the first of two main dish tortilla wraps that are low enough in calories so that you can enjoy a rich dessert without feeling guilty.

2 cups plain Greek (or regular plain) yogurt (use low fat for fewer calories)
1 cucumber, chopped into small pieces plus 1 whole cucumber (reserved)
2 tablespoons fresh dill (chopped or cut with kitchen shears)
1/2 teaspoon salt
1/4 teaspoon freshly ground pepper
8 whole wheat tortillas
3 cups cooked chicken, chopped (all or mostly white meat for fewer calories)
1 cup romaine lettuce, shredded
16 grape tomatoes, cut into halves
1 cup feta cheese (reduced fat for fewer calories)

4 to 8 firm Roma tomatoes (depending on size)

Mix yogurt, cucumber, dill, salt, and pepper in a bowl and put in refrigerator, covered, for 15 minutes. (You can make this several hours ahead if you keep it refrigerated.)

Divide the yogurt mixture so as to have enough to spread down the center of each of the whole wheat tortillas. (Tortillas can be eaten after heating in nonstick pan for 1 minute on each side, or just as they come out of the package. Divide the chopped cooked chicken and top the yogurt/ cucumber mixture. Add lettuce, a few grape tomato halves, and feta cheese. Roll up tortillas and secure with toothpicks.

Slice the Roma tomatoes and peel and slice the reserved whole cucumber.

Put one or two of these Greek Chicken Tortilla Wraps on a plate, surrounded by thin slices of Roma tomatoes and thin slices of cucumber. Grind a little more fresh pepper over the slices of tomatoes and cucumber.

Depending on how hungry you are, this recipe will serve 4 or 8.

DELLA'S ASIAN CHICKEN MAIN DISH TACO

Here is the second main dish sandwich recipe low enough in calories so that you can enjoy dessert without feeling that you've spent too much of your calorie budget for this meal.

2 cups cooked chicken breasts, chopped or shredded
4 tablespoons hoisin sauce
6 green onions (scallions), finely sliced
1/4 teaspoon freshly ground pepper
4 whole wheat tortillas
Optional (but good!): several watercress leaves for each taco

Mix the chicken, hoisin sauce, scallions, and pepper in a bowl until thoroughly combined. (Hoisin sauce is a great ingredient, found in the Asian foods aisle of most large markets, and it will keep for a long time in the refrigerator.)

Heat the tortillas, one at a time, in a large, nonstick pan over medium heat for about 1 minute on each side, just to warm them. Handle with tongs. (You can also eat them without heating, if you're in a rush, or aren't where you can cook.)

Divide the chicken mixture into 4 equal parts, and spread 1 part lengthwise down the middle of each tortilla. Top with several watercress leaves. Roll up and secure with toothpicks. Cut the rolls in half, on the diagonal.

If you want to serve these rolls warm, you can heat the chicken, hoisin sauce, scallion, and pepper mix over medium heat until just heated through (1 or 2 minutes). Then put the mixture onto the tortillas and roll them up. These must be served immediately, but if you don't heat the mixture these can be made in advance and kept fresh with plastic wrap or aluminum foil.

This recipe serves 4. Put 2 halves on each plate and surround them with a few slices of cucumber, tomatoes, carrot sticks, some grapes, or slices of cantaloupe, or slices of peaches, or orange slices — whatever you like that is in season.

This is a healthful, filling, low-calorie meal.

ABOUT THE AUTHOR

Melinda Wells was born in Georgia, grew up in Florida, and lived in East Africa and New York City. She now resides in Southern California with two big dogs and one bossy cat. Melinda loves to hear from readers. Visit her website at www.lindapalmermysteries .com.

We hope you have enjoyed this Large Print book. Other Thorndike, Wheeler, Kennebec, and Chivers Press Large Print books are available at your library or directly from the publishers.

For information about current and upcoming titles, please call or write, without obligation, to:

Publisher
Thorndike Press
10 Water St., Suite 310
Waterville, ME 04901
Tel. (800) 223-1244

or visit our Web site at:

http://gale.cengage.com/thorndike

OR

Chivers Large Print
published by AudioGO Ltd
St James House, The Square
Lower Bristol Road
Bath BA2 3BH
England
Tel. +44(0) 800 136919
info@audiogo.co.uk
www.audiogo.co.uk

All our Large Print titles are designed for easy reading, and all our books are made to last.